DOGS

OF THE

OLIGARCHS

a novel

By F.C. Fox

Deus Ex Machina

DEUS EX MACHINA PRESS

Deus Ex Machina Press

rm@exmachina.group

Publisher's Cataloging-in-Publication data
Fox, Forrester C.
Dogs of the Oligarchs / Forrester C. Fox.
1. Fiction

First Edition

Dogs of the Oligarchs is a work of fiction.

All of the central characters, incidents, events, and dialogue in the novel are fictional & imaginary. The views expressed by any of the characters in the novel are their own.

-    F.C. Fox, 2019

for Redmond,

Question what 'they' tell you;

Do Great Things;

And keep banging on those drums!

DOGS OF THE OLIGARCHS | Chapter List

THE TIP OF THE ICEBERG

❋❋

At first, I started noticing the little things.

And, at first, it was only one little thing here and then one little thing there. A word choice, a spin, a persuasion tactic. A subtle way to make the world seem like it was something other than what it was.

Sometime later, I started to notice all kinds of little things. Numbers, patterns, associations, word choices, stories didn't match up. Then, I noticed bigger things. Agendas, propaganda. And, of course, outright lies. Lies so big it is hard to fathom they could be untrue. I kept developing my lens and everything started to become crystal clear to me.

It took me years to realize nothing I was told could be trusted, unless I could see and feel it for myself. And even then, I urge caution.

It is impossible to know exactly why it happened. It just did. I know it's not an explanation. I know it! I'll try to explain. I mean, I was always quite perceptive. I always "got it." But, here's the thing. I only got the stuff I noticed. And it wasn't a lot. Everything went by me; in hindsight. It seems simple to point out, but it makes sense, right? And I missed so much! It wasn't that I didn't always see everything — that's an understatement. I missed almost everything. It's wild out there.

The things I investigated and learned about — from many sources, with Doctor Hogan Lowd, with Karen — and the things we saw, with our own eyes, would make the biggest conspiracy theorists ripe with envy. But we'll get to all that in due time.

Now, before, before I started noticing, I understood what I saw in my own personal way. That's a nice way of saying I thought I understood, but I didn't. Once I started noticing the little things, my understanding grew and I became ready to recognize bigger patterns and, finally, to see the big picture. And, the big picture is the vice-grip the 'system' has on humanity. Everything I'm about to tell you -- it all happened by chance. I could have gone through life as I always had, with blinders on; it was a few little occurrences conspiring to put me on a different path. After I was on a new path, it took a long time for me to figure everything out.

I came to be one of the world's biggest experts on the nature of the 'system.'

Meaning, I figured out there was a whole mass of ice — a colossus! — under the little tip of the iceberg I saw. The mass, guess what? It's the meaty stuff — the bulk. The block of ice. It's monstrous. Everything real, all of the levers of power and control, those are hidden under the tip of the iceberg. Most people never see them. I'm not certain they want to. And, the 'system,' like the iceberg, is hidden beneath. The iceberg hides its bulk by its nature. The 'system' does it by its design. Obfuscation and disinformation, combined with a heaping pile of distraction and propaganda. Shoved down the throat, by repetition. So, the tip of the iceberg is a lie by omission — just like the visible part of the 'system.' But here's the thing: it's hard to first start to identify the 'system.' It's hard to see it and many people never do. But once you see it, once you catch a good, memorable glimpse, things slow down and it becomes possible to start to piece the puzzle together. Things start to fit together and patterns emerge. Once I started to notice and isolate and understand parts of the 'system,' I gained the ability to see the whole thing.

The saying — "it's just the tip of the iceberg" — is one of my favorite sayings ever invented. It applies to everything, really. You have to go beneath the surface, or you might as well not even bother.

* * *

I used to fit in, pretty well. Things changed, somewhere along the line. A lot of people dismiss me, now, because I notice so much. It started with my brother Timothy posting on Facebook that I was chasing UFOs or looking for Elvis or Big-foot or whatever (I can't remember which conspiracy he cited first). I'll get to that story. Timothy is a simpleton and I don't want to get riled up, not right now, not at the outset. There will be plenty of time to rant, later on. Because of him, in large part, they say I'm crazy. Nuts! They say I flew the coop. They say the needle is not touching the record. They use the word "conspiracy" on their little digital postings. Not a little. They say it a lot. All the time! Conspiracy, conspiracy theory, conspiracy nut. It's their way of writing me off, entirely — because they don't want to address the substance of what I found. They don't want to investigate or question the 'system'. Their precious 'system'! They want the comfort of it, the complacency, the consumerism, the day-drunk buzz comes with every heaping pile of cheap corporate carbohydrates. Ignorance is bliss — you'll see. You'll see it's a defense mechanism on their part. They want to believe what they are sold. The propaganda is comfortable, even though it is harmful. So harmful! The official version of events - the 'system's' approved narrative - helps them to process and assign meaning to the things they see around them. They love the comfort of the industrial corporate world and they can't imagine modifying it, let alone living without it. They certainly can't imagine *trying* to break it down. For those reasons, I don't really care what they say. I don't care about Facebook, Instagram, Twitter. Those aren't real life, no matter what the masses think. They're not real at all.

These people, the ones determined to justify the 'system'

no matter what, are what the shadowy people in charge of this 'system', this permanent loop between corporations and the media and international governance — they are what these call cattle, or dogs, or slaves.

To understand how I got here — to New York, rampaging — with Ranald the Radiant and his brothers Eindride and Vilfred, the Steady and the Victor — I need to take you back in time. Trust me, everything fits together in the end. But I can't start the story with my search for Ranald de Radcliff. That would be just the tip of the iceberg!

Stopped Cold

**

I was born in 1982, in San Mateo, California — south of San Francisco if you didn't know. My name is Brandon Brooks, by the way. My father, Stephen Brooks, was a bookish accountant. Glasses, the whole bit. He is Anglo with a touch of German blood. Nice enough guy. His father, Roger Brooks, had been a pilot in World War II and did a variety of things professionally. Roger was his name, he wrote, he spoke. Roger was entrepreneurial and founded several companies, with the most successful one being a typewriter manufacturing business. Think of it, typewriters! At twenty-two, he married my grandmother, Patricia. She was European, a mix of a few different continental ethnicities that I won't list here. She was the daughter of a physician. When my father, Stephen, was twenty-six he married a stewardess named Dana. I will spare all of the literary pretension and simply say my mother died when I was six. She was in a car accident. It didn't kill her right away but it might as well have. She hung on for a few months but with blood clotting and strokes the end steadily grew nearer and nearer until it arrived one day. And then it was over. I don't remember much about my mother. A flash here and there and then some sadness and emptiness over what could have been. But that's life, I guess. I'm only giving you the background, it's not really an emotional topic for me anymore — how could it be after all these years?

My dad carried on. He re-married several years later and had another child — my brother Timothy — a simpleton. Timothy, by the way, lives his life on Facebook. Little posts with his opinions, with his gossip, updates to make it seem as if he is doing something (other than posting on Facebook). I grew up happy and healthy. My step-mother, Janice, was fine. Janice is a relatively thin brunette with a soft demeanor and kind eyes. We still keep in touch on holidays and the like; I talk to her more than I talk to my father. Not for any specific reason, she just keeps in touch more. I suspect she was as good a step-mother as a guy can ask for. Until I started noticing, I talked to my dad, Stephen, regularly as well. I think the conspiracy talk spooked him — he's one of those guys who thinks everything he reads on the internet is real.

I attended a Catholic grade school and the local Catholic high school as well. Serra High. The schools were fine, and I passed my time reading the normal books, spending time with friends, playing sports, chasing girls. Standard stuff, quite the standard-fare American childhood. I drove a Dodge. A Challenger I worked on myself. Fast car — loud. I got good grades and did well on standardized testing. In fact, I almost maxed my SAT test — I had a high scholastic aptitude and I also featured high levels of societal compliance. I attended Georgetown University in D.C. and primarily studied English but I also took a smattering of business classes. Accounting and such. I didn't know what I wanted to do — I thought I might go to law school and I might go to business school. I didn't end up doing either. Instead, I went to work in the corporate world. In the years which followed, I bounced around a lot. From corporation to corporation, from cubicle to cubicle. Always selling.

As that would indicate, I worked primarily in corporate sales departments. Keep in mind, this was at the tail end of the American empire. The changes started in '65 with the Kennedy Act — those had started to roost and the empire was crumbling at its edges. The best people left the cities as fast as they could. People stopped talking to their neighbors. Anyone could be "American" now, if they got the right piece of paper — but the corollary to this silly development was no-one was really American anymore. If everyone was, then no-one was, also. Think about it. Small shops and craftsmen were on the run, the mega-corporations had moved in to every nook, every crevice, of American life. Everything was a chain, a franchise. With the loss of the cities to the damaging euphemism, "urban decay," everything became spread out. Some people pretended not to know what urban decay was — others knew what it was and wouldn't talk about it. Those who risked talking about it honestly were called names, nasty names. People escaped into suburbia. But even there, corporate chain-stores, gas stations, convenience stores, fast food — all of these were ubiquitous. Bright colored signs pushing the same things but packaged and branded differently and with different advertising slogans. A non-stop barrage of advertising! Everything became nothing and nothing became everything.

I couldn't change it, of course, so I went with it. To be honest, I didn't even notice it when it was happening. I noticed it after it happened. The period of change, itself, didn't draw a single comment. From me, from anyone. I was busy, I didn't notice until it was already done. I suspect the same is the case for most people. The corporations just spread until they were everywhere. When you are busy with your everyday routine — your job — the changes around you can just creep up on you. It's hard to describe, hard to even acknowledge, that this type of massive change could happen around you, much of it in your twenties and early thirties. Of course, on some level, you notice these weird changes but there's nothing you can do about it, it's beyond your control. You shake your head, maybe, or grit your teeth... but you carry on. I had never known what it was like to know my neighbors, to be part of a community — those were my parents' neighbors we knew. So, in some ways, it was hard to recall what it was, in fact, we had lost when the mega-corporations took everything over. It was hard to recall, by design. For example, I worked in the 'system' and attributed the things I had to it - not the things I lost (which I couldn't see, remember). So, at first, I was fine with the cubicle. I thrived, in fact. I got a paycheck and I used it to do the usual. The things every corporate person does, you know.

Happy hour. New car. Ballgames. Gadgets. A wine collection. New furniture. New clothes.

I used all the terms you learn in the corporate world. I had them down. I was fluent, a master. I could compose the perfect corporate sentence, a sentence with a whole bunch of words thrown in so they, incredibly, say everything and nothing at the same time. I spoke of "return on investment," "velocity," "scale-ability," "agile deployment," "diversity and inclusion," "ally to the disadvantaged," "cost-effective," "at the end of the day." I could rattle off so many terms with such speed that my customers would struggle to keep up. I knew the right words and I steered clear of the wrong ones. But I would keep plowing forward — plowing the field and planting more seeds of need in the customers' dazzled mind. I was a dynamo. I sold a lot of stuff. It didn't really matter what it was, I could sell it. I always had a way to make my customer feel like they needed my product. And, often, they really did — at least in order to fulfill their own corporate-animal function at whichever global mega-corporation whose employ they found themselves in while listening to my spiel.

I must limit myself, however — for this is not a story about cubicles, it is not a story about product sales. In the end, it's not a story entirely about corporations or products. Those things are part of me, they are part of the modern world. The corporations I worked for were marketing power-houses. They manufactured and sold their products with tremendous success, with tremendous profit margins. When there was organic demand for their product — most often found when the product was addictive, provided a physical stimulus to the customer, or provided the ability for distraction and escape — there was simply no stopping the growth of the corporation. When there wasn't organic demand for the product, often times the corporation could create the demand for it through repetitive advertising. A well-tuned jingle, a memorable logo. A slogan, repeated over and over until it was beat into everyone's head. Until people had to have their product. Until people could not imagine not having the product. Until 'everyone was doing it.' In many cases, the person actually became the product. That may sound fanciful, but the brand could, in many cases, become equivalent to someone's identity. A brand is not a personality? Well, on some level, it may be true yet reality existed in defiance of this theory. This, no matter how useless and extraneous the product was, at its core. How I came to loathe the corporations and everything they stood for. Their tactics! Their repetition! Their depravity!

Remember, this is not a story about corporations or products. This is a story about truth. A story about a quest. A story about rejuvenation. A story about my journey.

I'm rolling through old memories, trying to think of the trigger — the first thing — that caused me to start to notice. I think it was early on. The way it worked was interesting. The facts are hard to decipher, because I have been noticing for so long it is hard to remember when I wasn't noticing. When I try to pinpoint an exact moment for my transformation, I have a hard time determining, through the haze of my old existence, exactly how things sharpened for me.

I have sifted through the retrospective many times, analyzing, thinking — trying to pinpoint the event. I go on tangents. There are so many alternative explanations. They run through my mind, twisting like a country road. When I get to a fork in the road, I take the fork every time, but then the road re-forks back to the same trigger. I have reached the destination, in my mind, and I understand when I started to notice. The event took place when I was working in sales at BigNet — an internet service provider where I was in charge of hi-speed commercial data sales. It was there I encountered a dose of double-speak so uninhibited it stopped my mind cold. My thoughts were a dove — cooing and bouncing along, happily — when it was snagged in a death grip by a bobcat.

The shock stemming from what I heard, there in the BigNet office, seems outsized in retrospect. It seems like it should have only sparked a disagreement, a point of contention. It doesn't seem like it should have changed my life. But it did.

It seems incomprehensible to me that it worked this way, that it had such an effect on me. But I understand it now, I understand why it did. During the conversation, at first, I had felt myself floating along, through another day in my native Bay Area. Probably thinking about the craft beer I would drink after work, or what movie I could watch, whether or not I should take my Audi through the car wash. Errands and the like. I was in a sales meeting in our Mountain View office, an area transformed from relatively run-down and innocuous, to an expensive — if still run-down — area full of corporate-types in ill-fitting corporate slacks riding below their silly button-down shirts. Something about the shirts, they were all very much the same despite some having triangle patterns, stripes, square-checks or solid colors, some draped like curtains and some more tight-fitted in their conformity. People might think the shirts were different, but they were all exactly the same. These people were riding the California tech-wave, or at least trying to.

It had been a particularly busy day, I remember. I was up early, around five a.m. I knew I was going to be busier than a one-legged midget in a butt-kicking contest. So, after I hit the gym I took a quick shower and grabbed my customary coffee. I was off, driving to the East Bay for my first meeting of the day.

The meeting, a sales call of course, had gone as usual. The familiar formula, you know, some small talk followed by a burst of information sharing (including pricing and the all important ask for the sale) on my part. When the time came, I rattled off, from memory, the data speeds BigNet could deliver, and raved about how the price was 'not an issue' because of the high level of inter-connected productivity the data-sharing technology would bring. And I made sure to emphasize the data network was 'always on' — so the employees of the company could do their work at all hours of the day and night and from any location. We compared notes. We chatted, we huffed, we mused. We discussed the client's information highway, their needs, how much of the personal information they scraped off the internet they needed to flow this way and that in order to mine the data for ad-serving and potential customer interactions. The ad-serving was key, as the corporation could shove product after product down its users throats (and make money doing it) through repetitive advertisement. It was all relatively standard stuff.

It was then, during the meeting, when it happened. It was a particular comment — one that cut through the ordinary sales meeting like an African Samurai — arrived.

Everything slowed down as my interlocutor, Lewis Frank, a data engineer working for a large communications and networking mega-corporation, said, in an offhand manner, "the more data we can get to and from more people, throughout the world, and faster, the better off we will be. Everyone will be better off."

Halfway through the line, I really focused in on his eyes and his face. It glowed in the bright, stale corporate light of the BigNet conference room. The expression on his face — blank — indicated he wasn't thinking deeply as he said it. He rattled it off, as

11

if it were fact.

What Lewis said, was this: "If we can use this data to build a more integrated, polite social structure, to bring people around the globe closer socially and politically — and, of course, economically, through trading and sharing products — the world will be a better place. A much better place."

A row of bright white tube lights glowed above us, shining down, creating a bland and hardened, enclosed corporate version of the sky. The electric light was emitted from the tubes, a constant stream, radiating down, splashing onto our heads, our faces, our bodies. I paused for a second. My hand moved first. I slid it about six inches towards the case containing all of my graphs, charts, narrative and pricing information. I moved it that direction, instinctively, towards the information I had used to close the sale. It was obvious Lewis would buy our data-push service — he said it himself, the world would be a better place. Then, without thought, my mouth moved.

"Why?"

I asked him a question, using one word. I said it instinctively, and it came out in a casual manner. Not disrespectful or combative. I certainly didn't have it in mind to damage my sale of the data-push. I wanted the commission from the sale, for sure. I didn't have anything in mind, I had questioned Lewis' assertion almost reflexively. I sounded curious in my tone; I was, all of a sudden.

We both paused, as if the question was a spirit entering the room and standing right there with us. Neither of us knew if the spirit was pain, uncertainty, doubt — or something much more mild and harmless. It was, after all, a simple question.

Neither of us spoke for a few seconds. In fact, neither of us even moved.

Then Lewis broke the silence with a forced chuckle, "Ha, ha humm."

I kept looking at him. I have no idea if it is true or not, but I imagined Lewis, like me, knew what he said had no basis in fact. His mega-corporation pushing data around the world had nothing to do with the world becoming a better place. He wanted to perform his duties at his job, that's all. To keep getting paid so he could pay his taxes and his bills. And I had set out to make my commission on the sale. We were two small cogs in the global capital-political machine, performing a small function to keep one piece of it involving the transfer of collected personal data, regarding millions of human beings, moving along.

"Well, I don't know. Doesn't matter anyway," I said, intending to clear the air. I was the one who had caused the angst with the impertinent question, so I tried to fix it by waving it off after the fact.

But, reader, know this: it was a simple question, looking back, that changed my life.

I have thought long and hard as to the reason for this. I mean, how does a one-word question in a corporate setting change me, or anyone? How is it possible? Was there something about me rendering me susceptible — vulnerable — to having all my previously held beliefs shatter around me like a vase thrown on concrete? Why were my ties to my previous way of life so weak?

It must have been this way, I reasoned, or the beliefs wouldn't have shattered. They would have held up. I would have gone on, as before, doing the same things. It had to be some sense of angst, a dis-connection from something important to me in my core — in my soul — something I hadn't even identified clearly. It was the same feeling I had when I drove to work, past a gas station, a fast food joint, a convenience store, a big box store, a gas station, a fast food joint, a convenience store, a big box store and then repeated the sequence over and over until I parked and walked into my cubicle with my plastic cup of semi-rancid, acidic corporate coffee with a burnt taste. Maybe the dis-connection — or something related to it — had identified me in some way (and not the other way around)? Maybe I was chosen for a reason? Maybe I had an obligation to notice? To bring about change.

It all seemed so far-fetched.

As you can see, I hadn't set out to start noticing, to start questioning things. I didn't set out to start investigating the 'system.' I hadn't yet taken any course of action that would change the way I spent most of the time given to me. My daily routine, so to speak. Heck, I didn't want to start questioning everything. In fact, all indications were I wanted to keep doing my thing, to live my life exactly as I had been before. But, with hindsight, I know what I wanted didn't matter anymore. The change was set in motion. Anyhow, thank you for indulging the lengthy explanation. It's important to me — it's important to my story - that was where it all started.

LAUGH IT OFF!

**

I was happy in artificial ways (promoted by corporate stimuli) and unhappy in natural ways (I suppressed the unhappiness). I was lying to myself. I lived a lie, and the punishment for lying was intertwined with the lie itself. Living that way was the punishment. Noticing things — fine tuning my awareness of myself, others, my surroundings, the world — noticing how the 'system' operated and reinforced itself became an every day thing. After the incident with Lewis, which I now recall quite fondly at times, moments like these started happening more often. One question, one simple "why?" and I was on my path. To be sure, I wasn't anything close to a full-fledged 'conspiracy theorist' at this point. I was nothing of the sort. And, I'm still not, if you ask me — even though that's what everyone calls me now (thanks Timothy). Why couldn't I ask a question? What was the power built into these assumptions, causing them to be unquestioned and unquestionable?

We'll get to it.

I recall the chuckle — Lewis' chuckle — as a watershed moment. It was the sound of someone so certain and yet so thoughtless in his certainty. 'Programmed,' if you will. Over-socialized. If there was a difference between Lewis and a corporate automaton — any difference at all — I certainly wouldn't be the one able to identify it.

His awkward chuckle echoed in my mind over the course of the night, even hours after the conclusion of the meeting and the data transfer sale. The chuckle replayed itself in my eardrums, while Lewis and I were far away from each other, as we had each long moved on to the rest of the day and early evening, to our food, our hobbies, our baubles and our respective friends or families or homes. Whatever the case may be. I have no idea what Lewis got up to after he finished his workday and it would be wrong and impetuous of me to speculate. It would be pure guesswork. I didn't ask him and I simply don't know. But I suspected it was standard-fare, late-stage capitalist-type activities.

For my part, at the time, I was seeing, casually yet quite often, a young woman named Erin. That evening, we had resolved — as modern couples do — via smart-phone to do something together, but we hadn't decided what the activity would be. Something. Anything. Focus. Drift. It didn't really matter, the point was to spend time together. I remember being tired of happy hour, tired of watching television shows or going to the movies. I suggested, via smart-phone, we do something more interesting than the things we always did. In my mind, my suggestion was for something fantastic, something far-fetched. Something exciting, even spectacular. Perhaps unprecedented? But the thoughts regarding the characteristics of the thing we might do didn't match up with any actual things I could think of doing, and Erin's responses indicated that she was in the same position. We had to do a corporate, semi-urban activity. We didn't know anything else. And if we thought of something, we probably wouldn't know how or where to do it. In the meantime, we kept exchanging messages on our smart-phone, pecking away at the screen like a skinny chicken gobbling up its feed.

The exchange that followed ended up being one of frustration. It was almost as if we both knew there was nothing extraordinary we could do, but we insisted on going through the process of trying to uncover an extraordinary thing hiding out there somewhere. Or maybe Erin had no such thoughts. I don't know. But the search was unrealistic, in context. We both had to be up for work in the morning. I had more data sales meetings and Erin spent her time booking travel and working on executive schedules for an entertainment company — her company (meaning the company that she worked for) made socially-engineered videos to sell to kids, and approached the task with the two-fold goal of generating money for sales of their product while pushing the most peculiar (even dastardly) behaviors they could scour up. Remarkably, the peculiar messaging still sold, no matter how obscure and unnatural their characters and story lines became.

I'll always remember Erin for her bubbly enthusiasm and also for her child-like good nature. We went back and forth with our messages, trying to coax a ground-breaking activity out of the discussion. Alas, there was none to be had. With time constraints and traffic constraints, neither of us could conceive of an activity to suggest even slightly outside of our norm. So, we ended up heading to a local corporate bar where I had a Belvedere martini, straight up with a twist, and Erin had a cosmopolitan. Then, we went to her place to watch re-runs of Grey's Anatomy and chat about our respective days at work, which, according to the conversation, were entirely ordinary. Of course, I told Erin about the meeting with Lewis, but not about the question and the chuckle. She wouldn't have understood. I don't mean it as an insult, but it's true. At the end of the night, which included our customary extra-curricular activity, I showed myself out, drove home and turned in for the night.

As I retired to my bedroom, I thought more of the meeting with Lewis than I did my time with Erin. This fact was predictive of future events, but I was too tired to think about things at the moment. At the time, for a few moments at least, I thought deeply about Lewis' absurd premise and my response, cutting that premise to the bone. Soon, I fell into a deep sleep.

INTO THE WOODS

**

My days of noticing and questioning had officially begun. That's a fact. Days went by, weeks, months. I stopped seeing as much of Erin over time. The shared cocktails ran dry, the television re-runs were paused. Erin didn't say anything, and neither did I. Nobody really cared, I guess. Judging from her Instagram account, which I still checked from time to time, she started to see more (socially) of one of the executives she worked for — a mousy, highly-compensated fellow named Carl. I had a nickname for him, which I won't share. I made several more sales at BigNet before changing jobs again in the early fall, as I seemed to do every year or two. I moved on to a different corporation, with a slight pay bump and much more work-related travel. This one was called EquiPark, a commercial real estate operation. I viewed the travel requirement as both a positive and a negative.

The disruption of my routine was negative; I loved my routine — it kept me sane.

But with the routine (and accompanying sanity) came the monotony. Tedious, persistent, aggressive monotony. I hated that! In my new role, I was able to get out of town and escape, for several days at a time, from the routine of my commute, the same coffee shop, the oppressive cubicle and the watchful eye of my boss. I didn't much care about the watchful eye — I was good at my job — it was the knowledge of being under the thumb of my boss combined with tendency to instruct me on something or other just because — not because I needed the instruction. It was as if he felt he should give me instructions and tips even though, often times, his face indicated he knew there was no merit to doing so. Nothing he said was helpful to me.

I often traveled to three places: Seattle, Charlotte and

Boston. So, in a sense, I still had a routine. It wasn't as routine as it had been before.

Now and then, during my travels, I made interesting acquaintances with people I met along the way. It made me feel connected to the world when I had these conversations.

One day, I was introduced to an interesting idea, quite by chance. The circumstances were as follows, I was at the airport in Seattle, traveling to make a sales call with one of our lending customers. A mustachioed fellow, twice my age, was enjoying an old-style rye whiskey — neat — next to me. I was sipping on a Belvedere martini with a twist. Presumably, he noticed my corporate outfit. His was less so. In fact, his gothic-skull belt buckle and old faded blue jeans rode over some worn motorcycle boots and was topped off with a half-tucked long-sleeve black shirt, no collar.

"Name's Owen," he said with a glance. I guessed he was genetically English. That was the look I picked up. I didn't ask, though.

"Brandon. Brooks."

I took another sip of my martini and glanced into the mirrored abyss on the other side of the bar. Liquor was everywhere, the bartenders hustled around making sales. This guy, this Owen - he had an enchanted presence — calm but peaceful, even joyful.

"You makin' a deal for the man?" asked Owen with a slight smile.

I couldn't characterize the guy, he had a calmness to him, but he clearly took delight in little things, in life. Not an ebullient joy (in your face), but rather a calm, focused contentment.

"Tryin' to, I guess," I replied.

"Industry?"

"Commercial real estate."

"Ah, capital."

The conversation went on for a while; Owen started going on about central banking, part of the conversation that stuck with me.

"You realize it's all the central banking? It drives your life, most people's lives. I don't even like to say it because they will probably pick up the conversation by satellite surveillance. Key words, brother."

"I don't know, man. I'm getting by doing what I can. Workin', you know."

"Think about it. Bretton Woods conference, man. Look it up on the internets. Realize the people who put it all together also write the stuff about it, though. You want to buck the central banking 'system?' So did Iraq, Libya and Syria. They got broken," Owen said, sipping his whiskey.

"Where are you headed, Owen?"

"Seattle. Then I'm driving east from there. I spend a lot of time in Wyoming."

"Sounds nice."

"Yeah, it'll be allright. The money controls everything. Here, there, everywhere. Think about it and do what you can with it."

"Maybe its true. Then what? I'm not a farmer... if I don't have money, how will I eat?"

"Everything you do feeds into the industrial machine. You can't say I'm wrong. I'm not saying it's an easy change – but the corporations need to be reigned in. And you have to look one step up the ladder to see the big picture."

The conversation continued on for a few more minutes, but that exchange was the highlight, the important part.

Owen paid his tab with the bartender. We exchanged pleasantries and he sauntered off — down the aisle and heading off on his long road to Washington and then Wyoming, via who-knows-where. I had no idea if he was right or if he was wrong. I sipped on my martini and thought about it. What did I know about central banking, about capital? Nothing much, to be honest. Certainly I knew about the interest rates in my deals, the purchases and sales and financings I set up for EquiPark. I thought of Lewis' chuckle and I thought about my question.

Maybe Owen was right. I was already noticing things more since my experience with Lewis — with the question. I sipped my martini again and thought about EquiPark. The thought hit me was this: who benefits? Who benefits from all these transactions we made? EquiPark, in a sense, sure. The property could appreciate. But it could also depreciate — the business was known for boom and bust cycles. Who was always there? Who made money, every day, from these properties, whether they went up or down in price? The lenders. That's who. And the governments, on the constant taxes on top of taxes. There were so many layers of taxation on every deal, in every day life. There was a tax coming and there was a tax going - countries have revolted over much less.

I thought more about the lenders. Time is their friend; their loans, properly collateralized, are notably low in risk. Every day, more money, more interest. Only at the highest levels can the corporation dodge its taxes. At the highest levels, they don't pay a dime. Think about that. The run of the mill people and regular corporations, they paid, constantly. So, the government and the lenders... and the special corporations... they benefited. They just threw a scrap here and there to the people spending all of their time making it work — and those people put everything they get back into the 'system,' anyway. I knew all this stuff from experience, I just didn't like thinking about it. I made a mental note to check into Bretton Woods.

I finished my travel with nothing out of the ordinary to report. My mind, a couple of days later, ranged back to the conversation I had with Owen.

I decided to go on the internet — the internets, as Owen call it — and research Bretton Woods. Why not? I spent some time reading about the conference, which took place in 1944 and was chaired by Henry Morgenthau. It resulted in the creation of a number of organizations. All of them had lofty organizational names. Their stated principles were very high-minded, ending poverty and such. I read about them all: The International Monetary Fund; the World Trade Organization; the World Bank Group, which was tied into groups called the International Bank for Reconstruction and Development, the International Development Association, the International Finance Corporation, the Multilateral Investment Guarantee Agency, the International Centre for Settlement of Investment Disputes. Orwell couldn't have named them any better.

The situation was murky! What are all these groups? What do they do? I read about them on my computer but by the end of the session I was more confused than anything. I had clicked around and, before long, I was reading a website discussing capital-based organizations — the organizations I had started reading about, they were really an interconnected web run by a small group of powerful people who had instituted global control of many of the world's governments. The website offered its opinion: any and all government activity is kabuki theater. Petty squabbles over -isms or -phobias or other non-issues are meant to distract the populace from the corruption, from the looting and pure corporate control of modern secular society. The real control was not in the government, it argued: the government itself was controlled. And the submission happened, originally, because of the binds of capital.

The binds of capital.

It was an interesting theory, but it was too much for me to process. Eventually, I clicked out of the website and went and poured myself a vodka soda. I turned on the TV and watched a movie, but I can't remember what it was called. My thoughts kept drifting back to the conversation with Owen. Underlying it all, the only thing I could be sure of is this: the 'system' is intended to foster the flow of capital — access to debt, essentially — around the world.

Why? Why couldn't capital needs be managed locally? I cursed Owen — halfheartedly — for asking me to look up this maze of organizations. My mind turned. Who ran these things? Where were they? Stated purpose aside, why were these tentacles extended throughout the world, basically unchecked? What was going on?

* * *

The next day, strangely, my brother (half-brother, really) Timothy made his first derogatory post about me on his Facebook account. Facebook was Timothy's entire life, and he posted with a religious zeal. He had seven hundred and thirty-nine friends on Facebook. Substantially more than the zero friends I supposed he had in real life. But this time, his post was different. Out of nowhere, he slammed me, posting the following message: "My brother Brandon Brooks spends all his time chasing ghosts around the internet. I'm ashamed to say he has become a kooky conspiracy theorist. Someone, somewhere, convinced him the world is controlled by a shadowy group of people who are subjugating the common folk to slavery, using debt and wages to accomplish the task. He'll believe anything you tell him. It's totally nuts! Everybody knows we have complete freedom here in the good old U.S. of A.! Next, he'll probably be looking for Bigfoot. Apple Pie and hamburgers for all!"

I didn't hear about Timothy's post right away - I didn't have a Facebook account. A few days later, my step-mother, Janice called me and asked what was going on with me after telling me about Timothy's post.

I was quite confused — it seemed like an incredible coincidence to have Timothy post on Facebook just after I researched Bretton Woods and viewed internet material outside of approved, mainstream sources.

An incredible coincidence, indeed! I had no desire to speak with Timothy, though, so I ignored the entire episode. I didn't want or need an explanation, and Timothy was free to post whatever he wanted to on Facebook. It didn't make any difference to me. It wasn't real.

Repellent, Low & Vile

✸✸

Somewhere in Antarctica

There was no red cliff in sight. Not only that, there was no red cliff within thousands of miles of the ice castle. It's not entirely clear where the Radcliff family came from... but clearly it wasn't this place. The ice castle was, in fact, more of a bunker than a castle. It was magnificent in its simplicity and characterized more by its humility and its practicality than by any manifestation of grand splendor. To the extent splendor was found in the castle — and it was — it showed itself in attention to detail. Ornate carvings were common in the bunker — so detailed and beautiful — and for this reason they were easy to gloss over without appreciating them fully. Beautiful materials, preserved by the family for thousands of years, but only for their utility. The most beautiful items in the castle — in fact all of the items in the castle — had a specific purpose. Spears for hunting food with magnificently fashioned metal, ice picks for spelunking in massive glacier caves with handles depicting Kings of yesteryear, vats of oil for frying food with beautiful, molded scenery adorning the outside — everything in the bunker had an important utility, and those living in it wasted no space or materials.

Inside the ice bunker, Ranald of Radcliff — a giant — had called the Council of Elders to order for the regular meeting of the full moon.

As Ranald waited for the other elders — his two living brothers, Eindride and Vilfred de Radcliff — he chewed on the body of a freshly-roasted and lightly-salted crabeater seal. At twenty-nine feet tall, Ranald held the roasted seal as a human holds a chicken wing. He was dressed in flowing robes created with animal furs. The sewing technique utilized to create the large garment was so skillfully performed, there was no way to tell where one fur ended and another began. The garment was seamless and it flowed all the way down from Ranald's shoulders to a few inches above the floor, which was a layer of stone. Massive letters were smoothly chiseled into the stone floor, spelling out Genesis 6:4. The differentiation between the lettering and the stone was very slight, and the lettering was hard to discern with the naked eye. Different types of stone — some gray, some charcoal, some black — all cut and set perfectly to give a solid, flat surface for Ranald and the other giants to stand or place furniture upon, and the Genesis reference was a source of great pride for Ranald, Eindride and Vilfred. A reference to their history, one of their acknowledgments in the Word, the Great Book.

Currently, Ranald was seated, on a massive throne-like wooden chair. The chair was sturdy and was replete with strange and somewhat fearsome-looking carvings of demons, angry witches, villainous sprites and other supernatural looking creatures — forces of evil, all of them, based on the depiction on the chair. With each bite, Ranald ripped meat and blubber from the seal's body using his massive teeth, and he felt nourishment as the bounty of nutrients was pushed down his massive esophagus and ultimately came to rest inside his ample belly. Ranald had done the same thing so often, for so many years — tearing the seal meat with his teeth and swallowing it down. One seal would fill his belly pretty well. Two and he would be stuffed. Ranald loved crabeater seal, it was one of his staples. He often ate as many as ten of them in a week.

Moments later, Ranald's brother Eindride strode into the chamber. He had a thick bronze band pulled around his forehead, which worked to guide his massive locks of exquisite dark-blonde hair back, keeping it out of his face, and pushing it toward the back of his head, from which it flowed down over his shoulders and all the way onto his back. The bronze band was adorned with an engraved inset showing a large man — a giant — clubbing a herd of men, women and children over the head while prior victims of the clubbing lay strewn across the ground. Presumably, those lying prone had been dispatched to another realm, killed by the giant wielding the club.

"Good to you, Ranald the Repellent," said Eindride, using his brother's nickname, an epithet borne out of affection even though it had a different sound to it.

"And to you. Did you have a refreshing hibernation, Eindride the Low?" replied Ranald, pausing from chewing on the crabeater seal, if only for a few seconds.

"I did. How was yours?" asked Eindride, blinking his eyes a couple of times and rubbing the right one with his massive right hand. His eyes fixed on Ranald's seal.

"Restless, as usual, my brother. Restless and long are a bad combination for the dock sleep," said Ranald as his long golden locks of braided hair flickered with light from the crackling fire he had staged in the pit under the open air section of the bunker, with a round hole directly above the fire to allow the smoke to rise and dissipate. Ornate carvings rimmed the hole, but the grooves and designs were so smooth and intricate they might have looked as if they had been inspired, divinely. But, on closer inspection, the carvings were seen to be demons, witches, trolls, goblins, ogres, angry spirits and other assorted monsters. Awful creatures which gave no quarter to anything good or decent. So, it was likely that the inspiration was not divine, but the opposite. "I have so much on my mind after the latest wake! Much to discuss."

Eindride seated himself next to Ranald. He struck his brother three times on the left shoulder — hard blows of affection. Phmmp! Phmmp! Phmmp! Ranald kept eating his salted crabeater seal, unaffected, but had a look of brotherly affection on his face as the hard blows connected with his shoulder.

"Break your fast, if you wish, my brother. There is plenty of seal on the salt rack. Goes down easy," said Ranald with a toothy smile. Meat and blubber was seemingly caught everywhere, between his teeth, on his lips, even in the side pockets of his massive cheeks. He was getting a lot of the food down, but much of it was escaping at the same time.

"I will, Ranald. First, I wish to quench my thirst with the grog of the dark heaven! Mauve, grog, now!" yelled Eindride, swiveling his head around to both sides, looking for the nook-Demon. "Where, by the Devil, is the Vile?"

"You don't need to make Mauve do everything, Low. I think he went to throw the rubbish into the deep canyon, anyway. The grog barrels are right over there. Go get one yourself. Only one or two before the meeting, Eindride. Keep your wits about you! Ha Hoo!" exclaimed Ranald with a deep laugh. "And I haven't seen the Vile — who knows what that boy got up to. Perhaps he is out somewhere making mischief, or perhaps he is still asleep."

"I'll go look upon him if he doesn't come out in a short time," replied Eindride.

Ranald, having finished eating the most recent seal, sat back. Eindride had returned with four barrels of grog, two stacked in each hand.

"I said one or two, Low!" bellowed Ranald, still chewing.

"I have deep thirst, my brother! I need to make this happen to replenish my insides. It will not affect my wits, Ranald, I am a very steady and stable presence, you know this."

Eindride the Low used an iron bar to wrench an opening

28

into the top of the first barrel of grog. He tipped it back and drank, hollering "To health and conquest!" before his mouth connected with the barrel. Most of the grog flowed from the barrel and into his massive mouth. Some missed the mark and streamed down his bearded chin. He drew from the first barrel until all of the grog inside it was gone. Then the second. Then the third. The fourth sat there, untouched, at least at the moment.

"Ahhhhh, that hit the spot!" said Eindride as he cast the empty barrels aside. A block-shaped, fifteen foot tall creature, flesh-colored but with a purplish tint, adorned with thick spiked-iron bracelets and anklets, clothed only in a waist band with a seal-skin pocket, entered the chamber, walking at a steady clip. The purple creature, a nook-Demon, walked directly over to a nook in the wall on the northeast side of the room. He stood in the wall-nook for a few moments before he realized Eindride had dispatched of the three barrels of grog. He walked and grabbed another full barrel. Then, he headed, methodically, in the direction of both of the giants, put down the full barrel and grabbed the three empty barrels, throwing them in the re-use bin, which sat next to the rubbish bin he had emptied moments before. The creature, the nook-demon, standing back in the wall nook after disposing of the barrel and bringing another to Eindride, rubbed the lone white horn on his forehead — and whipped his tail somewhat menacingly — as he returned to his wall nook and stood, expressionless.

The third brother finally joined the chamber. Vilfred the Vile walked in, without his usual rambunctious presence. He had a dazed look on his face, as if he had been continuing his slumber up until just moments before. It seemed he had not been out on the ice cliffs trying to spear giant petrel — the largest bird in Antarctica -for sport, as he sometimes did. He had not been getting into any other mischief — something expected from Vilfred, as he was a curious and adventurous giant, at least when it came to finding new and inventive ways to pass time and work on his hunting or his physical endurance.

"I've emerged!" yelled the Vile as he walked into the meeting chamber. "Another lengthy slumber, ended. I feel strong, but I have thirst and hunger."

Three of the wolvine — massive creatures showing twelve feet in height on all four legs — while laying about in the back corner of the chamber, perked up their heads, slightly. This line of wolf-demons were cast down from above with the Nephilim thousands of years ago and had been faithful companions to the giants for ages. They loved Vilfred the Vile because, of all the giants, he was the most likely to bless them with extra seared meat, which he did from time to time, but not today. Vilfred was too groggy to think of the wolvine. The wolvine were a lovable and playful species — they loved peace and coziness — unless their owner showed, through voice or visage, any amount of anger. At such times as those, the wolvine immediately displayed a savage level of ferocity rarely seen from any beast. They were, however, completely loyal to their owners, to Ranald, Eindride and Vilfred.

"It's time," said Ranald. "We have important matters to discuss."

"When do we start?" asked the Eindride the Low.

"As soon as everyone is awake and refreshed, we will start," said Ranald.

The Vile snatched a seal and started tearing at it with his teeth. He motioned with his free hand to the purplish creature — Mauve, the nook-Demon — who trudged to the grog rack and brought him a barrel after opening it.

Eindride, in the meantime, had knocked back the fourth

barrel of grog and was about to start working on the fifth. Ranald looked at him disapprovingly, but didn't say anything. Instead, he shook his head ever so slightly and squinted his eyes. Eindride, noticing the look, shrugged his shoulders as if to say, "I know, Ranald, but I'm thirsty my friend."

When he finished the seal and washed it down with his first barrel of grog, the Vile spoke. "I am ready," he bellowed in a deep, rumbling tone. "Let us begin the session of the Council!" He had a voice befitting his stature as a massive, fearsome giant.

IT'S ALL A LIE

✱✱

My life, during this period, started to change more rapidly than I had expected. Plenty of time had gone by since my relationship with Erin ended. We went through the awkward process of dis-entangling from each other. It took a week or so, but then there was no trace of Erin remaining in my life. Not on my phone, or in person. Of course, she scrubbed her Instagram account of all traces of me and she would, no doubt, be on to the next guy soon. It was as if she — and the related 'we' — never existed, except a little bit in the very back of my mind. And those were certain not to last forever, you forget what you want to forget and so on. Once a period of time had gone by — time spent un-knowing each other — I began seeing, socially, another young woman named Lexi. We spent time together quite often. A couple of times a week, at least. I think it was short for Alexandra, but — candidly — I never asked her and had no reason to be sure. It was unconfirmed.

Lexi was a fun compatriot. She spent her days working for a mega-corporation. She was in the Human Resources department, so she was focused on issues relating to the recruitment and retention of employees working for the humongous corporate conglomerate. The company she worked for was in the chemical business and had billions in revenue, globally. They sold chemicals for personal use under a variety of brands. The brands and products ranged anywhere from abrasive household cleaning products to facial peelers to chemical sunscreen sprays.

As I said, Lexi was fun, she almost always presented a cheerful mood. We had what I would characterize as a normal relationship. We hung out, we smiled, we joked around. We made small talk. And everything else one might expect.

"What do you want to do?" I might ask her via my smart-phone's messaging app.

"I don't know, what do you want to do? I get off work at five-thirty," she might reply.

"I don't know, let's come up with something fun," I might reply.

"Okay, whatever you want to do."

"Let's meet at the place where we always meet."

"Sounds good, Brandon."

After this exchange, we might end up at a local bar and drink a couple of cocktails during happy hour. We might grab sushi and sake. We might go watch streaming television — something funny, something dramatic, something mysterious, something with a criminal element - something we never really cared to remember after a few weeks had gone by. We were on to the next show by then. Who knows? The possibilities were not endless, but there were different possibilities nonetheless.

Over time, I noticed, very vividly, my interest level in conversations with Lexi diminishing. It had nothing to do with her. She was great. She was pretty, enthusiastic, fun to be around. I liked Lexi.

But it was as if I was thinking more and more about the 'system' I was living in. The 'system!' I'll come back to that. And it was as if I preferred my investigation to engaging in activities with Lexi. Just as my enthusiasm for Erin had dropped off towards the end with her. I wondered about myself, about my goals for relationships, for life.

I was still thinking about my groundbreaking "why?" with Lewis. I was still thinking about Owen and his comment about capital, about international finance. In fact, I would steal away time from my work at EquiPark to read further about these topics. The internet still had pockets of uncensored content. And, I became skilled at finding the uncensored content that remained. Many of these writings were esoteric, unfavored — critical of modernity, global capital, fiat money (which isn't real). These were dangerous writings, according to 'them.' I didn't know who, exactly, 'they' were. Not yet. I found myself spiraling down an investigative water-slide — zipping around corners and curves at a high speed, soaking up information and commentary — heading, hopefully, for a pool at the bottom, which, with a splash, would signify understanding.

In some ways, I was ashamed and frightened about what was happening to me. I wasn't doing the same things I used to do. The pastimes, the hobbies, the bars, the happy hours. I hadn't golfed in a few months at this point. And I used to, every couple of weeks. I was constantly looking for information, trying to piece together a clear vision of what was happening around me. How did these pieces fit together? It was a 'system!' But, down in the weeds of the 'system,' I couldn't get a clear view of what it was. My low vantage point kept me confused, my mind was spinning.

But this journey presented a dangerous personal situation for me, and I knew it. People who talk about the 'system' — who notice it, who define it, who point out its characteristics — are labeled, as I said before. The 'conspiracy theorist' tag attaches quickly these days. If you talk about the 'system' — if you say anything critical of it — you are labeled as one of 'those' people. If you're any good at exposing or explaining the 'system,' you're also censored by the 'system' itself. It's really simple. You're not supposed to notice things; you're not supposed to notice patterns. You're not supposed to question what has happened to American society.

When the shame and fright relented, as it always did, eventually, I would usually become wildly euphoric when I realized I was piecing together truths. I mean, the things I was finding counted for something. Truth matters! Right?

I wondered about everything. Even Lexi. Why was she bothering to spend her time working in a cubicle at some massive corporation? I mean the obvious answer is she trades fifty hours of her week for some money. That way, she can pay rent, buy food, consume entertainment. That's all. Should it be the way it was? Was there any other way? It seemed like everybody was doing it. She told me she was required to attend sensitivity training once a week — 'learning' to be sensitive to people who were different from her. These people were equal, but they were also preferred in some ways. They told her she could always learn to be more sensitive, to be more tolerant of differences. And so she was trained for this sensitivity, every week. These special people, they told her, needed to be elevated for their perspective, for their differences.

If Lexi looked askew at the corporate sensitivity hammer, she hid it well. She seemed to go about her day, and she accepted the way things were. Sometimes, for fun, I would lob in a test-question to probe Lexi's acceptance of her cubicle job.

"How long are you going to keep working at ChemFill?" I would ask Lexi.

"I don't know... I don't have any other plans and the benefits are okay," Lexi would respond, or something to that effect. Her eyes would look distant, removed, even forlorn as she spoke the words. She looked as if she was suppressing a feeling telling her something wasn't quite right. But she spoke the words anyway, albeit wistfully.

For me, my secret life (of noticing) quickly became an

entire anti-'system' demeanor. Of course, I was only anti-'system' in my mind, because I was still working at EquiPark and fully dependent on my commissions to maintain my customary semi-urban lifestyle and to pay my taxes. But I started shifting my appearance and my behaviors, a little bit at a time.

Sometimes I would despair about my little changes — I stopped cutting my hair every two weeks, not saying 'sorry' enthusiastically when I was slightly in the way of a co-worker in the hall — they seemed futile. But I reminded myself I had to start somewhere, and doing the little things were a way to start to de-program.

At other times, I felt I was making progress toward recognition. Steady progress. I kept questioning everything, always with a blunt "why?" or an "is this necessary?"

Even with this shift, my attitude stayed largely positive and I continued to dig in to my reading on the remaining free 'edges' of the internet. Lexi was often left on the sideline, presumably watching her television re-runs by herself as I spent my free time learning about the history of international finance and the globalist 'system' which, entirely by accident, came to the forefront of my life.

I clicked and typed as I navigated around the internet. Here was Napoléon Bonaparte, "When a government is dependent upon bankers for money, they and not the leaders of the government control the situation, since the hand that gives is above the hand that takes. Money has no motherland; financiers are without patriotism and without decency; their sole object is gain." Napoléon understood capital to be border-less, when controlled by forces without strong ties to the soil in which the capital was deployed. It could be used to manipulate and break an entire people. Beholden to money and consumerism, all was lost —

permanently. One lost the ability to control one's own destiny, to shape their family, to contribute to the shared values of their nation, which they once shared with people like them.

I continued surfing around. Here was Andrew Jackson, a rough man who understood the importance of the fight, "Gentlemen! I too have been a close observer of the doings of the Bank of the United States. I have had men watching you for a long time, and am convinced that you have used the funds of the bank to speculate in the breadstuffs of the country. When you won, you divided the profits amongst you, and when you lost, you charged it to the bank. You tell me that if I take the deposits from the bank and annul its charter I shall ruin ten thousand families. That may be true, gentlemen, but that is your sin! Should I let you go on, you will ruin fifty thousand families, and that would be my sin! You are a den of vipers and thieves. I have determined to rout you out, and by the Eternal, I will rout you out!" Jackson lost, though, eventually. He couldn't stand up to the relentless attacks brought about by those pushing their preferred capital structure. Jackson died; the 'system' lived on. The 'system' won, it persevered, it grew.

My contact with Lexi lessened in the coming weeks until months passed and we fell out of touch entirely, a mutual ghosting as it were, and my investigation into the 'system' deepened.

Months had gone by, again, and I found myself taking a long walk by the river — something I did quite often, several times a week, at least. I sat down on a rock at one point, enjoying the sounds of the rushing water, the birds, the wind rushing through the trees. It was wonderful to be alone in the park, alone with my thoughts. The sun shone hot upon my skin, but over the course of the entire walk at least half of it was shaded by trees and the intermittent exposure to sun and shade made the walk extremely pleasant. I continued on the walk until I reached my turn-around point and then started on the back-half of the journey.

I sat on the same rock on the way back — and was consumed with even more of a desire to understand the 'system.' If Napoléon and Andrew Jackson, men who had access to the highest levels of political knowledge, believed their respective countries were run, not by a democratic compulsion, but by capital — then it seemed as if my investigation — my new way of being — wasn't a waste of my time.

As I got up off the rock to finish the rest of my walk back to my Audi, I noticed a couple walking along, each holding a leash attached to a dog. The man, whose name turned out to be Rory, was a reddish-brown-headed guy with wild eyes. His hair was medium length and flowed in every direction. He had a pot-belly, which had overtaken the rest of his physique and become a point of emphasis. But, he had the markings of a man who had been fit and athletic — his movements, his frame. His companion, a black-haired woman with braids in her hair, had a pleasant look on her face. She went by the name of Lucille.

We made eye contact, so I commented, "I like your dogs. Nice day to take them out."

"It really is," said Rory, extending a hand and introducing himself and Lucille.

"I'm Brandon. Brooks," I said, shaking his hand and acknowledging Lucille with a glance.

"The mark of the beast!" exclaimed Rory.

I paused, then said, "What?" in a voice soaked with uncertainty.

"Lucille and I have been talking about the mark of the beast. Have you heard of it?"

"I have not."

"Sorry to jump right in on the topic," said Rory. "We were going over everything. They are putting microchips in people. They are developing implants to connect brains directly to your smart phone. Look it up. It's the mark of the beast."

I was taken aback, but I was fine. I continued walking along with them.

"I did see an article recently on microchips. Something these people are putting in their hands to be able to pay conveniently as they shop, and other things — unthinkable things."

"People love to shop," added Lucille.

"They do."

"It's the mark of the beast!" repeated Rory. "It's evil. It's the global cabal. People are so stupid and pliable they are marching along to the beat of their own destruction. Shopping along the way, buying junk they don't need."

"I mean, when you put it that way..."

"There's no convenience in putting devices in your body. A device in your head to control your phone? Pffft. Why not get rid of the phone, instead? It's the mark!" yelled Rory, his face bright red. He didn't appear angry, but rather, he looked excited and animated. He was one hundred percent invested in his commentary. The world around him did not exist to him, and I was probably just a fresh audience for him to say the same things he always said.

He continued ranting, "Devices in your body, think about it! Are you kidding me? ARE YOU KIDDING ME?" He was very animated and hollering, also laughing with exasperation. Was there something wrong with this guy? I mean, he had a point of course.

Melding with electronics was incredibly stupid. He was swimming against the stream, though. Whenever enough people started to adopt new technologies, the rest *always* followed the herd. The technology always grew and advanced, it never retreated.

We walked on, together. Initially, I enjoyed the company of the dogs and my impression was that Rory was too vocal, too wild for my taste. One of the dogs was a bulldog and the other was a mutt with some visible boxer characteristics, by the way. The couple, especially Rory, continued to be very talkative. The conversation moved off of the mark of the beast, shifting towards details regarding their lives, with Rory flapping his lips. They were visiting a couple hours south from where they lived, having driven down to see Lucille's mother. Rory blathered on and on. I wanted to dislike him, but couldn't. He was affable, and when Lucille chimed in she was good-natured and smiled a lot. So I engaged with them. When he had gone through their entire backgrounds, he shifted back to more esoteric topics. I was thrown off by the mark of the beast commentary, but when Rory kept going, it only took minutes to realize Rory was, in fact, a 'conspiracy theorist.' He couldn't help himself, and soon he was wildly veering from topic to topic. All of the pop-conspiracy theories also, to be clear. He touched on the moon — no one has been to the moon, he proclaimed. He touched on chem-trails. Demons. Third world immigration as a disenfranchisement scheme. UFO's. Flouridated water. Nine eleven. The NSA. Gun grabbers and false flag shootings. Globalists. Communists. He said those were, in some ways, two sides of the same coin. Vaccines. Aliens. Giants. Something about frogs. He went on and on, dominating the airspace for the bulk of the walk home.

At one point, time slowed down and I remember specifically focusing on his mouth, watching him articulate, so very clearly, a lengthy diatribe. "It's all connected! It's all a lie. No one gets into the globalist club without taking the mark of the beast themselves. No one. Not a single politician. No one gets into power in government, big business, big religion — unless they're part of the club. He's here — Satan. It's all Biblical. It's all a lie."

I walked on, rendered speechless by the barrage. In contrast to Rory, I liked to think before I spoke. I'm not saying Rory didn't think — ever — it's likely that he had been through these topics so many times he didn't have to, he was rolling on pure adrenaline. On this occasion, it was clear he was repeating things he had already thought about and decided upon. He was reciting from memory. He knew his topics inside and out. He was certain of them.

He railed for a minute against the Georgia Guidestones — which I had never heard of before that moment. Somewhat surprisingly, I was not annoyed with Rory's loquaciousness. I got a kick out of Rory and Lucille (when she chimed in). They were funny and open about everything. As I said, his hair and his eyes were wild. Overall, he was quite a funny looking fellow, somewhat bumbling in his affect, but endearing and clearly friendly. He wore these goofy tennis shoes, blue and red with no visible corporate branding. Generic shoes! He wore a plain watch and had no detectable smart-phone. I soaked it all in as he went on. I came to learn Rory and Lucille ran a little shop up in Sonoma where they sold old guitars and such. They told me the location and implored me to stop by the store to say hi next time I was up north.

His refrain, the saying he came back to at the end of a topic, over and over, was "It's all a lie!"

It's all a lie. Or some of it. Or none of it. I had to figure this out! I had to keep noticing until I knew what was going on. This journey had no end in sight.

Time for Revo-rution!

**

After finishing my walk, I stopped at the grocery store on the way home. I was trying to eat healthier and limit my intake of processed foods and sugars — while investigating the 'system,' I had been reading about the cozy relationship between big government and big food and I didn't like what I was learning. But I'll come back to that later.

I wound down for the evening with a snack and a glass of Oregon Pinot Noir. It was a nice way to end the day, in solitude with my thoughts.

Was it all a lie?

The night passed, easily. The next day was standard. And then a week had gone by, then a month, then three months. I still worked at EquiPark. I still was noticing things, on my own. I was picking up what I felt was manufactured corporate messaging. Once I started noticing the interplay between government, international capital and big corporations it became easier for me to categorize everything I saw. The propaganda and repetition was tiresome, but it was easy to see what they were doing and to analyze the interplay and the messaging. After all, I had been in the belly of the corporate beast for years. I knew what they did. I knew their tactics. I used them myself, on a small scale. I spoke that language.

Fearing I was becoming too withdrawn into my pursuits, I was fortunate enough to strike up a relationship with a rather interesting woman named April. April was a dutiful young lady, working in nursing administration at a local hospital. The hospital had actually been in the news recently for a very unpleasant reason. The hospital had hired a preferred, special person — a diversity-hire, intended to bring strength. The hire came in the form of a cheap Kenyan male nurse — yes, that actually happened — and, unsurprisingly, the hire went horribly wrong. You see, the man was found to be smothering the hospital's elderly patients with a pillow. He had knocked off at least a dozen of the patients, and the police (and therefore the administration) suspected the overall death toll might be staggering. I met April, in passing, at my local coffee shop and soon after we were messaging and spending time together. We had been messaging and talking for a couple of weeks and we had already gone out together a couple of times — I had to tear myself away from my investigation of the 'system,' but I managed. We had fun!

In fact, I had a date with April the next day at six-thirty. It was to be our third date, in person, and I had planned a trip to a small sushi restaurant and figured afterwords we could go for a walk by the river. Truth be told, what I often called a river was actually a creek. But it was relatively pretty, a small, natural escape, and I liked the small embellishment, it made me feel closer to nature.

When the time came to pick April up for the date, I felt a good energy in my breast. I sprung up to the door and rang the bell. It took a while for April to materialize, but eventually she answered with a smile on her face.

"Sorry, I was in the back room on the computer and I lost track of the time."

"Ha, that's okay. Anything exciting on there?"

"My friend Bob — we used to work together at a different health-care company — I love him but he's kind of a conspiracy nut — he sent me a link to a video about the giants living in Antarctica," April reported.

"No way? Giants? Like big people?"

"Well, I'm pretty sure its an entirely separate species. But sort of, yeah. I'll text you the link. I was watching that and then when I heard the bell I had to grab, uh, you know, all my woman stuff. Lip gloss and such."

"Yeah, you guys are high on the maintenance scale."

"Oh hush up," said April with a laugh.

"I thought we could grab sushi and then go for a walk down at the river. I love that spot and the weather is perfect. Sound good?" I asked.

"Sounds perfect."

"It's funny, on the same walk I ran into a couple who had all sorts of stories to tell a couple months ago. I can't even remember all of them, but they were enthusiastic about them. I bring it up because I distinctly remember he mentioned giants. He said they were mentioned in the Bible. He was a conspiracy nut too. Rory! He knew 'em all."

"Of course he did. Maybe he should meet my friend Bob over donuts and coffee. They can share some real doozies."

"I don't even want to know. Obviously. That's what needs to happen," I replied with a laugh.

We went off to spend our evening and I don't regret it. It was enjoyable. April was sleek and slender (a rare specimen thanks to the influence of big food and big entertainment), and she had a nice smile, bright eyes and an amiable personality. It was only the third date, but my brief acquaintance with her had already been most pleasant.

The subject of giants came up again, at the sushi joint. As we were seated at the sushi bar, things went from comical to absurd as the sushi chef, standing right in front of us, joined into the conversation.

"So... those giants in Antarctica... what do you think they do there?" I asked April, trying to stir the pot.

Before I could answer, I heard a shout from across the counter.

"Rumber. They rumber!" exclaimed the sushi chef, a handsome and dignified-looking Japanese man.

I looked at April and my eyes flashed. April, sat on her chair, in silence. We were both trying to deduce what the chef was saying. I had never heard of the word 'rumber,' but the chef was emphatically certain that the giants were 'rumbering,' whatever that may be. The scene became awkward as the chef could see, very clearly, we had no idea what he was talking about. His eyes blazed as he tried to get his point across the counter.

"Rumber!" he yelled, stomping around behind the counter.

April and I exchanged a confused glance when the patron to my left intervened.

"He's saying lumber. That's his accent. I guess they bang around, they lumber around doing giant things, giant activities," said the heavy-set patron as he licked the remains of a sushi roll off of the bunched tips of the fingers on his left hand.

"Yes, rumber!" exclaimed the chef.

"Oh! They lumber," I said. I was willing to take this at face value, because I had no idea as to what else they might do. I mean, it sort of made sense.

"Giants rumber in Antarctica. Big arms, big regs. Much activity. Hunt for food... make the chaos. But verrry tame for ... ummm... for maybe thousand year. No chaos town and city rike old time. Time for noise. They go take gord. Time for revo-rution!"

Chaos broke loose in the conversation, with everyone talking over everyone else.

"We don't even know they are in Antarctica, how can you take that as a fact?" said April.

"They rumbering!"

"How big are these... umm... things?" I said.

"How did this come up?" chimed in the patron sitting to my other side.

The conversation about giants in Antarctica roared for another minute. Then, with an uncontrolled laugh, the chef went back to cutting up fish. April put her hand on my arm and changed the subject. No more talk of giants, not tonight. She was telling me about a new movie she had seen recently (a romantic comedy I pretended didn't sound awful), when the door opened up behind her. A strange-looking family walked into the restaurant. It was a swarthy man and his stocky wife, together with their two children. One was a grimy, bespectacled toddler and the other was an infant in a stroller. The infant squealed and caught April's attention for a second. I saw a look — a gleam — in her eye. I used the opening to snare a piece of salmon sashimi from the center plate. The gleam in her eye retreated and, feigning horror, she looked on as I ate the raw orange fish right in front of her.

"Distraction is my friend. That's what you get," I said with a huge smile on my face.

April laughed, loudly. We finished the meal and went out to my car and drove to the river. We spent the next hour and a half walking and talking. Sharing stories and laughs. It was fun. I walked the line with April. If I was too attentive, I might find myself in a serious relationship. I didn't know if I had a taste for that sort of thing. Not on the heels of Erin and Lexi and everyone else. Not with the time I needed to dedicate to researching the 'system.' But I was very much taken with April, so I walked right up to the line. I had a track record of taking things only so far and then letting them fall off — but so did everyone else, I rationalized. Why should I be any different? There weren't different rules for me!

I had no idea what I would do here, this time. Was she special? I had no idea, but we had a good time. At the end of the night, I took April home. I arrived home and sent her a message saying I enjoyed the time with her. April responded, saying basically the same thing back to me.

I wasn't ready for bed, so I went on my computer and searched for information on giants. I was surprised to learn there were many references made to their existence, in no other place than the Holy Bible. Was that definitive on the issue, then? Giants existed, I guess. It's right there for all to read about. Three hours went by as I read every Bible verse I could find mentioning giants. It was a rich history, and I didn't know what to make of it. I found myself way off the beaten path of the corporate internet. I was on the un-regulated, un-censored portion — which was shrinking every day, but still around, for now. It was the part of the internet where you didn't know what was fake and what was all-too-real. Finally, I clicked off the last window, not sure how to categorize everything I had read. I staggered to bed, falling asleep pretty much right when my head hit the pillow.

Corporate Dog, Down

**

My hours-long detour chasing giants was a thing of the past. I was more comfortable re-evaluating everything, noticing connections and the tight loop between our government, the mega-corporations and our media-and-copycat-driven runaway consumer culture. It seemed more fruitful than chasing giants. Maybe I needed a soothing diversion with the giant story, a chance to break away from EquiPark and commercial real estate sales with some fantasy. It was a strange topic seeing as it was comical and Biblical at the same time. Either way, the giant exploration was over. I could not side with the sushi chef and anyone else who believed there were presently giants, somewhere in the ice, ready to cause chaos during a revolutionary rampage. I couldn't go that far.

I stopped at my customary coffee shop on the way to work and ordered a large iced Americano with an extra shot of espresso, five in all. I was tired because I had been up late reading about giant legends and watching videos regarding the same. The coffee brought a much needed burst of mental clarity and physical energy. I drove along my usual route at a steady pace. I realized something was different as I approached my usual parking space. There were masses of people gathered about, with signs and costumes. Some were masked and dressed in black.

"What in the devil is going on here?" I said to myself. I parked in a much more remote spot than usual, grabbed my bag and got out of the car. I walked to the nearest group of those who were gathered and asked one of them, "Hey, what's going on here?"

"Its a protest, man. We're protesting the government."

There were some federal buildings near the EquiPark

campus — so I guess the location made sense for this sort of thing.

"Oh. What's the protest about?"

"I already said, man... the government. And the corporations too, man. Get up to speed. Here's a flier," said the fellow, with a nasally voice. The man had a wispy beard, was partially bald and extremely skinny except for his round pot-belly. He had no noticeable chin. He extended one of his noodle-arms to hand me a piece of paper with some information printed on it.

I reviewed it, and it was a breakdown of where the different protest-groups were supposed to go. It was unclear as to what exactly was being protested, except government generally, which I surmised to mean circumstance, or they wanted access to free money of some designation or other.

The groups were divided into sections, with suggested locations around the area, as follows: students, families, women, labor & union, climate, anti-war & peace, anti-racism, anti-fascism, corporate greed, migrants and a separate (cordoned off?) section for another group that I don't want to get into.

It was a lot to digest. I walked on through the protest toward EquiPark. I wasn't happy with this inconvenience, this physical disruption of my workspace and my routine.

Despite myself, I stopped at one of the fountains where there was a pocket of protesters gathered with heavier density than elsewhere. It turns out there was an argument taking place at the fountain.

A creature of some sort, which I presume was a man — I could not be certain because it was masked and wore a cap — was arguing with what I easily determined to be a counter-protester. I did a quick look at the flier and determined the argument was taking place in the corporate greed section of the protest.

After a minute the argument was seemingly over, with the masked figure taking leave of the situation after a heated exchange of garbled nonsense. Their combined IQ did not reach over one-forty.

"What were they arguing about?" I asked an onlooker.

"Corporate inclusivity, man. We have to be lettin' everyone into the corporations. Everyone deserves a job, a fair wage. I mean, that's where it's at. A job, man! These corporations, they don't include all people. All races. All genders. The disadvantaged. Dumb people. People who are on the outside looking in. It ends up with wealth disparity that makes our social reality different than what our true potential reality could be with total inclusivity and equality. That's white privilege, man."

"Oh," I responded, quickly realizing I was speaking to another dimwit.

"The other guy was saying corporations were great and they brought us the products that we need, through capitalism. He was saying it's the corporations that make America great. He said America was always great, and his statement really lit the other guy's fuse. It looked like it was going to get physical, but suddenly the first guy walked away."

"Sounds productive," I said, facetiously.

I started to walk on, when, from behind me, I heard the loud roar of an automobile engine. I looked in the direction of the noise and saw a black Ford Mustang roaring in the direction of the group. It's trajectory seemed to be safely away from my direction, but in the interest of my bodily safety I walked as rapidly as I could, continuing on my path, looking over my right shoulder to see what happened.

The car headed straight into the crowd. I winced as it

slammed into two people in rapid succession. Rat! Tat! Thwack! One was a smallish creature, also a masked protester. The other was a plus-sized woman wearing a sweat-suit. She pinwheeled after the contact and landed head-first on the concrete. The noise was excruciating. A 'thwump' combined with a 'splashhh' noise as her head hit. I was too far to see what was on the concrete, and I certainly didn't make an effort to get a better vantage point. I was fairly certain the woman would not survive the impact. It was a brutal crash.

The door to the car swung open and the same counter-protester who had been in the argument a few minutes before jumped out of the car and sprinted away from the scene of the vehicular attack. He had a t-shirt on over cargo shorts and multi-colored ASICS tennis shoes. I tried not to make a value judgment regarding his clothes. Several protesters ran after him and tackled him while shouting "Murderer! Murderer!"

I stared in disbelief at the aftermath of the scene. I only stuck around a few moments, as I had things to do and I wanted to see about spending some time with April after work. I recapped the events in my mind. An argument between a corporate-supporter and a different type of corporate-supporter who wanted different people in the corporations ended in a car-crash homicide, assuming the plus-sized woman actually ended up perishing from her head injuries.

Kabuki theater? A convenient argument for the government to allow while the real corporate oligarchs and government kleptocrats laughed on the way to the bank?

It was definitely possible.

These men and women — all of them involved — thought they were arguing for an important agenda. They thought they were taking up for their own interests, their own small piece of access to the 'system.' But, as this incident showed, they are nothing other than dogs. Dogs belonging to the oligarchs who own the corporations. I say that as a lover of dogs. But I love real dogs, not this kind of human-dog. These human-dogs, they both fought and argued, in their own way, in full obedient support, in a submissive posture, to the mega-corporations and the vast, unaccountable forces of capital (the foxes in the fiat capital hen-house) that backed them. Yes, these corporate dogs had slightly different visions of what the worker bees at those massive corporations should look like and how qualified they should be to make their wages and get access to their benefit plans. But, overall, they both supported the same master, the global corporations and their controlling global capital. They never questioned the products the corporations were selling, their woke advertising (which one side approved of), their corporate agenda. These 'dogs of the oligarchs' accepted the actions of the corporations, no matter how damaging and demeaning, at face value — they bowed to capital, they bowed to money. And, embarrassingly, they were allowed only the smallest of scraps. They loved things — stuff, products — and the dream of having more things. They were fighting amongst each other, all the time, over access to crumbs.

They were good corporate dogs in this way — literally fighting in the streets to continue to operate within the corporate-government program of enslavement. This ensured the 'system' would carry on, with or without a few changes around the fringe - those didn't matter to the oligarchs. And now one of the dogs was likely dead, one of them was badly injured, and one of them would be headed to prison. Crashing into a woman intentionally, in that manner (and with her woke politics), could get him put away for a few hundred years. It was all so tiresome.

For me, life went on. Immediately. I walked into EquiPark, totally un-phased. I didn't care about the dead woman — or the other masked-person who had been hit — and I am not ashamed to admit it. She hated me, I knew it simply from what her friends reported had been said about 'inclusivity' — this always boiled down to having a deeply-seated, rage-filled animus against people like myself. They always hated the idea of people like me, and they hated the actual versions of us as well. They want our stuff and access to the things created by people like me. They wanted us dead, or broke. Preferably both. We can know this from experience and take their words at face value. I tried to shrug it all off.

Settled in the office, I slugged my way through a stack of paper on my desk, then some e-mails. Then some corporate reports. Then a conference call. Then more e-mails.

Eventually, my mind wandered. I became bored with my work tasks and I logged onto my internet browser. Giants? No way, no more giants. I took my quest — my quest to understand the 'system' — all the way back to the establishment of the federal reserve. I spent the next hour reading about it. But, my initial reading on the topic took me off on a tangent.

The Warburg family!

I spent another half-hour reading about a few of them: Max, Paul and James. Max Warburg was the first to grab my attention — the guy was a key figure in the degenerate, ill-fated regime known as Weimar Germany. I was careful not to get bogged-down reading about Weimar itself, not too much. The things that took place in the once-great country of Germany during the Weimar era were gut-wrenching. They made me sick if I read too much about them; a subjugated and defeated people being debased in the worst ways possible. A broken people wallowing in a darkness, a sickness — an evil presence created by what were clearly Satanic humans (judging by their actions). So I abstained from further reading on Weimar. I moved on to Max's brother, Paul. It turned out Paul was a key figure in the establishment of the federal reserve 'system' in the United States. Fiat money, money that wasn't real. Printed money. The 'system' itself was murky, the moneyed interests who created it spoke in generalities with a seeming strategy of boring any regular person reading about it into giving up — perhaps even boring them to death if they had to.

I read and read. Soon, it would be time to go home — I planned on messaging April on my way out the door to see if she wanted to spend a couple hours with me. Before I stopped reading about the federal reserve and the Warburgs, a quote from Paul's son, James, jumped out at me from the screen.

"We shall have world government, whether or not we like it. The question is only whether world government will be achieved by consent or by conquest," James Warburg had said, on February 17, 1950.

Wow! I thought 'world government' was a 'conspiracy theory?' What was going on here?

The setting was a hearing on revisions to the charter of the United Nations. I found his commentary to be alarming for a few reasons. First, the nation — a combination of blood and soil, creating a cohesive group of people — had always been superior for determining the destiny of a particular group of people to the vague concept of the 'world.' The world included all sorts of different people. Different sub-groups, often with nothing at all in common. People were vastly different and the concept of lumping them together indiscriminately seemed to me to be quite repellent and vile. So the content of what James Warburg said was off-putting to me. To say the least. That, combined with his personal connections to Weimar Germany, one of the worst governments the world has ever seen (through his uncle) and to the federal reserve (through his father), made it even more conspicuous. On top of that, James was a key financial adviser to Franklin D. Roosevelt, a polio-stricken demon who was President of the United States of America for twelve years.

These three men clearly played a key role in the puzzle I was trying to piece together. The attack on individual nations (world government), the rootless, Satan-inspired attack on human decency (Weimar), and the attempt to use global capital (federal reserve and world bank), wielded like a club through corporations, to control the world.

Was this conspiracy still a conspiracy if they admitted the plan? These were real men, these Warburgs. The federal reserve was real. Weimar was real — a lot of the details about Weimar were erased from history because of the events that followed it, the rise of Adolf Hitler and everything else. The consensus was that Hitler rose to power in a vacuum. But Weimar was still real, we can still know what was done there by that specific regime — the details of that history have not yet been totally erased. The United Nations was real. And this man, James Warburg, was openly advocating for international "world" government in a recorded transcript.

It was all right there. It was a provable truth. I had heard people call this very fact pattern a 'conspiracy theory.' How is that possible? I felt like an insane person, trapped in a maze.

But, even with this concrete discovery, I felt some despair, as I knew pointing these facts out, publicly, would still be labeled as a conspiracy. I couldn't say anything, to anyone, without being labeled and defined as a nutcase, a conspirator, a radical. The thought brought me crashing back down to earth. I re-centered myself, in my little work-space. It was time. I had explored and seen enough for the day. The corporate dogs, the Warburgs, all of it.

My investigation of the iceberg, the 'system,' was through for the afternoon. Reality began to assert itself, the pull of life, social life, human interaction. Before I could message her, happily, April sent me a message on my smart phone asking what I was up to. I told her I was leaving work and asked if she wanted to hang out for a while. Let's go downtown, we can walk around and grab dinner and drinks. She agreed.

We met up an hour later and cruised around the downtown area on foot. We were coming out of some bar or other after sharing stories over a couple of drinks when April, as she walked alongside me, began to shake her head slightly. She didn't intend for me to see the shake, as far as I could tell. But I noticed, and she continued with the slight shake for another second or two before she saw me looking and stopped.

I didn't know what to do, but she saw that I saw and, once I saw that she saw that I saw, I panicked. A tiny panic, but nonetheless. I blurted out a question, asking her if she was okay. A deadly question for a man to ask a woman, but it came out before I could stop myself. She answered, "You seem distracted, Brandon."

Now, of course, these are hard words for a man to hear. I took stock of the circumstance. I took a breath. I was distracted, I admitted to myself. The 'system' was revealing itself to me! I was noticing connections between global capital and our corporations and the effect they had on society. But I knew I couldn't explain it to April without branding myself as an extremist, a nut-case. And, worst of all, a conspiracy theorist. Rather than explain my side of things, I just kept the discussion at surface level. I inquired further, trying to figure out exactly what was going on.

"I don't understand, April. I thought we were having a great time?"

"We are, I guess," she replied, squinting her eyes a tiny bit. "What is on your mind?"

A sense of dread came over me. This sounded like a huge drag on energy if we were going to do a relationship deep-dive. I hated those! I had time for three things in my life — sales at EquiPark, April and my investigation into the powerful forces that had shattered our communities, our nation.

"Just work, I think. But I feel like you're elsewhere."

I knew, instinctively, I was headed towards a dangerous fork in the road with April. I folded my arms across my chest.

"I am here, April, with you."

"What do you want?" she asked, her voice tinged with sadness.

I had no answer to this question. What did I want? I was coming to realize I didn't want to do more sales — I had to, for now, but I mean long-term. What was the point? My mind raced, at least triple the normal speed. I was stumped. I wanted to know about how things became as they were. I wanted to know about the things that changed our culture. I wanted to know who the driving force was for these changes. I wanted to know who was in control. I wanted to know why men and women complied with the things we saw around us. Why did we accept the things that were pushed upon us, the things that I was noticing, in rapid-fire succession? Bad food, big drug companies, mega-corporations running roughshod, big chemical companies, social changes no normal person — no-one — wanted yet everyone always tolerated. Where did these things come from? Could they be stopped?

But April wasn't talking about these things! Silly Brandon! She was talking about "us." She was asking what I wanted with her, from her. She was asking if I wanted to build something with her.

The question came from insecurity, I supposed. Time was ticking by, I needed to say something. Hesitation was my enemy, in this case. April would take hesitation as scorn, as a lack of attentiveness, as a dismissal. I knew it in my mind, in my heart.

I was unprepared! I didn't know what I wanted with April, and making something up on the fly would be render me ridiculous. April was emotionally intelligent, and blabbering something out wouldn't play. It would be like throwing a million dollars on one roulette number and hoping it hit. Same odds.

"Okay, I understand. Let's have fun tonight and let's talk about it in the next few days? I love being with you, if that's what you're asking."

"It is what I'm asking. I'm a thirty-one year old hospital admin worker, Brandon. I don't mind working, I've proven that the last ten years, but it's not what I want."

"I understand," I said, grabbing April's hand and holding it. I guided her to the right. We went into a Thai restaurant — a vibrant place with diverse recipes, actually from Thailand. We enjoyed a spicy meal together and left the relationship talk for another time, but I could tell the topic would have to be addressed in the next few days. The way of the world!

RABBIT CHEESE?

**

Somewhere in Antarctica

The penguin rack was brimming at maximum capacity. Hung by their feet, the hapless birds waited patiently for their turn to be fried in a large boiling vat of whale oil. The majority of them did not seem too upset about their circumstances. They were not so in love with life as to worry about being eaten by the giants, it was just another thing to them. A few of them, though, did not want to comply, they did not want to become a snack. Unfortunately for the penguins, they were the perfect size for Ranald, Eindride and Vilfred to pop into their mouth, whole, for nice hearty portion of fat and protein.

Seared in fat (by Mauve) to the perfect temperature, Penguin was a staple for the Repellent, the Low and the Vile.

The giants sat at a massive triangular iron table with an iron stake through the center and a glowing reddish orb connected to the top of the stake. Ranald sat high. Eindride had crossed one of his massive legs over the other. Vilfred the Vile was, from the looks of him, still struggling to wake up completely. He slouched, with one massive shoulder leaning off the left side of the chair.

"Before we start, where are the females?" asked Ranald.

"They are all in their quarters," replied Vilfred. "My Gerd the Wide, my shining star — my love — probably eating a massive pile of pemmican mash topped with seal gravy. She drives me to the brink, that one. Inger the Inquisitive, no doubt writing in her journal, probably about her memory of the Grand Exit or reflecting on her reading texts from the degenerate human women who live only with cats. Runa the Believer, always worshiping and reading her Bible. Always."

"How are things with you and Inger, Eindride? Before the hibernation I recall a massive row..." inquired Vilfred.

"Well, things were fine this morning, better than they have been," replied Eindride.

"What was the fight about?" asked Vilfred, lover of conflict.

"She seemed to be feeling some vague discontent with our way of life. I didn't understand it."

"Vague discontent?" said Ranald, looking for more explanation.

"Yes, she wasn't happy, I could see it on her face. And it manifest itself in her kicking my shins, whenever she could."

"She kicked your shins? Impertinent! Did you spank her on her hind quarters?" asked Vilfred in a rushed voice.

"I didn't mean she kicked me literally, Vilfred. I mean she would take out her personal frustrations on me," replied Eindride.

"That's what I'm asking. What was the source of the unhappiness? Did you figure it out?" Ranald pressed.

"Well, it seemed she was taking no pleasure in life. In her chores and her duties. And it showed on her face," replied Eindride.

"I wonder why?"

"Well, you know, all three of them got that device hooked up. But Inger has taken the addiction to the content. She even asked Tyferius if he could help her set up an account on the human photography site they call InstantGram. I made sure Tyferius did not comply.

"I don't even know what any of that means!" interjected the Vile.

"You know, the thing — the device — we recovered from the human outpost and Tyferius connected to the stars. I can't stand it. But on the device, she would read."

"About what?"

"Phwwwt. Everything. But once, I caught her reading about something called 'emancipation,'" said Eindride, shaking his gigantic head.

"Ayyy, freedom," said Vilfred, nodding his head. "Freedom to do and say as you please."

"Yes, but from what? There is no such thing as true emancipation. If she did not do her feminine duties, she would not benefit from what everyone else does. Love is a form of obligation. Without those, she is not my wife; I have masculine obligations to her as well, husbandly obligations."

"And she sees wifery as slavery?" asked Ranald.

"The words she read on the device poisoned her mind. I don't run around claiming to be a slave, a victim, because I need to — with you, my brothers — catch our food and cut our firewood and keep discipline and order among the family. We do our part, we have for thousands of years. Everyone must do their part!" said Eindride, his voice growing more excited at the end of his speech.

"Who wrote the words, let's go smash their heads like pumpkins," said Vilfred, his face lighting up at the thought of violence.

"I asked Tyferius to spy on the device. He told me the subversive filth is written by a very specific band of human women. These human women, they live alone, in the cities, with only small cats and large boxes of wine — like modern witches. They complain about everything a human woman does in cooperation with a human man is to be called oppression. Over and over. They started this a hundred years ago, in earnest. Their goals are murky, perhaps only deconstruction of the family, the spread of misery — but of course they do not position it that way. Anyhow, perhaps there is no plan beyond that," said Eindride the Low.

The three giants mused in silence for a moment.

"Everywhere there is obligation. For the females and for us, the males. Both sexes play their part. Ours is harder if we are honest about it," said Ranald. "Perhaps they are mad about what happens when we are finished on any given day and we drink much grog and make merry. And there are other things, I'm sure, we do to them which make them feel we have the better deal. But things are as they are."

"They resent!" shouted Vilfred.

"Resentment can drive a giant to the brink. I am watching her carefully. I try to help her and get her off of the device whenever I can," said Eindride.

"It is a major disappointment for me. I mellowed the day I saw Runa," said Ranald, shaking his head. "It was near the end of the violent times, and there were still many female giants. I did less violence and I stopped looking at other females, she calmed me down — restrained me in a way. Even though some may not make the same observation, it is true."

"Ayyy. Well, in fairness there are no unattached females here and it makes things very simple. We have the nice opportunity to provide one-on-one discipline for the female," said the Vile.

"The fact remains, Inger needs a new outlet. I would love to get her more interested in cooking, or sewing. Something like that. Maybe cleaning? We are still arguing, and the toxins, written by those human women, float around in Inger's mind and need to be countered," said Eindride, with a slight frown.

"I still say smash the heads of the entire tribe of human women who wrote the garbage. Let's take the ship, find them, and smash their little bodies into a bloody pulp. We can erase their subversive garbage from existence. Problem solved," said Vilfred.

"It sounds more and more necessary," agreed Eindride.

"Ayyy."

"Enough about the females. How are the young ones?" asked Ranald.

"Games, no doubt. I have told them a million times not to play smear the reindeer but they still persist. The youngest one, Chasdon the Long, it seems as if he smears two reindeer a day for no reason. Sometimes he smashes them and sometimes he runs them through with a spear," said Eindride.

"This needs to stop. Our reputation is bad enough from the old days — from the ground battles after the Dark One lost the heavens to the Light and we were all cast out," replied Ranald.

"Let's not worry about it. No one is watching," said Vilfred.

"If this — smear the reindeer — is ever known by men, it will make us look as they expect we still are. We will need allies for our fight, human allies."

"No human is here in the cold, Ranald. When there is an expedition, we know about it. Nobody cares what we do, anymore. We are not a threat. I wish we were!" said Vilfred.

"Habit, Vilfred. Let's create habit for Chasdon and the others so we all do as we should do."

"Ayyy. When you put it that way, I don't disagree," said Vilfred.

"So, we can only kill animals we intend to eat. They are our brothers and sisters! If they sacrifice themselves for us, that is acceptable — ayyy, it is good and well — but for nothing? That is bad and cruel. There is no reason for it. Our destruction, from the Great Change onward, needs to be for good purpose. Tell the young ones to do something else. Build them a sled," said Ranald.

"I do, my brother. And I will tell them to build their own bloody sled. I am no carpenter or iron-smith by God! I'm a warrior!" replied Vilfred.

"Then against whom do you fight?" asked Ranald.

"That is the problem with being a warrior in this desolate place! I only see creatures not worthy of a fight. Even the white bear — a magnificent creature — does not have a chance against me. I won't fight him, I bear no grievance against him."

"Never-mind that. Tell the young ones so they understand and comply," stated Ranald, firmly. "If they don't understand, use corporal force on their hind quarters to get the message through, seven times."

"I will, it is settled," replied Vilfred the Vile, swilling grog from a fresh barrel that the purple nook-demon had brought him.

At present, the nook-demon was standing outside of his nook, by the multi-purpose fryer, a large, ornate iron cask that had obviously been hand-detailed after casting — it was thousands of years old and the craftsmanship showed. The nook-Demon had grabbed three fresh penguins and, after rubbing each of their bellies in a circular scratching motion for five seconds to thank them for the sustenance provided by meat and blubber — he dunked them, head first into the boiling whale oil. None of the penguins let out a peep, much less a scream. They knew it was their time. The nook-demon had a blank expression on his blocky face. He waited patiently as the penguins cooked through and then brought them to the giants, who popped them into their mouths, chewed and swallowed them down.

"Is everyone ready to start? Are you fully awake, brother Vilfred?" said Ranald, again, with a toothy smile.

"I am awake," said the Vile. "Haven't you heard me yelling? My voice echoes through the entire chamber. I fill the chamber with energy and life!"

"Very well, then we shall start. We have reached the time for action. We have been banished to this spot for hundreds of years... and while there is much to love about it — the endless supply of crabeater seal, the penguins... the beautiful white horizon of ice and snow, many times under a beautiful sky..."

"I love penguin poppers," interrupted Eindride, longingly. "Mauve, stuff the next batch of 'gwin with bear cheese before they enter the fryer, my demon-servant."

"Bear cheese?" ventured the Vile. "What is bear cheese? A, ha, a ha!"

"The cheese comes from the rabbit, Eindride," stated Ranald, matter-of-fact in tone.

"I thought it came from the bear?"

"No, brother. We don't have a bear."

"This is a mystery of the spoken word I will never understand!"

"Pampered rabbit, no milk for cheese many weeks. He spoiled! I kill rabbit but Ranald am NOT allow," mumbled Mauve.

A fat rabbit sat on a chiseled concrete block that was topped with velveteen pillows, under a chandelier filled with extravagant candles. It was surrounded by cabbage and other vegetables. It lounged on its back legs, leaning back with its ample belly protruding. Its face seemed to show contemplation and knowledge. Mauve turned to the rabbit, saying, "Make milk or stew, dumb rabbit-face. Patience am limit."

The rabbit seemed to scowl. It chewed on cabbage for a moment while staring at Mauve, as if assessing a threat. Seconds later, the portly rabbit's expression returned to a calm, knowing look. It chewed more cabbage.

While the grudge match between Mauve the nook-demon and the chubby rabbit played out, Ranald continued, "...While there is much to love about it, we have a purpose... evolved over time. Two thousand years ago, we were sent here to serve a certain master. The fallen one. The Bringer-of-Light who became the Prince of Darkness. He was our 'god', our master, our ruler," said Ranald.

"We did much damage for him in ancient times," said the Vile. "I remember smashing whole villages who banned his ways and rooted-out his supporters, with fire at the stake. When they burned one of his I destroyed the lives of ten of theirs with my iron hammer and my metal knuckles. I have many notches on the handle of my great hammer. You know this to be true, my brothers."

"We did great damage at the time!" said the Low. "The stinky men and their unwashed wenches lived in constant fear! They did nothing without looking over their shoulder. Those were the days. I was always surprised they continued to keep up the fight. Some of them would never submit, even to my club and your axe and hammer, my brothers."

The Repellent continued, "Do not look back so fondly, Low. Times have changed. It was once both necessary and, let's admit, we took great pleasure in serving him who gave us the ability to reign for him here on earth — the people felt abandoned by God. He reigned below, but appeared with us many-a-day. We were his favorites. But, for hundreds of years, now, we have been replaced."

"He gives us no quarter!"

"No benefits!"

"Our opportunities are few! In fact, they are none!"

"Yes. We have no work, let's face it. And with no work, there is no minimum level of support and everything we eat we catch ourselves! We have been abandoned by our master, who for hundreds of years commanded us closely."

"Why must we have a rabbit for cheese? We can't even get a goat! This is embarrassing and not worthy of our proud race."

Only Mauve glanced over at the rabbit. Mauve muttered, "Are defecate, lucky protected." The rabbit heard him and made a face showing discomfort.

"We had a goat, Vile — you ate it," said Eindride.

"No matter! It is gone," replied Vile indignantly.

"Well, one thing relates to the other," said the Low, not willing to drop the discussion easily.

"Here is what happened, brothers," said Ranald. "We have been out-flanked by his new servants who, through their clever fraud, do more damage than we ever could by force, and they do it every day — while we need to hibernate for half of each year to stay strong and virile. We know who these people are, we can notice patterns and name them. They hide in plain sight like lizards."

"They shall be named!" hollered the Vile.

"They shall, they will shrink back in fear when we first name them and then we will smash their heads!" echoed the Low.

"And, most importantly, we have the plan to defeat them, to take the source of their evil power from them. We worked it out with the Doctor," said Ranald.

"The drill will take what they have, which will become ours!" exclaimed Eindride.

"It will not work," disagreed Vilfred the Vile. "I don't care what plan you make. Something will happen and we will end up running amok. The plan will not hold, I am certain of it."

As the giants continued speaking, the nook-demon — Mauve — stomped over. Fifteen feet tall, square, heaviest in his shoulders and haunches — forearms the size of a log — a mass of muscle and metal spikes, with violent eyes coated, only once-over, with obedience brought about by fear of the giants' violent tendencies. One fearsome horn. A look in his eye of defiant subservience. His defiance fought against the subservience and lost, every time, every day. The nook-demon knew his frame and physical capabilities, while overpowering against most foes, were no match for the Repellent, the Low and the Vile. Not for a minute, not a chance.

As he stomped over to the giants, he had one penguin in each arm, and one he had attached to a hook on a chain-link rope around his next. He dropped one penguin in front of each giant and said "Much respect, enjoy penguin!" then walked back to his nook.

"Let us eat these squat, hearty penguins and then talk about the gold, the piles and bars of gold shall set us free," said Ranald. "Mauve," he continued, addressing the nook-demon by name, "bring us three more barrels of grog."

Mauve stomped off, bringing back the barrels a few moments later (saying "Grog to drink" as he delivered it). The giants opened the barrels and chugged the grog.

"Let us address and resolve on the plan now, shall we?" asked Ranald, addressing his brothers with a serious look on his face. "This is an important time, a pivotal moment in our history."

"It will end badly, my friends and brothers," said the Vile. "It always does."

PETTY DESTRUCTION

✱✱

When I dropped April off after the Thai dinner, my mind was heavy at first. But soon, I was in my digital comfort zone, on my computer — doing my research.

The video website — the one where I had watched the CGI rendition of ice-giants — served me with a pop-up notification for a video. I read the description. The video was about Michael and his angels fighting against the dragon. The battle, apparently, was ferocious. But the dragon and his angels lost. The dragon and his angels lost the fight, and were hurled down, from heaven, to earth. I wondered why I had been sent this notification — and then I saw one of the key words for the video was "giants." The artificial intelligence from the video site had, no doubt, served the notification to me based on my prior video investigation of these Biblical legends. Incredible, I thought. Were giants involved in the battle for heaven? Or were they only involved on the earthly side?

No matter! I was curious, of course, but there were other things I had on my mind of more importance. They didn't involve giants, and, frankly, they didn't involve April, either.

I wanted to go back to the Warburgs. My investigation had been so fruitful. Weimar Germany, the federal reserve, the adviser to FDR who backed one world government and the elimination of distinct peoples.

Was there more there? That family was an atrocity! A major stain on humanity, responsible for so many bad things.

There were more Warburgs. Otto Warburg became president of the World Zionist Organization in nineteen eleven. I knew nothing about the organization and what it stood for. I didn't even know what the word 'Zionist' meant. I looked into it, absorbing available information for almost an hour.

I was beginning to get fatigued when I came across the name of yet another Warburg. Carola, the daughter of Felix. She married into the Rothschild family — they had loads of money and gold — in nineteen sixteen, via Walter Nathan Rothschild.

I sat and thought. This family was an important nexus between governmental affairs and international capital. Federal reserve, world government, Weimar, ties to the Rothschild's money and open advocacy for United Nations or world government supremacy. Why had I never heard of them before?

I read, ravenously, as much content as I could find on this family. I filed away the knowledge.

Soon, I was worn out and dragged myself into bed. I slept soundly, waking early to get out to EquiPark. I performed my usual routine, stopping for coffee on the way to my office cubicle.

When I arrived, there was a note from a woman named Jazmine asking me to come see her in Human Resources when I arrived. I did. I found the office marked Jazmine and walked in.

"Hi, I'm Brandon."

"Oh, thanks for stopping by. I am sorry to tell you I've been asked to let you go from EquiPark."

I was stunned but managed to not show it. At least, I didn't think I did.

"Really? I thought things were going well," I replied.

"We had no issues for performance, but you missed two mandatory sensitivity training sessions."

"Sensi... I didn't even know I did. That's so strange. I'm sensitive to my calendar but I guess I didn't see the notices. Hmm, wow," I said.

"Well, you did, we track everyone's entry bi-o-metric-ally for those special sessions. Sensitivity and in-clu-siv-i-ty are the key — the most important thing — for EquiPark," said the woman, slowing herself down for words she found tricky to pronounce.

"I thought we bought and sold commercial real estate?"

"Well, we do — but the most important thing is we do it in a very respectful fashion, inclusive of everyone and with total deference to our past legacies of oppression."

"Oppression... I'm a real estate salesman. Oppression? And when was I not respectful?" I asked, showing only a touch of agitation.

"That's not the point. It's not about your actions, other than not attending the sessions. They were mandatory and there are no warnings for a topic as serious as sensitivity."

My eyes were wide. I had some money stashed away, so I didn't panic. Instead, staring at her hair, which was a garish, dyed blonde, I laughed.

"Ha ha. Okay. See ya, Jazzy."

I turned and walked out. My time at EquiPark was over. I had welcomed the drudgery and tedium of the work, because I made decent money. I had embraced my boredom, given over to it. And giving over to boredom let me sell plenty of properties. But I would find something else. I headed back to my office and looked around. It worked out well, because I didn't have too much stuff in there. In fact, I didn't grab anything other than my computer bag before I walked out to my car.

A few weeks went by, and I spent them not sulking, but in a flurry of measured and controlled activity. My days were full but the pace was not hectic, not at all. I went to the gym every other day, did a long walk by the creek in the afternoons, spent about an hour a day looking around for new possible jobs. My free time I spent understanding the world of international capital and the push for world government. Bernard Baruch, Josef Stalin's ties to the Rothschild family, the financing behind Cecil Rhodes' diamond operations, Olof Aschberg — these were all names and topics I spent time researching.

The whole sensitivity training firing gnawed at me. It chewed. It was galling, but EquiPark was interchangeable with any other mega-corporation, I figured. I had a few colleagues whom I liked, but no close friends working there. I figured it was best to move on.

My relationship with April went sideways for a couple of weeks, and then it was over. After the conversation we had on the night of the Thai food dinner, we never had the follow up — the deep-dive into our relationship status. Honestly, I didn't have the energy for it. My firing from EquiPark was a distraction, it was unsettling. The way I had interpreted the line of questioning from April was to say she wanted more from me, perhaps marriage. When I had slept on it for a couple of days, I reached a level of clarity on my thoughts regarding the topic, and I decided I didn't want more, not with April.

I liked her well enough, that's for sure. She was an entirely decent person with a good heart. She was cute, and cool. We shared a lot of laughs. But, in the back of my mind, at least, I didn't want to close the door on the idea of having a family. And April was thirty-one and planted, with roots, in a cubicle, mostly cleaning up the fallout from what big food and big pharma were pushing down the throats of the people. If it took a couple years to get her out of the cubicle, married and starting to think about a family, she would be pushing thirty-five years old. It just wasn't a fit for me. I didn't blame April for what corporations and industry (with their partners in the government) did to people, especially women. Big food did the damage to the people's health and big pharma feigned the "repair phase," mostly by pushing prescription pharmaceuticals on the damaged populace. April was a cog in their cash machine, doing their paperwork, tracking their profits. She had been propagandized to believe her job — which, let's face it, didn't pay all that much — was part of 'having it all.' She thought she had leaned in; from my vantage point it looked as if she got leaned on.

For me, she was too old — and she deserved the chance to find someone she could be with, long term. I was content to let our time fade away. I wasn't on digital media, so I didn't even have any public commemoration of the relationship needing to be wiped away.

That didn't happen, though, since she pressed me as to what was going on. I think she was looking for the follow-up conversation.

She called one day and we spoke for awhile. The key part of the discussion occurred when she asked me, "So, obviously I'm taking the hint... you don't want anything serious with me."

"I don't, April."

"Can I ask why?" she asked, emotionally.

"In the back of my mind, I was thinking I might want kids. I don't know how to say this so I'll just say it: I'm going to go younger, if I can find someone."

There was a long pause, and I thought I heard her sobbing.

"I'm too old?"

"Well, I didn't word it that way when I said it, but I'm going younger. If I can find someone right for me, of course. I know you will find someone, April. You're a lovely person."

A torrent of angry words came through the line. I won't recount them here. I parried for a minute and then excused myself, hanging up the phone and moving on with my day. The conversation took place on President's Day, so I also wished her a safe holiday before I clicked off the line.

With April and the hold-over conversation out of the way, I launched all the way into my research. I still enjoyed robust activity, both at the gym and outdoors. But I had time to research global finance for many hours, every day. Days went by like this. Then weeks. Soon, I had a thick dossier file documenting and organizing my filings. I spent weeks studying the Pan-European Union. It was strange, but I swear the content creators on the internet were trying to disguise the fact that this organization was the predecessor to the current European Union — the one bursting at its seams with unhappy, over-taxed citizens who had become surrounded with foreign influence, much of it from the third-world. The founder of the plan, Richard von Coudenhove-Kalergi, was a friend of Louis Nathaniel Rothschild — and Rothschild introduced Richard to Max Warburg, Paul Warburg and Bernard Baruch — names I had encountered previously and therefore knew much about their toxic ideas.

Words and thoughts swam through my mind — deformation, deviation, decadence, subversion, uncertainty, compromise, attenuation... catastrophe. Restoration and tradition were in there too, but these positive thoughts were outnumbered. They were swamped.

I ended the session when things got too heavy. Sitting alone, in front of my computer (again) — fretting about the 'system' and feeling somewhat melancholy about the state of human affairs. I knew I wouldn't end my investigation, but I convinced myself I had enough for the day. Putting the Warburgs and von Coudenhove-Kalergi aside for a moment, I decided to venture out for a drink. I went to my favorite bar — a hole-in-the-wall called Oswald's. It was grungy, a bit grimy. It had no frills, but I liked it. Instead of my usual martini, I ordered a whiskey, neat from the bartender, an older fellow named George.

Soon, I had struck up a conversation with a man sitting next to me (to be perfectly candid, he struck the conversation up with me). I had a strange feeling about him, as if I had met him before or there was something otherwise familiar about him. He was a doctor, he said, and he seemed to be a few drinks in. Or maybe he was just very talkative. He was telling me all about his brother — an explorer, apparently. The conversation went on, a one-sided affair, but I was enjoying it. The brother led an expedition into Greenland. He was a biologist and he went there to study the fauna. Almost finished with my third whiskey (which was one past my usual limit), I was ready to wrap up the night and get home, when the doctor — who told me Hogan Lowd was his name — pulled me closer to him and took a conspiratorial tone. Whether or not he was inebriated, he was quite coherent. He didn't slur his words and he expressed his thoughts very clearly. I wondered if the drink caused his inhibitions to be lowered, because he appeared as if he were ready to tell me something of tremendous importance. It seemed impossible that he had carefully considered his decision to tell me whatever it was he was about to say.

He puffed on his hand-rolled cigar a couple of times, producing a few billows of smoke. That was illegal, of course, but I gathered that Dr. Lowd had a special clearance to smoke at Oswald's. Or, he just did it anyway. His posture, even while sitting at the bar counter, was absolutely impeccable. He had the look of a classic southern gentleman. Yet, here he was in Northern California, sitting next to yours truly.

"I'm taking down the 'system.' The entire 'system.' At least if enough people join me," said Dr. Lowd.

"What?" I asked, looking for him to expand on the meaning of his comment.

"The 'system,' Brandon. We can break it. We're breaking it, with the little things."

"I don't know what you mean, Doctor," I said, with a quizzical look on my face. I sipped my whiskey. "Break what?"

"I founded a group, years ago, to work to bring the 'system' to its knees. I'm not bragging, but I'm a known anti-corporate."

I decided to project ignorance, I wasn't completely comfortable letting him know I too had been looking into the 'system' as well. So I stayed silent, except to ask him, very simply, "How?"

"Petty destruction! Petty destruction!" he hollered back at me.

I laughed, involuntarily. What a character!

"Ha! What in the heck is petty destruction?"

"Okay, look at it this way. We are at the end of the American Empire, it can't be sustained. No values. None! Look around! It's totally controlled by Globo — that's what I call the global corporate and financial interests by the way. To cremate the carcass of the American Empire — so we can begin to attack Globo — we do small acts to lower the morale of the remaining believers and overwhelm the 'system' with small costs and dysfunction."

"That's, umm, hilarious, I think," I said, staring at the doctor intensely.

"I'm deadly serious, Brandon. The 'system' is run by the corporations, the only thing they care about is money and servitude. You think Big Health cares about people? Think again. It's a factory. I became a doctor to try to help people, and all it did was help me see corporate corruption. They act in bad faith!" said Lowd, eyes ablaze.

"The money drives it all, hmm," I replied, thinking of my own study of global finance and its ties to aggressive, one-world government. The doctor was focused on the corporations in his rant. I could respect that, I had also tied them in, as the close connection to global capital was obvious, but I was focusing my reading on finance and the quest for neo-liberal world government and the dissolution of human differences, the dissolution of humanity itself.

"So, we take it from them!" he said, with the volume of a whisper and the emphasis of a shout.

"You steal money? I'm confused."

"No, they are too smart for that. Remember what I said. Petty destruction. We damage things where we can. If they fix the damage, it costs money. If they don't fix it, the deterioration adds up. When the deterioration hits a critical mass, trash starts to appear everywhere. The area gives over to people who don't have the capacity to manage industrial communities, everyone else retreats to reform a new community. The abandon city sucks more resources up because of the extra policing and welfare and the breakdown of housing and other buildings because the people who remain don't have the capacity to maintain the infrastructure. Drugs and violence, inevitably, creep in. Think of Detroit. Think of Baltimore."

"But that's a bad thing! How does turning places into a disaster zone help anybody? I don't get it. But your concept is so very interesting," I mused. I held my cards close to the vest. Of course, my research was purely theoretical and I had not tried to implement any practical measures of this, or any, sort.

"The disaster zone is not the endgame. Its a necessary step along a path to revolution, restoration... whatever you want to call it. But for that to happen, the American Empire in its current form needs to be swept away. We have to go through Petty Destruction to get to non-compliance and, ultimately, a new country after collapse. The hope is that at the end of the American Empire there is still enough will and energy among people — people like the Founding Fathers — so we can try again. It's a long shot, but it's better than letting Globo win uncontested. We want to bring about the end of commercial finance — on a mega-scale at least. For localized industry there should be a sane way to include debt as long as there are strict usury laws."

"I'm surprised your group has lasted this long when you tell random strangers what you are doing."

"Ha! You're sharp," replied Dr. Lowd.

"I'm serious. That stuff is not legal, Doc. Be careful."

"We're fragmented and dispersed. We communicate in person. They can't catch us. Even with what I said to you... if you went to the feds, I'll say I was joking, or deny it. No proof. Besides, you have the look about you. You're one of us, you're not going to report me," he said, recalcitrant.

"They have surveillance everywhere. Just be careful. What look do I have, by the way?"

"I have a sense about you. You are questioning the 'system.' I can tell," he said, pointing in the direction of his own eyes.

"Maybe I am... or maybe I'm not," I said, deflecting his lucky guess while wondering how it was possible. How did Doctor Lowd know that I was looking into things?"

"You are, you're questioning Globo. You are going to fight the 'system.' Call it a hunch."

I paused. The coincidence, this guess, was enough to throw me off. What were the chances? How did he get inside my head so he could do this little dance in there? A bit frazzled, I decided to re-center the conversation.

"So, Dr. Lowd, give me some examples of petty destruction, if you would. How? What?"

"It's all techniques we have come up with to damage infrastructure in ways designed to sap the corporate government's kleptocrat assets and are very expensive to fix or clean up. We developed an expanding super-glue compound we can use to destroy any federal, state or city machine that gets paid by credit card. It's a small tube and you squeeze it into the credit card slot — we make it from a simple compound and the cost to us is negligible. It disables the entire machine."

"You hit their revenue sources where you can. Mmm-hmm. A hit and run."

"We can freeze on-the-ground revenue and create massive replacement costs for an entire area with just a handful of operatives. And when they replace the machines, we can do it again. Another example, we have a little plug blaster..."

"A plug blaster?" I interrupted. This was becoming fanciful!

"Yeah..."

"That's incredible."

"Also remind me to tell you about air conditioners."

"Umm, okay."

"So, the plug blaster... we can use it to create potholes. Poke the sharp iron tip into the concrete, walk away, and two minutes later the blaster, working on a timer, makes a three foot crater in the street. Incredibly disruptive. We can make them for a nickel, each. Public services won't be able to keep up. It will bring down entire areas, financially. We started that part of the program about a month ago. Petty destruction."

"It seems like the first one would be an annoyance but they don't receive most of the money they take by credit card. The second one has potential, if you can do it on a mass scale without getting caught. There are a lot of cameras on the streets."

"We have methods to avoid detection by camera."

"What's the air conditioner thing?" I asked, feeling mellowed by the whiskey and quite intrigued by this character, this Dr. Lowd.

"Well, we can't have a proper revolution in large part because of air conditioners. They let people get complacent. They let people become overweight, because it is not a burden to carry an extra hundred or two hundred pounds when you can remain at a comfortable temperature, lolling about watching Netflix. Also, the natural heat deters runaway eating, it suppresses appetite. But, most importantly, with the temperature control comes too much tolerance."

"Tolerance?"

"Yeah. Tolerance for degeneracy and corruption. When the people are kept comfortable, they are pacified. They will never fight if they are comfortable. Think about it."

"So you want to take away air conditioners to start a revolution?"

"We melt them down, we have a unique device. We are just starting our attack on air conditioners. It has to be done."

I waited for Dr. Lowd to give me a sign he was joking. That never came. Instead, he went on, speaking in a low, conspiratorial voice.

"And here's the thing, Brandon. The point of Petty Destruction is, for sure, lost revenue and high replacement cost. But there's an overarching concept in play, we think it's very valuable."

"Oh? And what's that?"

"Non-compliance."

"Non-compliance," I repeated.

"Yes, when people see the Petty Destruction — when there are potholes every quarter mile — or every ten yards, however it ends up — on the roads, when they can't comply with requirements to pay things like parking meters because they are sealed shut with glue — they also start to think, 'why am I paying for this anyway?' They realize they already pay taxes and now they have to pay after-tax money to park their car — and they can't even do it because the city or county can't maintain the equipment. There's incredible frustration. It may stay below the surface, but eventually we hope it boils over. If they are also hot and uncomfortable in the summer months, tempers will run short, and we think it will happen."

"Doc, this is wild."

"Well, if people stop participating in the 'system' dictated to them by and for the benefit of the mega-corporations, by definition the 'system' will end. There is a requirement of mass participation."

I decided to go deeper into the conversation. Up until this point, I had just been listening with short responses.

"Wouldn't there have to be a layer on top of all the mega-corporations? Or is it a coincidence that they all act the same way and push the same talking points? Wouldn't it be a layer on top of the corporations that controls the governments by controlling the capital? Of course, the capital generated by the corporations feeds back through the loop. Tax the people as heavily as you can, leaving them enough money to service their debt. So, essentially, capital and the corporations own everything and all the resources — the money — it's all theirs. All of it, it's just a matter of time. Even if someone is holding on to some of it at any given time. That's the 'system,' right?"

The genial doctor nodded, "I think that's it. I just assume a layer on top of my discussion," he replied. "We have to get to non-compliance. We have to get to the non-compliance phase to take this structure down."

I felt dizzy — an interesting discussion combined with some whiskey — that did the trick.

"I wonder if it will ever happen. People seem miserable and content at the same time. I can't explain it... content in their misery with their easy access to big food, big entertainment and whatever their other distractions are... I don't think they will revolt. It's too easy to just go with it and whittle away time," I said.

"But... remember. That's why we hit the air conditioning. People wouldn't stand for the corruption if they didn't have air conditioning. That's the pacifier, along with junk food, alcohol, stuff like that."

"Wow!" I exclaimed.

We talked on for another hour, but the major points remained the same. I racked my brain to think about how Doctor Lowd had decided to approach me. How could he know about me? It made me think back to my brother's Facebook post — the one where it seemed as if he was spying on my computer activities. A wave of paranoia crashed down on me like a Tsunami — but it went away quickly as I assured myself these were coincidences. No one was watching my internet activities, I told myself. Right? Eventually, Doctor Lowd and I parted ways and I walked out of Oswald's to head home for the night. The takeaways from the conversation stayed close: Petty Destruction! Non-compliance!

NATURAL RESISTANCE

**

I spent a couple hours of each day, over the next couple of weeks, trying to find myself a new cubicle to inhabit. What good is a cubicle-monkey without a cubicle? I exchanged e-mails with corporate folks who had posted this or that job listing, things I found on the internet. I maintained the other parts of my schedule, going to the gym every other day and taking my river walk on a daily basis. I steered clear of booze and women, for the most part. It was a re-set, of sorts. In my e-mails to the corporate folks, I simply tried to pretend, for the folks I interacted with in human resources that I was an inclusive automaton. A corporate 'system'-supporting-drone born to push their lousy product. My resume went out right and left. It wasn't that I was desperate for a job — I wasn't. But I had time on my hands. I, of course, continued my investigations on-line.

The dating world kept calling out to me. But most of the single women I encountered in my circles were in their thirties. I didn't need to get right back on the merry-go-round. Looking back on my last half-dozen relationships, I couldn't tell whether I was the carousel or the carousel rider. Did it even matter? It would probably end in similar fashion, so I decided to hold off for a while.

My investigation was plugging along, and I got lost, again, in the world of international capital — on the internet — for a couple of hours that night.

I fell asleep a little while later and then a few days went by until I found myself in the office of a new corporation, interviewing for a sales job. The meeting moved along at a brisk pace, possibly owing to the amount of caffeine I had pumping through my body. I had two large espresso drinks prior to heading in, and I was jittery.

It wasn't nerves, it was purely chemical, coffee-induced. Since the only reason for my taking the interview had been a slight case of boredom — I wasn't bored with my investigation but I didn't feel that I could justify doing it full-time, since there was no goal attached to the pursuit and I had always been a goal-oriented person.

This job would be sufficient to fill some time, and still there would be plenty of time to notice things and investigate the 'system.'

The interview ended up going well, with my primary contact at the company being an odd, yet relatively cheerful plump fellow with a high-pitched voice and rosy cheeks. Their corporate office was extremely casual, and the fellow was wearing a NASA t-shirt, shorts and sandals. His outfit made me thing of Rory who viewed NASA (and almost everything else) as a scam. Anyhow, I could tell the man was very sensitive, if you know what I mean. I didn't ask, and he didn't tell. And the interview went on like this. The company — a drug maker called MindSmash — wanted me to do something different than my pure sales jobs in the past. They wanted me to spend half of my time in the sales department, and half as a liaison with the marketing department. This was new to me, and I didn't mind the concept. Why not open up a fresh perspective? Expand my horizons?

The offer came in a week later and, after some back and forth we agreed on terms. I was to begin the following Monday. Things went swimmingly at first. I had a little office, it wasn't even a cubicle. I went through the list of assigned leads and made my sales calls. As I said, MindSmash was a big pharmaceutical company. It was owned, in large part, by a big-money family out of Chicago. The chairman of the board was named Justine Pratter (he used to be known as Jeremy Pratter). The company sold all types of drugs.

Their biggest categories were anti-depressants and pain-killers. A little break from the human condition.

I was assigned to study the interplay of our sales tactics with the marketing for the anti-depressants. The company had an overall anti-depressant use rate of one hundred and ten users out of every ten thousand Americans. Not bad. That purchase rate generated a lot of dollars for the parent corporation. The task we faced, however, was to raise the number from one hundred and ten to two hundred and twenty. They wanted us to double the users of the psychotic drug!

I began intense studies of our sales tactics and understood them well. It took me another six weeks to gain a deep understanding of the marketing side of things. I went through all of the print ads, the television spots, the radio clips. I also looked at the digital campaign. I formed an opinion and typed it into a detailed e-mail to the head of the marketing department, with a copy to my direct boss. By all measures, it was a good e-mail. My reasoning was sound. I provided evidence and comparisons for my claims.

It didn't land well with marketing, though. I couldn't put my finger on it, as to the question of why. Everything I said was laid out clearly, and I was right. There was no connection from product advertising to the call to action to buy from our peak sales demographics. Instead, the marketing sat at the fringes, pushing behaviors which most of our customers had no interest in — things I assumed were of interest to Justine Pratter. I received a curt response to my e-mail saying it would be reviewed by the director of marketing, Miranda Hoffman. Afterword, a couple days went by where I didn't hear anything.

Then, on a Wednesday, I got a notice from the director of marketing herself, letting me know she would be visiting our office the following day — she asked me to cancel anything else I may have had scheduled in order to accommodate the hour time slot she requested.

I complied.

I wasn't worried about the meeting, not at all. I had everything in a tight row — I knew my data, so I would see what the lady said and then react calmly with facts. Instead of focusing on my drug-peddling job, I decided to continue my on-line research into the 'system.' But, unlike most of my prior sessions, this one wasn't very productive. I ended up clicking on one wrong link, somewhere along the line, and I was very quickly catapulted from a website where I was reading an article about Bernard Baruch to one called "Birds Aren't Real." Birds, they claimed, were CIA drones. First giants, now drone-birds? It degenerated from there, I was rolling down a digital hill, clicking links about the illuminati, JFK, the moon landing, chemtrails, toxins in food ... and on and on. A couple hours later, I didn't know which way was up. Eventually, having passed a sufficient amount of time, I got in bed and went to sleep.

The following day, I had settled into my office and was going over my sales reporting. I was so engaged in the data I lost track of the time.

My eyes flashed upward from my computer screen when I heard a voice say "Is that Mister Brooks?"

"I am, call me Brandon," I responded, folding down the lid on my computer. "You must be Miranda."

The lady, Miranda Hoffman, barged into my office like a bull — sandals with a small heel, maybe an inch and a half, gold slacks, blue blouse — her hair was brown and tied into a bun, her eyes were brown as well. Her face was oblong, and she wore two rings on each hand, with nothing occupying the fourth finger on her left hand. The poor lady was in her early forties and all indications pointed toward spinster.

She sat down without invitation, and she sat heavier than her physique seemed to require. It was as if gravity applied more to her than most everyone. I took note, but obviously didn't comment. She forced a smile by squeezing one eye slightly shut, lifting the left side of her mouth and raising the eyebrow of her un-squinted eye.

"Okay," I thought, without saying a word or moving a muscle.

"Brandon! I received your e-mail. I wanted to come and discuss it in person, thank you for taking the time to meet with me."

"Of course, Miranda. It is no problem at all."

"I thought it was a good e-mail, very thorough."

"Well, good. I was worried because your response seemed short," I replied. "I was worried I missed something or had a flaw in my methodology."

She folded one leg in what was a strange position, under the other leg. I don't know how to describe it, but it wasn't the usual crossed leg. She pinched her face and glanced at a printout she held in her left hand.

"You weren't wrong about anything you wrote. But we don't advertise here in the approach you advocate. Your e-mail was basically talking about straight-up, descriptive advertising and targeting the lifestyle of our main demographics. We do tangential advertising here. We advertise on a tangent."

"Oh. What is advertising on a tangent? I don't know what

that means."

"It means we don't focus our advertising primarily on the product or on our main consumers. Those people will buy the product no matter what. Doctors, our foot soldiers, drive most of our prescriptions. If someone is feeling a little down or has some pain — Boom! The doctor takes the opportunity to jack them full of our medications. And the medications are addictive and indefinite in term. Have you ever heard of someone getting off anti-depressants? Ha! So, we get a revenue stream for the life of the subject. It's pure gold," said Miranda. "It's a cash cow."

"That's uhhh, well... okay," I said, uncertainty dripping off my voice.

"So, we have been tasked with advertising tangentially, which means we run ads about social issues that are important to our stakeholders — our owners. It's a hot-button list, you can probably figure it out from our Twitter feed. We're pushing social change, not drugs. The drugs push themselves, through addiction, and the network of doctors are incentivized appropriately. We are a behemoth. We aren't going away, no matter what we put in our ads."

Suddenly, it was as if I was removed from the room, entirely. I was surprised at her blunt nature. Of course, I had noticed our advertising had little to do, directly, with our product — other than mentioning the product brand name. The advertising copy pushed obscure lifestyles, people with debilitating natural characteristics, random social issues which were unpopular with normal people. Now I realized why. The drugs sold themselves in different ways, and the mega-corporation had a different agenda with the repetitive messaging they always pushed.

Why, though? I asked myself. Was it misdirection? Did they want to promote these things in the name of tolerance to deflect from the fact that they were selling billions of dollars worth of damaging drugs. Was it more nefarious? Was it a plan to kill people, legally?

I re-focused on Miranda; I stopped hovering above and re-entered the room.

"I understand, Miranda. We're pushing something else because we want to, not because we don't realize we're doing it. I was assigned to do this project, that's why I did it. It wasn't my idea," I said, pretending to deliberate as I spoke even though in reality my thoughts were clear and pre-arranged.

"I think you did a good job. But that's not the strategy sent down from the top. Essentially the ads are to hammer on the random person watching the ballgame or whatever. I'm not going to say we're gas-lighting them — but we do push behaviors they would never entertain on their own. Breaking boundaries, training minds. Making the unfamiliar — even the repulsive, familiar. It's a repetition strategy. It takes years to break down the natural revulsion to some of the stuff we push. But we are years and years into it. It always works; people can't resist forever."

"Is it fatigue?"

"Yes. They resist and then one day they just break. It's proven, time and time again. We're making progress, along with our brother and sister companies. Barriers are breaking down because people are giving up — they give up and accept the propaganda — they choke down their natural resistance to the stuff we're pushing."

For a second, I was going to pretend to go along with Miranda. I was forcing my face to look contemplative — like I was deliberating and agreeing with her comments.

But then, something happened. I stopped forcing myself to

do anything. MindSmash was not for me, not anymore. To be blunt, I snapped. I stood up from the chair, from behind my desk. "I'm out of here," I thought.

"Hey Miranda, you know what, this job isn't for me. I'm done here," I said, grabbing my bag and walking by her without further comment. Her face registered as quite shocked; she was a corporate creature — she gave her life, her best years, to the corporation and, from the look on her face at present, she could never contemplate what it would take to quit her job. On the way out the door I sent a message, from my smart phone, to my boss containing two words: 'I quit.'

I didn't feel any tinge of regret as I walked out of the lobby towards my car. I drove straight to the dive bar — Oswald's — the one where I had met Hogan Lowd a week or two before. I sat down at the bar, next to a woman. The bartender was filling a beer and then made his way over to me and said, "What are ya havin'?"

"Rye whiskey... on the rocks, something with a traditional style," I responded.

The whiskey arrived and I sipped it once. Then again. I finished it and ordered another. I stared ahead across the bar. What was becoming of me? I had quit my job over some normal corporate behavior. Established corporations did that all the time. Social molding. Pushing the things they wanted to push, different behaviors, transgressing old human limits and customs. Overcoming the human impulse toward revulsion, when appropriate.

"Hitting the booze," I guess. What was I doing with my life? I had turned April away for no great reason. Now, I had quit a new job on an angry whim and headed straight to the bar. I didn't want to admit it to myself, but I was hoping Dr. Lowd would show up. On the heels of the meeting with Miranda, I was in the mood to talk about Petty Destruction, or any other wacky form of counter-subversion that came up.

DESPERATE BY PROXY

**

Dr. Lowd's impeccable posture first advertised his identity when he walked into Oswald's, the dive bar. Bearded, wild-eyed, eccentric looking in general — but with his shoulders thrown back and his head held high. Gray hair up top, styled down and to the right like a classic gentleman. I knew right away, without even seeing the features of his face, it was him. I wondered for a second if I could find him here on any given day. What a way to go through life!

Our eyes locked for a glance and he walked directly over to me.

"Brandon Brooks. Good to see you again, so soon."

"And you, Dr. Lowd."

The bartender walked over, asking, "What are you having today, Doc?"

"Sparkling water, my friend. I can only imbibe the good stuff two or three days a week, that's the rule."

"A crying shame. One water, coming up, Doc."

It is difficult to express the thoughts I had as I looked over at Dr. Lowd. I felt an unrealistic, almost mad, expectation telling me this man would be the one to break me out of my malaise.

I was still fascinated by his guess — or mind-reading — about my investigation into the 'system.'

One thing was certain: my cycle of corporate jobs, temporary women and distracting pastimes were not working for me. I needed more. This need, more than anything, drove me into deep corners of the web to read about forbidden topics. But pinning my hopes on a strange Doctor I met in a dive bar?

Ridiculous! "What is wrong with me?" I thought. "Is this really my life?"

Still, the expectation persisted as Dr. Lowd settled in and started sipping on his water, which he seemed to relish.

My glance stayed on him and I noticed a ring on his middle finger, left hand, with a red stone, rounded, in the centerpiece. It shimmered in the electric light from the beer and liquor neon signs placed around the bar. I observed every little detail of his ring. I was enamored with this character. Dr. Lowd and his concept of Petty Destruction, potholes and blown-out air conditioners.

The whiskey was affecting my mood — I hadn't had too much, obviously, but it was lightening me up, into a feel-good stage — the sweet spot. I embraced its effects. The negative events taking place between the last time I saw Dr. Lowd and the present moment were basically forgotten. I didn't care about MindSmash, not one bit. I was fully in the moment.

"I have no illusion that you will join the Petty Destruction team, Brandon," said Dr. Lowd, avoiding small-talk. "You're slated for bigger things. For the real deal."

"Yes, no offense. I admire the concept and do not have high-regard for the 'system' — in fact, I quit my job today — but I don't think PD is right for me. I don't know why, it's just not a fit for me."

Dr. Lowd paused for a moment before responding.

"We all have to fight the 'system' in our own ways, Brandon. The problem is, the fighters are too few and far between. The consumers, the people who buy into the 'system' out of some sense of blind conformity — they outnumber us twenty to one." After another pause, he added, "Probably more like fifty to one. Ah, probably more than that even."

"Well then, what hope do we have? They can pick us off, marginalize us. They can just call us crazy, or hateful, or whatever. They wear us down with constant media, repetition. The numbers aren't there. People get tired of resisting the bombardment. They get worn down. They give up."

"It's true."

Another pause.

"Then what?" I asked, taking another small sip of my whiskey.

"Well, we probably need a miracle. But those happen, you know," he answered, with a wink.

As he finished speaking, Dr. Lowd pulled a pocket notebook out of his light coat. It had a pen strapped to it, and he placed the notebook on the bar counter. He took a sip of his water, scratched his chin through his white beard — for only a second. He looked at me, then looked across the counter and sat there, on his stool. Staring forward.

The calm feeling I was enjoying only moments before abandoned me. It exited. I felt agitated, anxious. I was on the verge of something I couldn't quite grasp. I tried to reach it, with my mind, and it escaped me every time.

To combat this unpleasant sensation, I took a sip of whiskey, larger than normal. I emptied the glass, in fact. The bartender looked at me and I signaled for another one. I had no intention to drink wildly, but two whiskeys seemed like a minimum requirement for this mood, whatever it was. I needed something to jar me out of a rut.

My second whiskey arrived and I took a sip. I relaxed, again, a bit. My agitation and feeling of unrest waned.

Finally, Dr. Lowd spoke again, in a hushed tone, but with a deep voice, saying, "Last time we spoke, you told me you were investigating the 'system.' But you didn't say a lot. What are the things that have intrigued you?"

I considered my answer carefully.

"I've been focused on international capital as a driver of societal and governmental behavior. It was a couple of conversations I had that started me down that path. One with a former co-worker where he said something as a throwaway and I asked him 'Why?' in reference to an unfounded assertion. The other was a conversation with a guy at a bar, like we're talking now, in the Seattle airport. He had strong opinions about global capital — he seemed like a prepper or a cowboy or something. He was different. Those two things started me down the path. By the time you told me about Petty Destruction I was already looking into things — as you had guessed. Other things have come up as well — other, far-fetched conspiracies. The moon, UFO's, giants. Not from me, from a guy I met."

"A lot of those other things are psyops, they are distractions. They are meant to be edgy but it's really just a way to channel energy into silly pursuits."

"Yeah, that's my thought."

"If people are focused on aliens and the supernatural and science fiction — or even the moon — they take their eye off the ball. The government counts on distraction."

"I don't believe any of it."

"I'm not saying it's all false, I hold firm that it's meant as a distraction. If those things exist — and they may — there is still no known way to harness them for change. That's why I'm focused on what I am, the thing I told you about. Petty Destruction!"

"Results," I agreed, "are paramount."

"Don't discard the other stuff. But focus on what you can change. That's the problem with it. We're at the mercy of those things to reveal themselves. But don't close your mind off from them, in case they do. If you have a chance to harness something like that, it could change the world."

"Yep. And I think that's what is making me feel unsettled. I've been doing all this work looking into the tentacles of global capital but I don't have any power to do anything about it. I trace the web and it makes me feel helpless."

"I know what you mean. I felt the same way for a long time."

My perceptions sharpened. I knew I had to channel my work — my life — into accomplishing something. Noticing wasn't enough. I could point out links between capital and government and corporations and families all day, every day, and never accomplish a single real thing. Agony overtook me as I thought about being the guy with an opinion on everything and a back-story explaining why the world is as it is but nothing, achievement-wise, to hang my hat on. No accomplishments, no original thoughts, no decisive action. I hated 'that Brandon.' A fruitless being spinning tales of woe and failure. Gutless, staring into the abyss as everything remained a degenerate, soul-less corporate strip-mall wasteland around me.

Two things happened, right at once. My phone buzzed with a message. I was about to check it when three striking young women walked into the bar (that was the second thing).

One of the young women caught my eye and caused a ripple of warmth to run through my body. Then a second time. Was this the same movie I always seemed to live in? She looked younger than my most recent ex-girlfriends. Was it madness to keep pursuing this stuff? Was it something else? She had long brown hair, and from the looks of it, it may have been straightened. The young women chattered amongst themselves and looked at their phones.

Against my wishes, I kept staring at her. Mischevious but good-natured, cheerful unless pushed too far, graceful, bad-tempered, cheerful, awkward, graceful but not dainty. I imagined all those things, since I had no way of knowing anything about her. But she held my full attention. I noticed a little scar on her upper calf, but had no way of knowing it had been caused by an ice-skating accident, when she was kicked at pairs practice a few months before her thirteenth birthday. It was eight inches above her shoe. She wore a full skirt. I forced myself to look away, as I didn't want to continue to stare at her — and get caught — I couldn't let myself be the creepy guy down the bar.

Out of nowhere, Dr. Lowd said in their direction, "Ladies, put your phones down and come on over here. There's someone I'd like you to meet."

I swallowed. He had 'old-man-wingman grit' — charging straight ahead, no tact, fearless, no misdirection, no game — and not a care in the world. A boomer-led charge into the fray in age old matters of the opposite sex. I had no idea what would happen, but I was holding on to my figurative hat.

"This is Brandon Brooks. A man you will hear about in the future."

It is hard for me to describe the level of apprehension I felt at the Doctor calling the women over in this fashion. As if through a haze, I watched — let's face it, horrified — as the women walked over. Strangely, the whole gambit was working. The girls had an odd air of familiarity with Dr. Lowd. I couldn't put a finger on it.

Did they know each other? What would he say? What billing would he give me and how would I dig myself out of whatever he was going to say.

My eyes lost their focus as I was trying to keep my head from exploding. On the one hand, I don't want to make it seem like this introduction was the end of the world. No matter what happened, I was just meeting three young ladies. Yet, the unpredictability of Doctor Petty Destruction made my balance go off, even if only for a second. I thought I might fall off of my stool. There seemed to be a looseness between my rear end and the stool — to which I had been attached firmly moments before.

I took a sip of whiskey and sat still. Dr. Lowd created this mess, I would let him get out of it.

"And how are you lovely ladies doing tonight?"

"We're great, it's Cynthia's birthday so we're out gettin' wild and crazy. And how about you?" said the one who initially caught my eye.

"Very well. Very well. I'm Doctor Lowd, by the way, and as I said this is my dear friend Brandon."

I could have sworn I saw Dr. Lowd wink at the brunette, the one I was (I'm embarrassed to say) checking out. I couldn't figure out what in the heck was going on. It was all so strange — I liked the uncertainty which came with Dr. Lowd, but being a part of it was also unsettling.

"It's very nice to meet the both of you. That's Cynthia. I'm Karen. She's Gabriela," said the brunette, indicating her friends with a gesture of her hand.

"Wonderful to meet you. I am happily married, I must report. But this Brandon here, he is quite the eligible bachelor," said Doctor Lowd. I had no way of knowing that his wife, to whom he was married for almost fifty years, had passed away two years ago. It would have made the comment even more endearing, and it would have probably given me the chills, had I known it.

"Never mind my friend, he's always up to mischief," I chimed in, trying to mitigate the damage of looking desperate by proxy.

"Ha ha, it's okay," said Karen. "You're kind of cute, so it doesn't bother us to have an obviously crazy guy inserting himself into our night. Wild-eyed, you might say," she added, looking at Dr. Lowd and smiling with a show of something on her face I couldn't quite place. "At this rate, the good Doctor will have you hitched in no time — any day now. I'm sure you're incredibly thankful."

I laughed, detecting sarcasm and subdued my embarrassment to a manageable level. I noticed the way Karen's hair fell down around her face, and liked it. It has been claimed that it is a universal truth that a man with sound footing in life (I think she meant financially) must — always — want a wife. Jane Austen, I think.

Did I want a wife? The proposition was dubious. Actions speak louder than words, and I had never gassed myself up and driven, with intent, in that direction. Not with any determination or dedication. Objectively speaking, I must not have wanted one.

"We'll have to see about that," I replied, with an exaggerated shrug, raising my shoulders for a little over a second and then letting them drop.

Joking about the relatively aggressive introduction seemed to make everything better, right away. The conversation veered off to more palatable topics. Nobody talked about the weather, thank God. It would have been an awful sign. Instead, we chatted for ten minutes, with everyone relaying where they were from and something about themselves, in an interesting fashion.

I acquitted myself rather well, I must say, despite the shaky beginning caused by the metaphorical bomb set off by Doctor Lowd. As the conversation wound down, I caught Karen taking a quick glance at me, confirming my estimation that nothing had gone wildly wrong.

Dr. Lowd, probably sensing the young women would move on soon, decided to pull the emergency brake in the moving car and see what happened.

"Brandon here is hot on the trail of aliens, UFOs and giants — he's investigating the 'system.' That's how I found out about him. He'll be an international sensation. Brandon, get Karen's number so you can update her on her progress."

My eyes were wide, but I smiled, almost laughing off the awkward, hard-charging approach from Dr. Lowd.

"I wouldn't say I'm on the trail of anything," I said, trying to deflect. "I'm just a guy at the bar. Good old Oswald's."

The other girls had moved on to the bathroom or further down the bar, or wherever. I hadn't noticed because I was focused on Dr. Lowd's commentary — I almost couldn't believe the whole thing had happened — and checking Karen's reaction to it. Karen, looking at me once more, grabbed a napkin from the bar and took a pen out of her purse. She wrote ten digits on the napkin, handed it to me, smiled, and walked off after her friends.

"Okay, Doc, well that's one way to do it," I said after Karen left.

"You have to go after what you want, otherwise it will never happen. I helped you."

"How do you even know I wanted her number?"

"I saw you looking at her when she walked in."

"Oh, and that's all it takes?"

"You're a man — and I notice things. Thank me later. Where were we?"

"Who knows? You're doing petty destruction, I'm investigating global capital. We're both trying to change the 'system,' but the 'system' is winning. Every day, it grows bigger and stronger with the cycle of wage-slavery and distraction and we're here at a bar drinking whiskey and soda water and trying to wish it all away."

"So do something."

"I told you, I like petty destruction — I appreciate it and I respect what you're trying to accomplish — but it's not for me."

"Do something else."

"Like what?"

"Find a way to fight against what you see, your own way. And call Karen, she seems great," said Dr. Lowd, adding a wink, which I guess was a common thing for his generation.

A few minutes later, we wrapped up our conversation and shook hands.

"You can find me here most days. And here's my contact information if you need to reach me digitally," he said, handing me a business card. "You know, e-mail, text, whatever. You can even call if you want."

"Thanks, Doc."

When I returned home, sleep came relatively easily after a couple hours spent on the internet. On the platform I typically used to watch videos, I was served an advertisement for a video called "Giant Rampage," which I watched. It was a five minute video of people, pretending to be giants, role-playing in the snow while speaking in old-style, dated and a loud-style of formal-sounding English. It was the last video I watched, before sleep took over, and my dream was full of giants and war drums — they were rumber-ing!

MENTAL WARFARE

**

Somewhere in Antarctica

The grog went down easy. Too easy, in fact. Mauve kept bringing fresh barrels whenever one was emptied. The giants were swilling the barrels down in massive gulps. Now and then, they popped a penguin into their mouths, but more grog went down their throats than did penguins. It would take a lot of the mash to incapacitate the giants with drunken-ness. But that had happened before! Thousands of times, in fact.

The orb in the center of the triangular table started to glow with a more reddish intensity. It seemed as if the light, coming through the open-aired section of the ice bunker, was striking the orb at the perfect angle, causing the glow. It had a translucent quality to it, combined with a red-intensity rarely seen in any type of gem-stone on earth.

"The pleasantries are out of the way, we must get started with the council meeting. We have important decisions to make," said Ranald the Repellent.

"I have had the proper amount of grog. The perfect amount! Imagine it," said the Vile. "I feel good, but I am not schnozzered. I am present. I am here in full."

"Let's make this fast," said the Low, allowing himself a massive belch after the comment. His attitude, which had previously been one open to new adventure changed as he felt the effects of the grog. He was comfortable, he felt good where he was. "I don't think we should make changes. What is wrong with our lives here? We enjoy the clean, natural terrain. We are free from interaction with humans. The Dark One has left us alone for hundreds of years. He is busy with his army of progress. They work digitally with the images they send down from the clouds. We are antiquated. We are obsolete. There is very limited use for mashing and rampaging these days."

"It is a real skill which Satan's new workers possess," added the Vile. "Our video — the one Runa the Believer created for us with Tyferius — we were able to send it into the ether many months ago and it has been viewed less than ten times. Satan's workers make videos that are watched many millions of times."

"Our video has certainly not 'gone viral,' as they say," agreed Ranald, his voice booming slightly less than usual as he spoke of defeat, ineffectiveness, failure.

"It is not meant to be," said Vilfred the Vile. "The Dark One's new favorites... they have all of these things under their control. They can suppress or censor our video if they like. The material they don't like is banished into a nasty black hole where it never comes out. It is disallowed from the computing structure by the Dark One's corporate slaves and it is as if the material never existed in the first place. The same thing will happen to our stupid video. If it gains popularity it will be smashed and removed. Do not put your hope in that silly video, my brothers."

"It was a miracle that we could get the video made and into the ether," said Eindride. "We are not a technical people, we all know this. Credit to Runa and the young one for even getting that far. We must be proud, even in defeat."

"We are not defeated! We don't need the video production to be widely viewed," said Ranald. "We only need the right viewer."

"Ay, then there is hope," acknowledged Vilfred.

"There is always hope."

"But what is the plan? Why not stay here? What is wrong

with our lives?" asked Eindride the Low, echoing his earlier comments.

"I am tired of the same penguins... The toxins in their brain make my mind fuzzy," said Ranald.

"You want penguin?" interrupted Mauve. Several penguins on the rack wiggled, only slightly, when Mauve spoke the word.

"No, I was saying I am tired of eating penguin, Mauve. I am tired of crabeater seal, the same grog, the icy terrain. It is true, it is beautiful to look at, at first. But I have the terrain imprinted in my memory already — the beauty of it. I will never forget it. We belong in a castle on the warm sea, where we can roam more freely and wear less furs because of the natural warmth from the sun, for three-quarters of the year at least. We belong in a temperate climate. Our warmest month is not warm, not at all — it hovers in the negative temperature realm."

"We are moving for the weather? That's ridiculous, Ranald. Wear furs to stay warm and be happy," countered Vilfred.

"Enough of the back and forth. I want to go visit with the Wide. I need to patrol her Pemmican intake, it is becoming too much for me to bear. Their is a strain on our bed frame. She weighs nearly as much as I do, and is much lower in height. Let us hear the plan, evaluate it, and decide!" hollered Eindride.

Mauve brought three more barrels of grog and three more penguins (even though none of the giants really wanted them) to the table — making two trips.

Ranald rapped his knuckles on the table. Rat! Tat! Tat! Rat!

"Here is the plan. We will take the ship and head north to the city of New York, sailing by the wind. With weapons and armor, we will take the gold from the building they call the Federal

Reserve. The Doctor is going to help us recruit a human partner with our video. This will need to be a special man. We need him to create human accounts for us, to facilitate our new location. We will have him convert the gold reserves into human money. We will purchase our new land on the coast of Italy. We cannot let mankind know we are active again — we cannot take the land by force, we must purchase it legally..."

"Leee-gally," echoed Mauve, seemingly practicing his language skills.

"...in compliance with human custom — this man will serve as our proxy. He will be rewarded handsomely," finished Ranald.

"This is far-fetched!" interrupted the Vile, bellowing.

"We have done harder things!" exclaimed Eindride, still sitting on the fence, but starting to like the idea of adventure.

"What if this man converts our gold to human money and keeps it for himself?" asked Eindride.

"What if I smash him with my fist, using overwhelming blunt force?" retorted Ranald.

"You are not smart, Ranald! All this, why? You are pretending to be an intellectual. It doesn't work," stated the Vile. "You could wear spectacles on your face and you still would not look learned."

"When we steal the gold from the Federal Reserve structure, we will benefit in many ways. First and foremost, we can enjoy warmth and sun. An ocean without massive blocks of frozen ice. Our friends, the crabeater seals and penguins — they will thrive in population with us removed. They will roam more freely on the land and in water, not worrying about being snatched and fried. They have shared so much with us to keep us strong and healthy. Most importantly, we will get revenge on the Dark One for replacing us. We will work for the Prince of Peace," said Ranald.

"Insanity!" hollered the Vile.

"We cannot be saved, we have done too much," claimed Eindride.

"I have studied the matter and that is not true — Runa has read many things to me. Years of study. We can find salvation through a new belief in Him. All things are possible through Him."

"Humbug!" bellowed the Vile.

"It's true," insisted Ranald.

"There is nothing — NOTHING — more ridiculous than the three of us turning to the Prince of Peace. He will never have us. No way."

"No, many things are more ridiculous, my friend. The Dark One has taken the humans too far. I never minded destroying them physically, but I don't appreciate the mental warfare. It is worse than anything, they do not deserve this."

"A charitable Ranald, what a ridiculous thing. A bad joke."

"It is self interest, I will not lie, and I can only hope some day it turns to true belief like Runa has found. I am working on it. I hope He has this in store for me," said Ranald.

"None of it matters if we can't recruit this man you speak of. We can't purchase land without human accounts. And no one cares about our stupid video; we will not find this man," said the Vile.

"Ay, we can't do it on our own. Moreover, we haven't set sail in ages. We need to make sure the ship is still seaworthy, my brother," added Eindride, looking out for the practical components of the journey.

"We will have the help of Mauve and his brothers — I will make a deal with Mauve to keep him loyal to us, for life. And the man... we will find him and he will help us. Have a little faith, my friend and brother. We will be fine," said Ranald.

"Bah! Faith! You cannot be serious!" shouted the Vile. "Ranald the Repellent speaking of faith, now I have heard it all."

"I am. And it will work. Have faith," replied Ranald.

"This will never work. The plan is a bad joke. I don't even know what the entire plan is and I know it won't work. It will end with us running through the streets aimlessly, destroying everything we can. It always does!"

Ranald stared at Vifred. Eindride relaxed in his chair, letting his brothers sort things out. Ranald didn't say anything further, so Vilfred continued, "We start with a plan and then instead comes chaos! The chance we will successfully steal this gold and sail it to Italy is beyond the pale," said Eindride. "It's not going to happen."

"Stop the negativity!" bellowed Ranald, slamming his fist on the triangular table. "Stop it, now!"

The nook-demon, Mauve, turned his purplish head slightly to the left to check in on the conflict. He smiled. The giants went around and around arguing in this manner for another hour — the entire conversation will not be relayed here. Several times during the rest of the conversation, Mauve, listening in as usual, laughed, and then muttered "Destroy!" to himself. Soon, however, the matter would have to be called to vote; a decision would have to be taken.

* * *

At the exact same time as the conversation was playing out in Antarctica, my brother — Timothy — was typing on the keyboard of his Chinese-made home computer he had purchased at Costco using debt financing. His fingers were sticky because he was wolfing down 'Chipotle Ranch Doritos,' three or four at a time. The chips were made by Pepsico using genetically-modified corn which was turned into a mash and fried in canola oil.

Timothy licked his fingers until they were mostly free of the seed oil, salt and preservatives they had accumulated and then he continued typing on his digital Facebook account.

"My brother Brandon is convinced that Elvis is still alive! Apparently, there is no conspiracy theory that is too wacky for Brandon Brooks!" He fired off the post. A few minutes later, he checked his smart-phone. There were already ten replies mocking me by name — Brandon Brooks — for various 'conspiracies.' And, Timothy had received $50 on one of his digital money transfer account — sent by the Zürich Operation Group. He was expecting the transfer, and when he saw that it arrived he licked his lips, pocketed his smart phone and walked out the door, heading to his car.

CASH COW

**

I awoke with a start, thinking I was late for work. It was a Saturday. Of course, I wasn't late for anything. I had quit work. And all my corporate jobs had allowed for weekends off. Waking with that particular sensation was wrong, then, on two levels. Overcoming the short flash of panic, I lay in bed for a few moments, relaxing. Eventually, I decided I would go out shopping, I needed a few essentials — toothpaste and other bathroom supplies, stuff like that — and wanted to buy a new pair of casual shoes as well.

I took a shower and combed my hair back. I felt the presence of something looming in the room as I prepared to leave. It was just a feeling. I couldn't pinpoint what I was thinking about, what I was feeling. This feeling — a spirit? — was a strange sensation, seemingly hanging in the air. Not knowing what it was, I ignored it. What choice did I have?

For the moment, I made sure to gather the things I needed for my trip. Keys, wallet, smart-phone. I was ready to go shopping, but by the time I was almost ready to head out... that moment was over and another one came. And this one, it packed a punch.

A train of thoughts smashed through my mind's wall. My resistance to thoughts, my ability to close my mind to ideas I didn't like — I couldn't do it any more. I worried — was this permanent? — had I lost my ability to filter and discern? The thoughts flooding my mind were of a certain type. It was all the conspiracy stuff. The things that had to do with my investigation into the 'system,' for one, but also more fanciful conspiracies. The trigger was a quick flash, in my mind, where I recalled the ridiculous video I fell asleep watching. The one with the giants, rumbling around in the ice. They claimed to be in Antarctica. Bellowing about a revolution and carrying weapons — axes, clubs, hammers. The production quality, overall, wasn't great, because the costuming was over the top. The iron bracelets, the massive-looking clubs, the huge iron helmets sitting on top of braided hair. The large furs draped over their bodies. They looked too awesome to be realistic. Someone was trying to hard on that one, I thought. The voices, they boomed!

I continued to consider the video for another moment. For a five minute video, they actually had a meaningful budget for computer-generated imagery. I mean, they had penguins in the videos which looked like pigeons standing next to the men dressed as giants. They did well with the digital effects! But I'm not sure of what the rest of the messaging was; I'm not sure of the point. I have no idea.

The rest hit me as well. Not only the giants. All of the things, all at once. All of the theories, they tore me up, they thrashed at me, they tore at the inside of my mind. I couldn't categorize them fast enough, it was a flood of information. The monetary system, the ties between governments, the federal reserve, corporations and central and world banks. I was spinning!

I recalled a quote I had read during one of my investigation sessions: "The international bankers swept statesmen, politicians, journalists, and jurists all to one side and issued their orders with the imperiousness of absolute monarchs." The quote was from David Lloyd George, Prime Minister of the United Kingdom and he was speaking about the Treaty of Versailles.

So... that was the Prime Minister of the UK saying that bankers, essentially, controlled the world? I mean, if you boil the quote down to its essence that's what it says. Why would he lie?

I was overwhelmed, I lost track of the truth. A financial cabal setting global policy? Was it possible? But, arguing that was a 'conspiracy' according to the media, according to everyone. How could the Prime Minister say that — but I can't believe it to be true?

I kept spinning.

The conspiracies had become, for me, like a group of sirens, singing. All of a sudden it had happened — maybe the day I quit MindSmash? They had light brown hair, green eyes, red lips, nubile bodies. The sirens sang to me, they caressed my feelings. These things, the very things I had been noticing and discovering for months now, they were a contradiction. On the one hand, they were fragile. At times, I dismissed them, thinking the web of connections was implausible. It drove me insane — I don't like to admit it, because I have this theory about starting to question your sanity — once you start, my theory goes, it is hard to stop. It's like noticing. There are no brakes on that ride — when the roller coaster leaves the station you go where it takes you, nowhere else. One day, I could think one thing was true with tremendous certainty. The next day, the certainty regarding the same very thing was gone. I would worry that I had imagined it all — or that someone was pulling the wool over my eyes by cherry-picking facts and quotes to make things appear other than as they really were. It was madness!

I would try to dismiss the thoughts. I would try to recall my old way of corporate thinking, of not worrying about things such as this. But then, invariably, the siren would start singing again. What was true? I had no idea anymore. Many things seemed to be both true and spectacular lies at the same time. The world swirled around me.

My thoughts blended together and became a muddled grey-zone. I snapped out of the zone for one reason — my phone rang — it was my step-mother, Janice, calling.

"Brandon?"

"Hi Janice."

"How are you, Brandon?"

"I can't really complain. Is everything okay?" I replied.

"Oh yeah, it's fine on our side. Stephen said to say hi."

"Oh good. I was worried because I haven't talked to you for awhile and it's kind of a random time."

"It is. Well, Stephen said you exchanged a couple of messages and you said something about quitting your latest job. He was worried about you, so I thought I would check in."

"Oh, that. Yeah, I quit MindSmash. I'm fine. It wasn't for me. I quit in the moment."

"I see. Well, you have to trust your instincts."

"I try to do that. They asked me to do something. Then I did it. Then they told me thanks and you're right but we're not going to use what you said. So, I got frustrated. I started questioning their advertising strategy and they admitted the focus of their advertising was not the product. They admitted they were pushing other stuff. I don't even want to go into what the 'stuff' is. You probably know, though. It was MindSmash — I'm sure you see their product advertising if you watch television."

"You know we watch a lot of television. Your dad loves his shows."

"Uhm-humm. So yeah, that's all. They call it tangential advertising."

"Well, we wanted to check in and make sure you're doing okay. Do you have something else lined up? For work, I mean."

"I haven't thought about it, Janice. I've been in a cubicle pushing product for so long things became a blur. I've been working on an investigation in my spare time. I don't know if I'm going to do anything with it. I guess the only options are to write a book or start a podcast. Who wants to do those things, though?"

"Err, uh, yeah. Is that what Timothy is posting about on Facebook? We were all confused about his comments. And all the people joining in below his posts. What are you investigating?" asked Janice.

"I don't pay attention to Timothy and his ridiculous Faceberg account... never-mind that clown," I said. I was highly irritated and a bit surprised to learn that Timothy was posting about me. I hadn't spoken to him recently. I continued, "I started to read and think about the ties between global capital and our government and how those two groups fit together. You know, how they use megacorporations and mass media to control and modify human behavior. They make false things seem true through repetition and propaganda."

Janice was silent. I froze for a second. I realized it was probably a concerned silence, so I kept speaking, attempting to diffuse the situation: "Don't worry, it's not conspiracy stuff. It's not aliens and UFOs and giants and stuff. I'm not into wild stuff. I'm looking at how big money, big government and the big corporations work to control things. It's interesting, that's all."

There was an awkward pause.

"Okay Brandon. We were worried about you, mainly your dad. You know how he prioritizes the nine-to-five. The nine-to-five comes first."

"I appreciate it. And I do, too. I had to get out of MindSmash, though. It wasn't for me."

"Don't be a stranger, Brandon. I'll talk to you soon."

"Thanks for calling, Janice, and I'll talk to you soon. Tell my dad I said 'hi.'"

I hung up and sat there, staring at the wall. I felt like a loser. I quit my job pushing pills — a steady earning opportunity — because I didn't like a conversation about their advertising. It was rash, impulsive behavior. A moment later, though, I wavered... taking my own side. I didn't like the actual advertising and I didn't even like the product. I didn't want to be a pill-pusher, on any level. Why bother? That's not me. I wavered back... thinking "doesn't everyone have to work for companies they don't like?" Was there something wrong with me? Had I become too impulsive, too impatient?

I walked out the front door, locking it behind me. Then on to my parked car. The walk over was pleasant, it was a beautiful day: the warm sun glowed with a pumpkin-orange tint and the cool breeze meandered about like drunken squirrel. The path to the car was partially shaded by the big-leaf maple tree off to my left. The alligator-green leaves on the tree shivered due to the breeze. A number of typical neighborhood noises filled the air. There was still a mid-morning haze hanging in the air.

When I left the house, I had no plan as to where I was going — my enthusiasm for shopping had waned. I didn't really need any of the things I intended to buy, not immediately. I still had a couple squirts of toothpaste, I reckoned. And I didn't feel like going to a bunch of stores. Not anymore. I walked out of the house, anyway, without a plan. Should I go for coffee? Then the gym? My river walk? I thought of heading to the bar to talk to Dr. Lowd, but quickly realized he wouldn't be there for at least six or seven hours. I reached the car and unlocked it and got in. I always thought of myself as independent and self-sufficient. Between the time I hung up the phone with Janice and the time I walked out the front door, I fell into a mild depression. I was aimless. Even when

I had jobs, when I had sales goals, when I had a busy daily routine.

Now? I had no aim. I was floating along.

I got in my car and decided to head to the river (which was actually a creek). Thinking of it as a river made me feel better about myself, about my day — so that's how I categorized it. Either way, it was a beautiful California day, and spending it by the river kept me calm, and also allowed me to feel separate from the structural and social problems the state faced after years of deterioration.

After driving and walking a mile and a half up the trail, I sat on a little wooden bench for fifteen minutes. I walked on after seeing a path heading to the north. It forked to the northwest and the northeast. I had always taken the northwest fork, because that path followed alongside the river. For some reason, I decided to take the northeast path, which I followed for ten minutes until I reached higher ground, where I looked out and noticed the trail dead-ended into a pair of soccer fields. Men and women — adults — were out playing on the field. I decided to watch for a few minutes.

I wandered over to the field and was struck, immediately, by one player on a team wearing white t-shirts as uniforms for their recreational league game. It was remarkable how quickly this man was able to stand out as a negative example, illustrating all of the things that have gone wrong with humanity in recent, modern times. I gathered the man's name was Nolan — one of his teammates had called it out while he possessed the ball, asking for a pass.

Nolan probably worked a non-descript corporate job, just like the cattle at the protests outside my office. Nolan, judging by his appearance and demeanor, was keen on consumption. Nolan was an unfortunate by-product of the entire 'system' I was coming to question. His identity, his humanity, had been entirely subsumed into corporate consumerism. Two things led me to discern this, quickly. These were his physiognomy and the words he spoke. I do not want to sound harsh, and I have tried to keep this description to a matter-of-fact tone. But this Nolan, a cash cow for the corporations, needs to be described for the point to be understood.

He was under six feet tall and quite over-weight, probably eighty or eighty-five extra pounds of greasy fat was carried on his bloated carcass. He was obese. This was, quite clearly, a man who spent his money on big food and big soda and big beer – and whatever else the big corporations pushed on him. I mean, it would be impossible to develop Nolan's physiognomy without being a heavy consumer of corporate, processed food and high-calorie beverages. So, the corporations were making money from Nolan on the front end. They would be paid on the back end as well. Think about it. If Nolan wasn't already on a variety of pharmaceutical drugs, he would certainly be soon. Insulin, blood pressure, cholesterol, erectile dysfunction, you name it, Nolan would most certainly consume a drug for it. No doubt he watched television and other types of entertainment non-stop and this, went my theory, caused him to purchase whatever other products were advertised incessantly during his television and digital-media binges. His red-brown hair sat above a bad hairline, receding at the edges. He probably bought a product for that, too – without result. The coup de grâce, for Globo, would be if the corporations could get him on hormone drugs for the back half of his life, a non-celebrity Jenner. A final humiliation (although he wouldn't realize he was being humiliated) on top of everything else. Nolan, for the corporations, was a puppet on strings. Dance, boy! Jump! Kneel!

The icing on the cake was his mouth, which never stopped moving. He called out to his teammates, barking out ridiculous instructions (they didn't help). When he wasn't doing one of those things, he was complaining about the officiating — along with his friend, a dullard — also fat — sitting on the sideline, soaking in misery. Nolan had an opinion on everything. He was the 'cash cow,' the man who had no skills and no value (unless you were a global corporation, in which case Nolan had a steady value — he provided profit). Of course, Nolan had no self-awareness. I shook my head, bemused. Nolan probably thought his jogging around — LARPing as a soccer player — moving his hefty body to and fro around the field and taking a few ill-fated kicks at the ball for twenty minutes of a rec league game, qualified as strenuous exercise. No doubt Nolan would celebrate his completion of the game with a macro-brew or ten, an estrogenic nightmare which would contribute more to his man-breasts and beer belly. He probably wasn't even smart enough to drink his gallons of beer to numb himself from his meaningless bugman existence. He just drank it because the corporations pushed it on him with their advertising — he thought it was fun. A fat American who would go into debt to buy cheap plastic junk (or whatever) made in China — he was the epitome of the modern American soy-and-carb-fed nu-male.

Almost immediately, I grew tired of marveling at the pathetic Nolan — the cash cow who never had an original thought or performed an original, meaningful action in his entire life. I turned and walked back to the path, following it down the incline, back in the direction from which I had arrived at the soccer fields a short time before. Walking steadily, I made my way back to the bench, but this time took the fork back to the northwest and walked along the river in quiet solitude.

When I got to the next bench, inspired partly by Nolan, I rocked out some push-ups, three sets of twenty. I made a mental note to do more later and to remember to hit the gym the next day.

Had there been a pull-up bar in sight I would have done some of those, as well. I sat down and spent the next couple of hours thinking. After the push-ups, thankfully, I didn't have a single further thought about Nolan. There was no helping a man who was so far gone, who had given over to full and complete corporate control.

I thought, I stared at the live-stream of the river water, I looked at the blueberry-candy sky. I relaxed. The setting provided merciful escape, free from heavy thoughts. It was a pleasant session, seeing as I didn't dwell on the 'system,' my future — I just lightened my load. I thought about many things, but it was a whimsical time with positive energy, not intense at all.

The third time I checked the content of my smart-phone — over an hour into my time by the river — I saw a missed call and a text message. The call was from a number I didn't recognize. When I looked at the text message, all it said was "WYD? Karen."

It was the young woman from Dr. Lowd's bar. It felt good to receive a message from Karen. A surprise! It also countered the quite severe feelings of isolation I had been having (without admitting them to myself). Even before I quit my job, I was going through my entire day with only superficial contact with others (even people I was 'close' to). It made me feel good to have some attention from Karen. She was mysterious and, on top of that, she was very attractive.

"I'm sitting by the river enjoying the day. Not doing much. WBY?"

She responded immediately, "Let's go do something."

I didn't feel like playing the game, so instead of trying to come up with something unique to suggest as an activity, so I replied "What do you want to do?"

"Let's go to the mall."

Karen didn't strike me as a mall type. I paused for a moment, with surprise.

"Okay. I was actually thinking about grabbing some new sneakers."

"Pick me up when you can. 633 Hargrove."

I was only mildly interested to see how far away this particular dead end was — a road like this always seemed to end with one. No matter! I liked Karen in the brief time we talked at the bar. So, I felt hopeful, as much as anything, as I got in my Audi and navigated my way to her address — with precise help from my smart phone which guided (and tracked) my every move.

I pulled up to her house, but before I could hop out of the car and go knock on the door, Karen walked out. She was wearing a striped jumpsuit. I was struck by how athletic and carefree she looked. She carried a small bag with her. She was a pretty girl.

Getting in the car, Karen asked, "How was your picnic?"

"Ha! I didn't have a picnic."

"I know, I just like that word. Your walk, or whatever?"

"It was good. I do it a lot. So... like usual. I saw the crane I always see. I named him Herbert."

"Are you okay?" she asked me with feigned urgency.

"Yeah, why?"

"Herbert? Ha!"

"I don't know, I never thought about it, it just happened. And what's wrong with Herbert, anyway? What would you call him that's so great?"

Karen scrutinized my face, trying to figure out if I was trolling her.

"What are you looking for at the mall?" I asked.

"Don't know," she said.

"Oh, okay. Sorry for the intrusive question," I replied, sarcastically.

We rolled down the road, chatting and making progress toward the mall.

"I like your outfit," I volunteered at one point. Part of me was telling the truth, and part of me thought the outfit was kind of funny and I wanted to see what she would say about it. I couldn't decide.

"Oh, thanks. It's comfortable."

"Looks like it."

"Yours needs an upgrade," teased Karen.

I found it hilarious that Karen was willing to roast me for my t-shirt, old shorts and sneakers (without socks, which I swore I would never wear again) — she had met me just a few days before. I went along with it.

"Wow... Ha, well, I've had this t-shirt for about five years. Maybe you have a point."

"I was kidding. Guys who have to try hard are ridiculous. They look stupid."

I parked the car, taking note of the location. I hated losing my car in parking lots, it led to too much frustration. For the next couple hours, we enjoyed each other's company and the pleasant weather. Talking, walking, shopping. The mid-afternoon California sun shone down, it glistened with the typical blues and yellows, and a dash of sparkling orange. I bought a pair of simple, flat sneakers and a grey t-shirt. Karen helped me pick both. "You happy now?" I asked her, referencing the t-shirt joke. She didn't buy anything, herself. I got the sense she wasn't even really shopping.

When it was clear we were getting to the end of our tolerance for shopping, we sat down at a coffee shop and each had an iced espresso drink. Karen had a strange way of keeping the conversation focused on me. She zeroed in on my interests, my thoughts, my likes, my dislikes. I realized, in real time, that she was very elusive. I didn't know anything about her, but she had me talking in circles about all sorts of things. She even got me going on the 'system.' I covered Bretton Woods, the Warburg family, international finance, global government, propaganda and the convergence of global communism and hyper-capitalism in the form of runaway consumerism. She probably thought I was nuts!

I decided to try to regain my foundation, keep more control over the conversation and stop ranting. It was hard because I had so much to say about these topics.

A couple of times, I caught myself staring at Karen as she spoke, without following her words — they were probably circular anyway, she never seemed to say anything revealing. Each time I caught myself staring without listening, I had to shake my head slightly to snap myself back into the conversation. We finished our drinks and looked at each other.

"You have to get back home anytime soon?" I asked. It wasn't an artful comment, but it would have to do in order to wrap things up at the mall.

"Yes, I need to do a few things around the house. I'm not in a rush, but yeah."

"I've had fun. We should do something again."

"I'd like that."

We strolled back to my car. As I walked around to the driver side, I noticed a big hole in the concrete, on the road behind and to the left from where I parked. I didn't notice the hole when I parked. It was about three feet deep and four feet in diameter at the surface.

"That's strange," I said, to myself more than anything.

"What?" asked Karen, since I said it loud enough for her to hear.

"There's a big hole in the road behind the car. I didn't see it when I parked. Did you?"

"A hole, what? Ha!" she laughed. Then, seeing as I didn't laugh, she went on, "A hole, hmm. No, didn't see it," said Karen, looking straight ahead without even making an effort to locate the hole behind us.

I maneuvered out of the spot, careful to avoid the damaged part of the road. I dropped Karen off and then returned home. When we had reached her house, at the end of the ride, we shared a few words — saying goodbye — and a quick touch of our hands plus a moment of eye contact before she exited the car and went inside. Nothing more.

Rag-tag Push-back

**

Two uneventful days went by, which brought me to Monday. When I was a corporate guy, Mondays were my worst nightmare. But now, it was just another day... another chance to investigate. That night, I had a familiar dream. The dream always alarmed me. It was definitely a 'system'-related dream, but I couldn't completely understand why it kept recurring. In the dream, I am always surrounded. I am always outnumbered. I also feel threatened. The men surrounding me are all wearing business suits, carrying briefcases. It is clear to me that the men are armed, but I never see an actual weapon. They never do anything, other than gaze at me, silently antagonizing me. Watching, staring. It is suffocating, and in the dream it is as if a tremendous amount of time goes by. Years. I never do anything. I'm surrounded by these business-men. In one of the dreams, I checked my pockets for a weapon. I had the urge to try to blast myself out of the imprisonment. But there was no weapon to be found. The dream went on and no matter how hard I struggled against my state of paralysis, I couldn't move my body.

I woke neither early nor late. Right down the middle. I hated that dream and tried to banish the aftermath of it from my head. The only message I could take away from it was one of helplessness, impotence, despair. It was as if I was surrounded by the dogs of the oligarchs — or, actually, the dog-trainers, the higher-up types — and had no real choices in my life. Even the ones I made were not really a choice, because everything fed through the corporate-government filter. I poured myself a small jug of coffee and logged onto my computer. I disregarded any thoughts of shaving or showering. I was intending to spend the entire morning investigating the 'system,' drinking black coffee and trying to figure out a plan of action. What good was life without action? A life of thought? Ha!

Besides, we had already lost the battle. Before shutting down my computer, the last quote I read was from one of the Founding Fathers, Thomas Jefferson: "If the American people ever allow private banks to control the issue of their currency first by inflation then by deflation the banks and corporations that will grow up around them will deprive the people of all property until their children wake up homeless on the continent their Fathers conquered... I believe that banking institutions are more dangerous to our liberties than standing armies. The issuing power should be taken from the banks and restored to the people to whom it properly belongs."

According to Jefferson — who was no idiot — the battle against the 'system' was already lost, it was already over. All that we had left to do was to cry and gnash our teeth. Could someone change things? It seemed impossible. So in this manner, the morning slipped away from me and apprehension and helplessness turned into full-blown despair. My investigation seemed worthless. The battle was over. What's more, I was setting myself up to be lampooned as a 'conspiracy theorist,' the exact thing my half-brother Timothy was posting about on his ridiculous digital accounts. My thoughts, when I tried to lay them out in a linear fashion, were an embarrassment. I didn't even feel like a real person anymore.

Suddenly, I had to get out of my house. It felt too restrictive. But to where? The shopping plan from the day before had been a disaster. I had no idea what was unspoken with Karen on the ride home. I started to question everything about Karen. In fact, when she sent me a message on Sunday asking what I was up to, I didn't respond. How convenient was it, really, that she just happened to walk into the bar when I was there? How fearless was

Dr. Lowd, as a wingman, and how did he close her so effectively? I mean, really, a few days later and I'm out shopping with her?

I had nothing to do. No job. I didn't feel like hitting the gym this early, I wanted to do that in the afternoon, around lunch time. I needed to get away from my research, I didn't want to sink in digital quicksand. I felt enclosed by circumstance but at the same time, I felt some freedom. I could still do what I wanted, right? I could get in the car and go wherever I wanted, as long as there was a road and I had gas in the tank.

I had no argument to the case I was making in my head. So I drove, north. I went through San Francisco on 19th Ave. The city had become more and more dirty over the years. This is not a sociological story, so there is no reason to document the societal ills and rampant degeneracy I encountered as I continued on my drive. "Better not to, I don't want to hijack my thoughts. Let it roll off. Just let it go," I told myself as I saw one particularly distasteful scene after another. It was bad, better to ignore it, let it roll out of my mind. Soon enough, I was cruising across the Golden Gate Bridge. It was late morning, and traffic wasn't bad — it was a picturesque scene, in fact.

I'm not sure exactly when the thought entered my head, but it was somewhere north of the bridge. Maybe as I was heading through Ross, San Anselmo or Fairfax. But I decided to go all the way up to Sonoma, and I was going to look for the store up there — the one run by that guy Rory and his girlfriend — or wife, I couldn't remember — Lucille. Remember, Rory was the conspiracy theorist I had met on my river walk some time ago. It was an odd thing to do, but why not? What else was I going to do — go look for Dr. Lowd or wait for Karen to contact me? I didn't want to play games. The idea of dating in my thirties was less appealing than ever. What if Karen was cool and then she suddenly became nuts? I didn't know her mom — and if her mom was nuts that meant she would be too. I mean, I hadn't even really talked to her. What if she would, out of nowhere, go on a binge and talk about her landlord or her work (if she worked, I had no idea), or her everyday chores, or packing a bag, or medical issues or whatever. What a mess! I wanted to pull the parachute, but I didn't even know why. We had only hung out alone the one time. And, if I was honest, it was fine. We had a good time. So what was this rant? What was this turmoil? What was the issue? My head was spinning again and I felt slightly insane.

I kept driving and a while later, I was in Sonoma county. In terms of the shop belonging to Rory and Lucille, I had no indication of where it was located and I didn't even have a name for the store. I may have been on a fool's errand. Eventually, I made it into town.

Why was I doing this? I shook my head with a momentary wave of frustration. I drove down the road, thinking I had wasted my time for no reason when, all of a sudden I heard a loud banging coming from my left. Bam! Bam! Bam! I was startled and looked to my left. I saw his hair! "Ha!" I laughed, without thinking. It was Rory, banging on the door of an old pickup truck. He looked as if he was trying to pry it open. The road was lightly trafficked, and there was no one behind me, so I stayed at a complete stop and rolled down my window.

"Rory! Rory! What are you doing?"

Rory looked in my direction. Of course he had a conspiracy t-shirt on. I'm not going to even go into the design or the topic, it's too much for me to bear right now. Too raw and controversial. I can't do it.

Rory paused when he heard me call his name. I could see uncertainty on his face as he looked in my direction.

"It's Brandon! Brandon Brooks! We met by the river, I met you and Lucille."

"No way! Park and come on in, dude!" said Rory. His eyes were wild.

I parked and walked towards Rory. Rory, with a goofy smile on his face, stopped whatever he was doing with the old truck — all the banging — and led me into the shop. The shop was called "Parker's Mortuary" — I had no idea where the name had come from and I figured Rory would tell me whether or not I asked. So I didn't.

Rory was fidgeting and shuffling as we walked in. He was such an amusing character. Lucille, snuck up behind us and then ran her fingers down my back like a rake, three times. It felt good, with her long nails giving the right level of intensity for the back-scratch. When I turned, she had a big smile on her face and hollered "Brandon!" as if we were old friends. she hugged me, like a hug from a cartoon. I couldn't help but appreciate the warm greeting.

"This is so groovy... you came by! I mean, we really meant the invitation but of course we didn't think you would really come. It's a hike to get up here from south of San Fran. Let's rock out!"

"I know. I didn't have anything to do. It feels like forever driving through the city. Stuff has gotten real bad through there. What happened to that city?"

"I know, we try not to go down there much. This is our spot!" exclaimed Rory.

"Well, I know. I love it." I replied, looking around.

"Check it out, man. So how have you been?"

The store had a good energy. It was eclectic, there was stuff everywhere, but it didn't seem like it was over-crowded. It was all-right. I soaked in the environment while I responded to Rory, "I mean, I've been good. I can't remember where I was working when we met, but wherever it was I'm not working there anymore. I think MindSmash. Actually quit my job a short time ago."

"That's a great step. Don't let anybody smash your mind, bro — you gotta think for yourself. What have you been doing?"

"Well, nothing. I went to the mall with a friend. I work out. I've been sort of looking into some things on-line..."

"Looking into things on-line!" Rory hollered with a big smile on his face, glancing from me then to Lucille then back to me. "Ha! That sounds like a recipe for disaster!"

Lucille laughed. I did too.

"Well, maybe it is. I'm all tied up over the connections between global government, global capital and our mega-corporations. I actually snapped and quit my job over sort of the same issue."

"What do you mean?"

"Well, I was brought on to tighten up this company's advertising program. When I made my suggestions, the woman basically told me 'hey, look, we're not really advertising the product. The product sells itself. We're doing tangential advertising.'"

"Ha! What in the world is tangential advertising?"

"Yeah, I kid you not, that's what she called it. They were pushing behaviors — things people wouldn't think were natural — they showed the other stuff repeatedly, because the product sales came from elsewhere. It's like a psy-op. I don't even want to go into what it was. Unnatural stuff. Harmful stuff."

There was a pause.

"Well, if you think about it, a lot of companies do that. They're playing the long game," said Rory. "The corporations are so strong they can push fringe behavior in their advertising and there is no penalty for it. I think it's called being woke. They sneak in things people generally want no part of until those things are normalized. People eventually give up and take the mark of the beast, because of the strength of the propaganda."

"It works," said Lucille. "Repetition works. Repetition is their game."

"We're still paying for letting these people run wild for so long," I said. "I don't think it can be fixed. It's all lies."

"You should read the list."

"What list?"

"Dr. Lowd's list."

"Wait, what? You know Doctor Lowd?"

"Pfft. Who doesn't?" asked Rory.

"Well, I had never heard of him, then I meet him at a bar, then he introduces me to someone I spent time with yesterday. Now, everyone knows him. What is going on here?" I asked with genuine exasperation coming through in my voice.

"Oh yeah, Dr. Lowd is well known. He was the biggest name in anti-corporate activism for a lot of years. He's underground now, all sorts of rumors, though. Petty destruction, non-compliance."

"Wow, uh — well, I did not know that. And I didn't know everybody knew about that stuff."

"Where have you been? Everybody who questions the

'system' knows who Dr. Lowd is!" teased Lucille.

"Well, I guess I was so deep in the cubicle I didn't know about all this stuff. It never even occurred to me to oppose the corporations. They're out there, selling stuff, all the time."

"It's not only corporations, but I think Dr. Lowd does focus a lot on corporate behavior because they hide in plain sight. You can see what they are doing – if you care to look and analyze it. They created confusion through repetition and took away our absolutes. They took our absolutes with lies. Without absolutes, you spin like a top."

"We've got a poster around here somewhere from one of his rallies... Lucille, do you know where it is?"

"It's in a frame on a wall somewhere, Rory. You can find it just as easy as I can, quit being so lazy. Walk around, you can downsize your belly."

"Lucille!"

I was startled for a second, but when I looked up I saw them both smiling and glancing at each other. They were playing around. I remained at ease. We all looked around for the poster, and then Rory spotted it and pointed it out.

I walked over to it. There was a boot, stomping on a stereotypical fat-cat corporate guy, who had a bag of money and money bulging out of the pockets of his suit, which strained uneasily under the man's layers of blubber. The poster had the listing of the date and the location for the rally (It was in San Francisco about twelve years ago) and Dr. Hogan Lowd was listed as the keynote speaker, along with two punk bands performing a free concert. I guess that was before punk went corporate like everything else. All of it took place in Golden Gate Park.

"Wow, this was a big deal! I never heard anything about it."

"Well, unless you were paying attention there's no real reason you would. I mean, the corporate media only covered his rallies begrudgingly. They only covered them because so many people showed up and the alternative press was writing positively about Lowd. So, they tried to reign him in with character assassination, blaming him for things he didn't personally do."

"Like what?"

"Well, one of his supporters fire-bombed a carbohydrate factory. The guy's kid weighed like a million pounds and had diabetes. And he loved the refined sugars and carbs the company made. The dad had some weapons expertise, and he was able to rig a sophisticated chain of bombs inside the factory after hours, using a stolen key-card and a janitor's outfit. Took out the whole operation. They blamed Lowd."

"I see. The Doc probably wasn't against the destruction, though?"

"Of the factory, nah. But the guy took no precautions and many of the workers were killed. Those guys were pawns, not puppeteers. Lowd would not advocate careless killings. The factory workers are pawns, not villains. Unless they're woke, that's a different story."

I stared at the poster for a while. It had some sayings, or rules, listed throughout the poster. I read them all. I thought about them, carefully, as I read.

1. Corporate Power will be retained and it will grow unless it is taken away by force.
2. Never trust the motives of a corporation.
3. If a corporation is pushing a product on you, it is almost always bad for you.
4. Make the corporation admit what it is doing. Make it

admit what it is selling.

5. Reduce the corporation's product to it's core description. Then ridicule it.

6. You can never hurt a corporation bad enough to account for what it deserves.

7. If you allow a corporation any wiggle room it will seize more.

8. If corporations are allowed to buy politicians, the politicians will be corrupt in one election cycle – and it's irreversible.

9. If a corporation has to kill you to make money (the slower the better, though), it will kill you.

10. When you threaten a corporation, always fulfill the threat as soon as it comes due.

11. If a corporation is pushing a social 'issue' or 'lifestyle', it is most likely something that no one actually wants in their life.

12. If a corporation tells you something, the opposite, or something close to the opposite, is likely true.

13. A corporation that sells addictive products with no redeeming qualities should be subject to the harshest of punishments, including physical destruction.

When I saw the poster, it seemed as if the light dimmed in the shop. I don't know why. The dimming effect produced a sort of mental haze causing me to question my ability to reason and discern truth. What if this was just the other side of a propaganda coin, anti-corporate garbage as opposed to the usual corporate promotions. I stared at the poster, and I realized Dr. Hogan Lowd had been a well-known anti-corporate activist. He was the real deal! In person, he struck me as a bit crazy... but I kept staring at the poster and I read the statements twice. Was he wrong? Where's the lie? Rory and Lucille were looking at me, gaging my reaction.

Now, I was feeling paranoid. All of this was a strange coincidence. Was I targeted by Rory and Lucille? Did they follow me to the river and then feign as if they bumped into me by chance? There was no way they knew about my visits with Dr. Lowd until I told them today. Unless they were lurking in Oswald's the same night I met Lowd and I didn't see them. "Stop it, Brandon," I told myself (in silence). There was no way they knew I would be at the river the day we met. There was no way they manipulated me into finding their shop today. This was all chance.

I needed to find some meaningful clarity. Too many thoughts — and a voice — were swimming around in my head. If the 'system' was really so bad — so corrupt, so damaging to human beings — why didn't more people notice it and fight back? I mean, Dr. Lowd, Rory and Lucille? That's a rag-tag team trying to push-back against many, many millions of corporate consumers. Perhaps the 'system' was not a problem and I had just lost my mind.

This feeling was overwhelming. I lost my confidence — I had to be all wrong! The 'system' was fine — it was me there is something wrong with. Why can't I enjoy the products and the corporate entertainment like everyone else? Television and macro-brew? Fast food. Just all the stuff they churned out for the consumer? I had done that before — before I started noticing.

I could feel my heart thumping as I continued to stare at the poster of Dr. Lowd's event, then I started to look around the shop again.

"Everything's fine," I said, finally. Dr. Lowd can't be right. The corporations make things we need, they make things we want. The corporations are fine. This sentiment was so strongly programmed into my mind, it crept back in without invitation. It was hard to get it out.

Rory and Lucille were staring at me. They each had a look of sympathetic concern on their face. Rory shook his head and huffed out an exaggerated breath. Lucille went to the refrigerator, without asking, and brought me an unsweetened green tea.

"Here," she said as she handed me the bottle of green tea, after she removed the cap. "You're probably thirsty after a long drive."

TORCH AND PLUNDER

**

Butter-yellow rays of sun kept streaming in through the large bay windows at the front of Parker's Mortuary.

"If you can't see it yourself, if you can't feel it — and if you never thought it through completely, but you feel like it was pumped into your mind — you can't trust it. It's not real, man. All that stuff, everything you're told, it's not real," said Rory.

"All the digital content? It's not real. It's propaganda," added Lucille.

I sipped my green tea. This was heavy for me. Was there a middle ground between questioning everything (like Rory) and questioning nothing (like most people)? I wanted that.

"I don't know, man," I said. It's a cliche, but you can't always get what you want, and I knew I couldn't. I had started questioning everything and I feared — I knew — I couldn't stop.

"You have to let it go. You had so much invested in the 'system,' Brandon. You hate what you see," said Rory. "You don't like the fact that you got conned."

Lucille stared at me while Rory spoke.

I noticed her soft skin and friendly eyes when I glanced over at her. Rory was still speaking but I somehow lost the feed of his words as I thought for a second about Lucille. I was happy that she and Rory had found each other. They seemed like a special pair, perfect for each other. But what about me? Was I going to bounce around, alone forever? Should I reach back out to Karen, since I had been ignoring her for two days now?

But pay attention to what happened next.

I started processing Rory's words again, after the interlude where my mind wandered.

"...The people fight for scraps instead of changing the status quo. You understand the oligarchs want everyone locked into massive amounts of debt so they have no choice but to commit all their time to working for the oligarchs' corporate interests. They are okay with the masses getting some table scraps — even with the occasional nice house here and there. Who else is going to pay the taxes to feed back into the 'system' and let them push more of their products and their propaganda?"

"Tax revenue doesn't even matter with fiat money, Rory. You know that," said Lucille. "They make it out of thin air. That's just another mechanism to keep the people enslaved. The money is fake. It's all lies."

"Rory! If things were so bad, people would cause a change," I said, for my own benefit as much as for the others.

"That's what you don't understand, Brandon. People can't even see how bad it is — they can't see the oppression, the corruption — it's on such a massive scale people can't even process it. And even if they caught a glimpse of it, they have to get through the next day — they have the routine — they call it the grind — and they have to do it. It's prescribed; it's baked in. You realize the people who have an interest in the status quo also happen to control the propaganda spewed out of the media and corporate advertising? You realize everything you think you know, they teach you?"

"You're having the argument every which way."

"Slap me and call me Sammy!"

"You're nuts."

"You want to see it, Brandon, but you won't let yourself. You said yourself you were investigating the 'system.' Find any corruption yet? I mean, come on. Find anything that looks a little fishy?"

"I've seen some things. I think global capital controls most world governments through corporations and their media partners — products, including services, and the underlying propaganda — they apply money and debt to these things and control behavior. Humans have a herd mentality — think about it. How many people do you know that are truly unique? These governments put their boot on the throat of the people. And the levers they use are obvious. They condition them to control themselves and make them unable to exert themselves outside of the herd."

"That's a good thought. You're not constrained, Brandon. But it's not an original thought. Been said a million times."

"Well, I'll be..."

"Some people are so dependent and so far gone they can't even entertain that thought, even if they were spoon-fed it. But there's a difference between being unconstrained and being original. And the thought of corporate slavery and monetary debt... is not new. You didn't come up with that idea. Great men are original."

"I know, I pieced it together, but I read plenty of quotes from people who were on the trail of what was happening in society. People have been noticing this for a while. High-minded people in important positions. Those people have a perspective allowing them to recognize, to notice. People, patterns, facts. Normal Joe and Betty don't have time to think about this stuff and they may not even be smart enough to comprehend it. Their mind is battered with the information pumped into it for too long, too many years."

"Buried in corporations. Buried in advertising. They don't

know which way is up."

"It's sad, it's like a new species. It's not even human."

"Corporate man."

"What is corporate man like?" Rory asked me.

I hesitate, so he answered his own question: "Whatever the corporations tell him to be like!"

"Ha ha ha!" everyone laughed. I took a sip of my green tea.

Lucille stirred, out of the three of us, she was the only one seeming the slightest bit uneasy. Not in a bad way, but seeming like she had something on her mind that she wanted to get out in the open and she was struggling with it. That was my impression, but it could have been anything.

How peculiar life is! A short time ago all I had was corporate sales and now look what I am onto! Wide new area of exploration. The layer on top of the corporate products, the sugary, salty foods and the cheap goods — the layer of corporate entertainment — was poison. At least I saw it now. It wasn't too late for me. But what would I do with the information? When I thought it through to the end, the same fear pinned me down — that I would investigate forever, captivating my thoughts with interesting and true factoids and anecdotes — and then I would die, knowing all this stuff but entombed in the corporate dystopia I had uncovered but had no ability to change. It was mentally debilitating.

Rory started the conversation again.

"So, what do you think of the shop?"

"I love it. It's got a good vibe. Nice energy."

"Yeah, it's not part of the rat-race. You shopping for anything?"

"Nah."

"I was teasing. Nobody shops here. Let me ask you something, Brandon. You've been at this for months, you've investigated many things. You may not be ready to admit everything is a lie..."

"You always say that, Rory, but what do you mean? What does it really mean?" I asked.

"Basically, everything you are told is a complete lie. The corporations and the government create and disperse the lies — the people parrot them. It's a circle. It's all..." said Rory, before I interrupted him.

"You sound angry when you say that, Rory. You shoot yourself in the foot when you run around saying everything is a lie because then everyone can attack you. You seem unhinged when you say that. That's when they zap you with the conspiracy theorist tag and then it's over."

"Well, yeah, that's what they do to you. I just don't let it bother me. I continue to conspire," said Rory with a smile.

"Who is they, anyway?" I asked, with sarcasm in my voice. As I said it, I glanced from Rory to Lucille and noticed she looked concerned. Or maybe that was my imagination kicking in.

On the wall over her left shoulder I saw a David Bowie poster from the Thin White Duke era.

I couldn't get over the hump, like Rory had. I couldn't give in to blanket statements. I struggled with Rory's argument. How could everything be a lie? I didn't want to be dismissed as a crackpot. I had done a lot of things with my life — I had worked at big companies and sold prominent products. I didn't want to throw all of it away for the Loch-Ness Monster or to argue about radiation making the moon landing one hundred percent impossible for humans.

"You know who they are. 'They!'" hollered Rory, smiling.

Lucille, who had been pretty passive, interjected, "You came here because you were seeking something. A different way, a different path. You've been doing your own research. But you can't get there. You've met Dr. Lowd. You met us by chance. Give over all the way. Give over all your preconditions and preconceived notions. It's like Rory said, you are not fully constrained. But in some ways, you are still dependent on your old framework. You operate inside it, you don't question it, you don't question how to change it. As long as that is the case you cannot conceive of what needs to be done to tear it down. If you don't know how to tear it down how can it be replaced?"

I had the same feeling I had many times as a child when I would stay with my grandparents in Palo Alto. My grandmother would make these cookies (part cookie, part cracker) — it was some sort of a traditional German recipe, I think. I hated them! She would walk over with them in a bowl, her feet plodding along inside her slippers. I knew what was coming — those cookies! I wanted to pass, to say no, to turn them away. But I never did. I always ate the cookies. I hated them! The taste! I loved most cookies, but I resented these. It was, to be clear, the only thing that bothered me about my grandmother, a wonderful woman.

And here I was, with Lucille and Rory — two random conspiracy theorists I had met by the river — and they were lobbying me to cast aside all my beliefs, to free my mind from the pretensions that had been poured inside my head since I was a little kid. Throw them all away! I didn't want to, I wanted to hold on to the comfort of everything that I knew, the comfort of the corporations and the way the sterile suburbs interacted with the decayed, violent cities. But like eating the cookies — I knew I was going to do it. I knew I was going to drop everything and rebuild my thoughts from nothing. The groundwork had already been set. My research had already taught me too much.

"Okay, I'll tear everything down, I'll do it. What do I have to lose?"

It felt exciting to say that I was ready to free myself from my constrained — my programmed — way of thinking, but how could I be certain I could accomplish it?

It happened again, I questioned my sanity. Was I insane? I felt light-headed.

"You have nothing to lose, Brandon. You have to give over to it. There is so much to gain."

"Everything is so uniform, so entrenched. When you drive around, you realize everything has been strip-mined by the global government. Everything is gas stations, fast food, strip malls selling chain products. There is no local culture anymore. Everywhere could be anywhere, it's all interchangeable. You see that, right?"

"For sure. They stamped out the unique diversity of little communities, little areas, with the global kind of diversity. Low-paid wage slaves from wherever working for some mega-corporation. The people who live in the United States now have nothing in common with one another — except the ties of the global corporations they consume from and work for. It's a disaster."

"It's sickening."

"What can be done about it?"

"I don't know. Doc thinks 'petty destruction' and 'non-compliance.' I'm not convinced."

"It's not enough. We love Dr. Lowd but it's not enough.

They simply ramp up the advertising and increase the taxes — the petty destruction can take down the quality of living but it never rouses anyone from their slumber. The 'system' will survive anything like that. People notice and move on. After a while, they don't even notice the damage, they ignore it. They look past it in a zombie state, pacified by mega-corporate products and entertainment — staring at their smart phone. Petty destruction doesn't inspire anyone to do anything, not one thing."

"Uhmm, so things carry on as before."

"It makes the Globo-Corps stronger. They entrench. They get to add a victim complex to their aggressive posture. There's nothing more powerful than a rich, aggressive victim. Someone who can cry out in pain as he strikes you."

"Well, what then?"

"Torch and plunder."

"Torch and plunder? Seriously?"

"Yes."

"Really?"

"What else is there?"

"Nobody's doing that."

"Recently, at least. There have been civilizational recoveries before. Demons have been expelled from societies before. Don't be so certain this 'system' is permanent. We have to fight."

The idea of attacking the global mega-corps was ridiculous on its face. The corporations had the sanction of the state. They had the capital. They could bring to bear the power of the police force on a moment's notice. But for a second, I indulged my fantasy, suggested by Rory. I gave in to the possibility of a different type of world. I gave into the possibility that a corporate techno-kleptocracy did not have to be a permanent condition! I gave in to the desire to do something great. Torch and plunder. Torch and plunder! For a moment, I ceased to be Brandon Brooks, corporate sales-man. I was no longer a corporate dog, a corporate jester being kicked or mocked by my betters, the men who made the decisions about what to do with the money generated by the sale of products and the massive haul from taxation and re-taxation. They could put a tax on top of a tax on top of a tax, all auto-deducted and efficiently pumped into the globo-techno government coffers. I floated above my usual status, in the realm of possibility. I became strong, with a desire to do great things. I was radiant, powerful, robust, sturdy. I felt freedom to go with this strength — I was somehow unbound from the corporate tether. For a moment, at least.

But the freedom was based on nothing real. I would have to create my own freedom. What would I torch? Where would I plunder? With what army? I crashed back to earth only a few moments later. I had no exact notion of how long the ecstasy of the possible lasted. My thoughts were flashing so fast at the time that my perspective of actual time was lost.

"Sounds like a death wish," I said, after the ecstasy of the possible had left my mind. "You're gassing me up, man. Nothing is going to happen, nothing will change."

"It's better to try — to do something — than to go on like this, surrounded by big food, big tech, big pharma, big government, big chem and big media, among others. Better to go down fighting."

"Rory, stop with the gloom! I know it's bad. I said I would break down my thoughts. I will. But I don't want to go negative. Too much negativity all the time — that can't be overcome. It saps energy. It destroys people. I've seen it happen."

We spent the rest of our time together musing about many topics. We shared anecdotes and theories. We schemed, we ranted. We railed against the 'system.' We conspired! But no decision was reached with regard to any specific action. The oligarchy was safe and would remain in position to tighten the vise.

FISTS LIKE CLUBS

**

Somewhere in Antarctica

"Stop the negativity!" bellowed Ranald, standing up from the triangular table. "For many years we have stayed here, freezing our tails off..."

"We don't have tails, Ranald!" yelled Vilfred, swilling grog and laughing. To accentuate his line, Vilfred rattled and rapped his massive iron rings on the triangular table. This brought great distress, this time, to the rack of penguins, since sometimes Vilfred did the same thing to let Mauve know he was hungry. It seems that the penguins had grown a bit tired of accepting the fate of the boiler, at least if their noises were any indication.

The rack of penguins let out a cacophony of murmurs and squeals!

Mauve, the nook-demon, who loved literal humor — and was proud of his spiked tail — laughed heartily. "Humph, Harrumph, Ha Ha, Muaaahhh!" He stared at Vilfred and realized that the rapping of the rings was for emphasis, it wasn't a request for fried penguin.

"Silence, I am speaking to our plan. We have been trapped here for almost hundreds of years. We need to make some plans and we need to make some decisions. I will have no more interruptions! As much as I respect and love the sacrifice of the Crabeater Seal and the humble Penguin I will not ask them to sacrifice their flesh for us for much longer. We will be making a change! We will be leaving the cold."

"It won't work!" yelled Vilfred.

"SILENCE!" bellowed Ranald, smashing his fist on the

table. "By God I will have you in the vault!" Ranald pause, then continued, "We all know what happened with our ancestors, back at the time of the great enchantment. They took human wives. They birthed our relatives, our brothers and sisters, who, like us, worked for the Dark One. They ran through everything doing violence, as did we my brothers, as did we! We ate through their supplies and we took everything they made available to us and everything they did not! The destruction that followed cannot be cataloged, the devastation, the lawlessness, everyone turned against everyone else. Our brothers and sisters, our relatives — the ones who went to the tropics, they were killed by a plague like none the world had ever seen, wrought, first, by a vile man and an unsuspecting monkey and spread through unnatural, unspeakable deeds. Their bones are entombed! We came here to escape the great plague — as you remember. But it was never meant to be permanent! Oh no! We stayed because we became obsolete. Weapons of a war that is no longer being fought in the old style. So here we are. But we are still breathing! We are all that remain, you, Vilfred, you, Eindride and me — plus the females and the young ones. There are no more of our kind, besides our humble outpost."

"You don't know that, Ranald. Other giants may have escaped to the cold... to the north, perhaps," said the Vile.

"I don't believe it. And trapped here we are! Forgotten, by the Dark One, we used to be his favorite toys — oh the damage we could bring to bear! Fists like clubs! Hammer-time! Axes and clubs! Our path was always filled with blood! With Un-righteousness!"

Ranald continued, while Eindride and Vilfred looked on with familiarity and a splash of boredom. Their faces indicated they had heard it all before.

"But the Dark One tired of our skills, of our particular form of brutality. As you know! He was able to access his victims more easily through a different set of violent arts. Less bloody, for sure. The mind-trap! The mind-bend! He was able to unleash and capture his victims, binding them to a life of service through messaging only. Propaganda! It's so easy over a long time frame, and then the humans reinforce the behavior amongst themselves. We became obsolete. No more smashing and bashing and rampaging and pillaging! The jingles, the repetition — the things that bind the people to his ways, to his new modes and orders. It was genius! It was beyond our pay grade, but I understand why he chose a different approach — think of the efficiency. Giants running around bashing villages into submission is one thing. Controlling people with electronic messaging, pacifying them with evil material and sub-standard nutrition, with social and personal degradation... with population bombs from the most backwards and desolate places on earth... evil genius. The wedge!"

"Ay, the wedge! Remember the magnificent Cathedrals the Christians used to build?" asked Eindride, casually. "I have to admit, those were magnificent structures. Fun to smash, when we worked as we did. But they always rebuilt them. The humans and their spirit..."

"They always came back no matter how much pain we inflicted on them," added the Vile, licking his lips.

"Maybe that is why Satan changed his strategy..."

"Ayyy."

"The Dark One has divided them from the Prince — mentally. I watch the videos Tyferius pulls down from the ether, there is a bland nothing-ness, a disgusting landscape, a strange void combined with evil undertones — degeneracy brought about by Satanic subversion — filled with corporate music and a trash economy, a trash world existing in full replacement of the splendor of the old human communities and buildings."

"Trash World!" yelled the Vile.

"Nothing upon nothing, with nothing only replaced by something when it is trash and serves an evil purpose."

"Trash world!" yelled the Vile, swigging from his grog barrel.

"No goods are artisanal! There is no true craft, no craftsmen, no-one who transcends the base level of humanity to make something glorious, something magical."

"How do you know?"

"I just told you. I watch the videos Tyferius the Troublesome brings down from the clouds!"

"You know nothing of those videos. They can fake anything. People could say anything and you would believe it! You are stupid."

"They are real. Belly up!"

"Nay! Calm down, the both of you," interjected Eindride.

"I don't think you are understanding me. The Dark One convinced the humans to stop making fabulous, glorious — permanent — temples to the Righteous One — instead they became drab and interchangeable, bland, embarrassing, shameful and low."

"You don't know."

"I do know, I have seen the videos Tyferius pulled from the ether."

"I told you, Those can be fake!"

"They are nothing of the sort."

"So what! Enough of this! You have no point!"

"I have a point, Vile. And I will show it to you," replied Ranald, patting the sword that was strapped to his hip.

"You only like to hear your stupid voice you big lug!"

"Bite your tongue or belly up!"

"Humph, Harrumph, Ha Ha, Muaaahhh!" laughed the nook-Demon. He loved the conflict!

"I am forced into this speech because you never think of anything independently. You and Vilfred, I love you, you are my brothers, but if you are left to your own devices you will do nothing. We will be here a thousand years from now, eating fried penguins and drinking grog. And freezing our tails off!"

"Humph, Harrumph, Ha Ha, Muaaahhh! No tail on you but big spike on my tail! Regal!" chimed in Mauve. Ranald gave Mauve a harsh look — he would often overlook Mauve's laughter but Mauve wasn't supposed to speak out. Mauve frowned and looked at his feet, muttering "Hmm-mmm."

"This area has been good for us," continued Ranald. "We survived the plague because of it, the G-A-F hybrid bacteria-virus could not survive the cold. Without this land, we would be dead like all the others of our kind. Except for the possibility of one other rumored outpost, somewhere in the frozen north."

"Humans put that on video for the views. They have a way to get paid in gold for posting original content. It's not true."

"For the last time, Eindride, you don't know!" yelled the Repellent.

"The G-A-F bacteria killed everyone of our kind, except us," Eindride said, holding firm.

"Either way, it was long ago. That risk has subsided, it is gone. I am warning you, if we stay here, forever, we will be here forever! If we never leave, we will never leave," said Ranald.

"You say the same thing then you agree with yourself and act like you said something special! You think you are smart but you're not! You are dumb like the rest of us! Fill your mouth with a penguin instead of these stupid words! Are you a giant or a jester?"

"Humph, Harrumph, Ha Ha, Muaaahhh!" laughed Mauve, anticipating a brawl.

"Silence, Vilfred. We know what has happened in the human societies — the Dark One has emerged victorious. He obliterated culture with some clever word games," said Ranald.

"You say this all the time. The words mean the opposite, or they mean nothing. Blah, blah, blah. Who cares about human culture?" retorted the Vile.

"I'll say it again, Vilfred, so you can learn something. His servants created digital propaganda to mush many different cultures together — the better cultures were not allowed to criticize the worse ones, because of brilliant concepts he introduced. Hate speech and equality. If you criticize bad cultures and bad people, its 'hate speech' and you are against 'equality.'"

"But humans are all different, right? I don't understand equal," Eindride chimed in.

"Ayyy, they are different, of course. It was just a word puzzle. It conflates different versions of the meaning of the word equality," said Ranald.

"You didn't make up these thoughts, Ranald. You are parroting someone. You buffoon, you couldn't think of this on your own," heckled the Vile.

While the Vile was speaking, one of the young giants, Chasdon, walked into the council meeting. He wasn't supposed to, but he was curious about a question he had for Ranald and couldn't stand waiting.

"Ignore him, Chasdon. He says these words but he won't fight and he won't listen."

"What are you talking about?" asked Chasdon, forgetting his original question.

"The work of the Devil, young Chasdon. Truth was silenced, across the board, and the Fallen One elevated the worse above the better, the ugly above the beautiful, the bad above the good. And he controlled the governments and corporations to suppress dissent and resistance. Only approved views and behaviors were allowed — and the views the Dark One approved of were, of course, the worst ones. He loves degeneracy and evil!" said Ranald.

"Of course he does," replied Chasdon.

"Some of the people could see it happening, but they had been outmaneuvered. The fight was lost. Disagreement with the Devil and his secularism became 'hate' — and 'hate' was branded as always bad. Even if the object of the hatred deserved much worse, like being smashed by a club. All the Devil has to do now is tighten his surveillance and censorship and use his grid to remove dissidents and no-one will ever question his global reign again," explained Ranald. "And that is what he is doing."

"He copies these words from somewhere! Look at him. The fraud!"

Ranald and Chasdon (and Eindride) seemed to ignore the Vile.

"Things always change. Why can't they change back? Why

can't someone run the Devil off?" brave Chasdon chimed in — running the risk of a spanking for speaking in the council meeting without approval.

"Well, it's a good question, Chasdon the Long. You are a smart young chap. Here's the thing: God can't fight back against the Devil if he has no army. Everything will be uniform, every man will be a bug-person capable only of consuming simple, degenerate media and corporate food — no soul," said Ranald.

"Why do we care about the stupid humans? Let them do what they want!" yelled the Vile.

"Even when we were working for the Devil, we respected their arts. Did you ever hear stories of us smashing the David? We didn't smash museums, libraries, symphony halls. Only very rarely did we smash their Churches. Now... all of those things are replaced with a cheap digital culture. It's all trash... especially the music. It's impossible to describe how bad the music is in trash world," said Eindride.

"Without outside influence, the people will continue to conform and accept the global corporate technocracy," said Ranald.

"But who cares?" asked the Vile.

"Well, it is important to us, now. We changed sides, remember? The Dark One doesn't need us anymore. His system enforces itself! We might as well make ourselves useful."

"Runa says its deeper than that. She says its never too late for us, even with the things that happened in the old days."

"Aaaaah! I don't care!" Vile bellyached.

"Well, the people didn't care, either. And for this reason their heritage, their traditions, their cultures — that's why they have been replaced with trash world. So, maybe you are like them, a bug-giant instead of a bug-person. You don't care about being worthless, you have no purpose except to eat and drink grog."

"Okay, okay, let us pretend for a second that you are a philosopher and not a mindless oaf — even though you are a mindless oaf. What should we do, Ranald?"

"Okay, I will go into more detail later but in broad strokes, we shall sail to New York, drill under the federal reserve building, steal their gold from their vault and make our way to Italy. We shall set up a new castle there and escape the cold. After we do all that, we shall work to bring down the Dark One. We will spread the Word on the world wide web of internets."

"How are you learning all these things, anyway?"

"There is a man I trust. He writes of these things on the world-wide interface I mentioned. I have learned to access it with the projection machine set up by Tyferius the Troublesome."

"Ah, I see. So we put all our faith in this man, whoever he is. This will end badly, it always does."

"It is the right thing to do, I am certain of it."

"How will we get into the vault in this building, this gold reserve?"

"Remember the expedition into our territory — it failed, they brought the big ship and they all froze? One of the kids found the ship much later..."

"Yes, I remember."

"Well, one of the things we recovered from the shipwreck was a drill, a drilling apparatus so powerful and so advanced in its capabilities — we will have no problem going through the upper ground at the reserve and taking the gold. The drill is heavy, but

Mauve and two demons are strong enough to pull it..."

"I thought the young ones broke the drill on the glacier?" asked Vilfred.

"Ha! Never! No glacier could break this thing. It breaks through everything, like it is going through jelly!" claimed Ranald.

"Speaking of jelly, I wish we had some!" said the Vile.

"We can have all the jelly we want when we get out of Antarctica, my brother."

"Never mind the jelly, we don't even have real cheese. We have a rabbit for cheese, and the rabbit won't even make any."

"Stupid Rabbit. I make stew," muttered Mauve.

The rabbit lounged on it's perch, sitting on its haunches, but did not move its face. It's ears perked up and its eyes turned to the left toward the giants, peeking to see if there was any cause for alarm. The rabbit made a nasty face at Mauve and then returned to chewing cabbage.

"The drill — it can cope quickly with all layers of stone, wood, or metal between the air and the gold, including the iron vault itself. The drill has a diamond-encrusted head which could go through the walls of the Devil's home itself."

Mauve turned his head when he heard Ranald make this particular reference to the Dark One. It brought back memories for Mauve, a simple-but-focused creature. Mauve had also worked directly for Satan. He had no independent moral compass, but saw his future, his fortunes, as bound up directly with the brothers'.

"How can we carry this drill?"

"It fits on the ship. Then, Mauve and the other two demons will pull it in front of us, on a sled — one with wheels, not blades."

"I am work hard, eighteen hour days," said Mauve.

Ranald sat down. He leaned back. Vilfred stared straight ahead. Eindride breathed slowly, then took a sip of grog — a small one this time, not the usual chug-a-lug.

"I don't see why we should do this," said Vilfred the Vile. "But at the same time, I don't see why we shouldn't. It is decided, then. I will vote with Ranald in favor of this plan. Make it unanimous, Eindride. Give your assent, we are a team."

Eindride, who usually purposely worked to come across as less intelligent than he was, didn't do so now. Instead, he paused, then spoke slowly in a low, rumbling voice, "One thing. Who is the man, the one you say writes on the magical projector?" he asked, looking at Ranald with an intense stare.

"The man is Doctor Hogan Lowd."

"Is our trust in him well-placed? Have you communicated with him, directly?"

"Ay, it is and I have. He started us down this road."

"Now we know who Ranald copies his words from! He admits it!" exclaimed the Vile.

Eindride spoke, ignoring Vilfred's constant criticisms of Ranald, "Okay, well I vote with you, my brothers. I vote in favor of the plan. First the gold! Then to Italy!"

"Ayyy!" they all cheered, despite the dissent voiced during the council meeting.

"We leave tomorrow! Have the kids check the ship and I will have the females load the food and goods, on penalty of spanking! Mauve and the demons shall load the drill. Vilfred, do

DOGS OF THE OLIGARCHS | F.C. FOX

not forget to leash the wolvine first thing in the morning for transport to the ship. Tomorrow we sail!"

"Ayyyy!" a celebration echoed throughout the chamber. Everyone swilled more grog. Mauve's tail moved from side to side. The rabbit had a confused look on its face (no mention was made of bringing the rabbit), but it ate cabbage anyway.

BLACK HOLE

**

I left Rory and Lucille's shop after a while. Walking out the door and into the beautiful Sonoma sun — yellow rays which weren't strong enough to break free, out on their own, to create a bright yellow blaze; instead, they were overpowered by the blue from the sky as they bounced and floated down to eye level. Surrounded by beautiful light and trees — with a few birds singing — I felt a momentary elation which proved fleeting. Why was I — slowly but surely — leaving the safety of my corporate sales world? Why would I throw it all away to fight a 'system' I didn't understand and I couldn't defeat?

I was safe in my old world. Corporate sales, commissions, apartments. A date here and there, nothing serious. This move, dabbling with the Rorys, Lucilles and Doctor Lowds of the world — it was less predictable. I was out of my routine, out of my element. Out of my turtle shell. What if I liked Karen? What if I went and did something with her, something traditional, something permanent? With that thought, I felt as if I had actually lost my mind. Stop it, Brandon Brooks! What was I thinking? I was immune to those kind of pressures. I had decided long ago that I didn't want anything more than a few dates when social media was involved in the equation. I didn't want to be serious with anyone who lived a digital life on those platforms. And, every girl — every one — did. A pretty girl without Facebook and Instagram? Pffft. That's a fish, without water. I could be with them temporarily, but in the long term, social media was a non-starter for me. I didn't want it in my life. The content — the ebb and flow of content — on those platforms was not for me. Dating a girl who allowed herself to be contacted by random e-people for a dopamine hit? Nope. It was insane! Hard pass.

I got in my car and drove south — still in a haze — there was a contrast between my car, my Audi, which was ripping along the Northern California roads, tires gripping and sometimes squealing on turns taken at a particularly aggressive angle while traveling at a high rate of speed and the general tranquility of the Northern California weather.

The drive home was nice, it was uneventful. The rest of the day, then the rest of the week, went by. I don't like to focus too much on my own personal unpleasant experiences, but what happened next caused several more weeks to go by while I existed in something of a blur. I didn't get much done in any regard. My investigation, my hobbies, the gym — they were all put on hold. I passed time by watching movies. I was filled — my internals, my internals — with a stinky wind and a dirty rain, I felt like a hunchback tethered to a church bell — except my tether was to the commode and ringing the bell was malodorous rather than melodious. I cursed my circumstance! I couldn't concentrate on anything, including my research. I didn't think of the 'system,' of Doctor Lowd, of Rory or Lucille, of Karen. The thought of pursuing another sales job did not even cross my mind. I focused on my health and keeping my food down. I would proceed in a fog from my bed to the store to the couch — with many stops in between, at the place I will not name here. It was a rough few weeks. For the most part, I was able to stay positive. I focused on eating fresh foods and drinking clean liquids — no alcohol (no trips to Oswald's) and, although I was not capable of completely eliminating caffeine (a personal weakness) — I managed to limit caffeine to one coffee drink, taken in the mornings.

Eventually, this trial, this tribulation of the stomach — it passed. And I promise that by relaying this fact, using that word, that I do not intend to make a pun. It was over, and I felt like myself again.

Life came back into focus. The haze lifted from my mind. The people I had ignored for those several weeks when my stomach refused to settle, I started seeing their communications again, on my smart phone. Some missed calls. Messages on a variety of messaging platforms (I had six of those on my smart phone). I thought desperately about going back to how I was before this 'period' of my life started. I wanted to un-notice everything I had learned. I didn't want to know about the 'system,' not anymore. I sure as eggs didn't want to fight the 'system.' Taking my normal drive and seeing the landscape full of gas stations, fast food restaurants, chain stores and billboards advertising this or that — it was too much, too prevalent, too entrenched — there was no entry point to challenge it. It would grow and grow and grow until every part of the world looked the same. People living in small apartments providing a small service to the 'system' while consuming the products it pushed. The unspoiled lands would all be purchased and owned by a select group of oligarchs. The riches, already heavily concentrated, would concentrate further, the tax and consumer mega corporate government loop. How could I combat that? I couldn't. I wanted to go back to sales, to work activities. I didn't want to know about all of the things I had been looking into. I hated this feeling. I wanted to fit in, again.

That's what I told myself, anyway. But it wasn't true, it wasn't real. I didn't want that, I didn't want to fit in, eat fast food, drink soda and take their 'entertainment' right to my face until I finally died, weak and powerless.

I wanted to fight. I wanted to fight against Globo to the death, if I had to. I would not comply with it, a rotten, corrupt, degenerate 'system.'

It only took a few minutes after the wave of doubt passed for me to admit to myself that I would fight. I had to figure out a way to get better at fighting them. Dr. Lowd's answer was Petty Destruction. I didn't love it. Too much risk. Globo had too many cameras. Their minions were everywhere, watching, ready to report back to the founders of their dark religion. They would do anything to harm people who fought against complete subjugation to Globo and their new ways of living. If you go the petty destruction route, all it took was getting caught one time — while blowing up their stuff — and they could take away your freedom. Globo had a whole industry — the 'legal system' — which utilized indentured servants to enforce their arbitrary rules — the ones that preserved the system were enforced while everything else was ignored. And once you're in the 'criminal system' part of the bigger system, you have punched the tar baby so to speak. Few have escaped it. They can do all sorts of stuff to you to track you, to change your bio-mechanics, whatever. They can drug you in jail, even murder you if you're dangerous enough to their interests. Jeffrey Epstein, the Israeli operative who blackmailed politicians and the wealthy, he's a perfect example. They killed him, right in his jail cell. I didn't think petty destruction, or anything like that, was worth the risk. With the personal dislike of petty destruction (I admired people willing to do it, but the details weren't for me, I thought it was a reckless tactic), I was faced with a choice: harness Dr. Lowd's concept of non-compliance to bring about change; or, come up with a concept of my own to attack Globo. Whatever I chose, I needed something that was a real weapon.

While I was in the haze with my digestive issues, the contact from my family had been ramping up. Not feeling well, and focused on recovery and returning my stomach function to normal, I had ignored them. That only emboldened them! Their fingers dialed and typed. It was so aggravating. I rolled my eyes as my smart phone antagonized me with sounds and other notifications.

My step-mom Janice called me half a dozen times and sent

ten messages. My dad chimed in with a call and a message. My aunt lobbed in a phone call (I suspected that Janice put her up to it). My half-brother Timothy, the simpleton who posted hysterically about me on Facebook, even messaged me asking where I was.

I had ignored them, but then, my step-mom called again. Feeling better, I figured I had to get the call out of the way. I answered.

"Brandon, my goodness, you disappeared... how have you been?"

"Janice, I'm fine. I was having some problems with my stomach and I didn't feel very talkative. I'm sorry. I'm fine."

"Oh... are you okay? We are all worried sick about you. Nobody has heard from you and no-one has heard whether you have been able to lock down new employment. A nine-to-five."

"Yes, I feel like I'm pretty much recovered. I don't know what it was, maybe some food poisoning or something. Whatever it was, it lingered and it took me a long time to get right. I've been watching what I eat and taking probiotics and a couple other supplements. I think it was a turkey burger that got me, I'll be off those for a couple of years. And no, I have been focused on my gut I haven't been working on finding a job."

"I'm really sorry to hear that you weren't feeling well. I'm glad it sounds like you're recovered. That's great."

"Thanks, Janice."

"I told your dad about our conversation last time. You know, the one where we talked about your investigations. He's been ranting about your being a 'lousy conspiracy theorist.' And, Timothy keeps fueling the fire, once a week with a new post on Facebook. Like clockwork. Think about calling him. He misses you. He's worried about you."

I rolled my eyes. I hated when I did that — it was the expression of a teenage girl. It made me feel powerless and immature. But I could already see what was happening, I was being categorized and branded — immediately — for taking even a short-term different approach. And this was happening amongst my family, people who love me. It had been a few months since I quit MindSmash, and not having a "nine-to-five" in that time was enough to set everyone off. To set them against me.

Janice and I wrapped up the conversation without saying much more. Just the usual pleasantries. I let her know that I missed her (I genuinely did) and to say 'hi' to everyone and I would check in soon.

But the snowball had already formed and was rolling down the hill. According to my family, I was now known as a full-blown conspirator. People were posting responses to my brother Timothy's weekly posts, each of them making a different crack about the moon, frogs, flouride, big-foot, lizard-people, tinfoil hats, chemtrails or whatever. There were over thirty replies to the original post, from people who had never met me, mocking my 'views,' which they invented.

I guess it was an interesting time to be accused of questioning or investigating the 'system!'

There may have been, still, a part of me that cared what my brother Timothy thought and what he wrote on his precious digital tablet — the most important part of his life. There had to be, because each time I heard about his posts I felt agitation, even some anger. But, that part was negligible as those emotions always subsided quickly. If I had seen the posts with my own eyes, I hardly think I would have even responded to Timothy. I didn't have an account on Facebook. I had no real interest in that stuff, nor did I care much what Timothy thought or said.

The next day, feeling better, I drove downtown, into San Mateo. I didn't have anything on my list to do, except to drink some coffee. Although days had passed since I recovered from my set of stomach problems, I hadn't really resumed going to the gym, not yet. "Just a few days more," I told myself, "And I'll re-start my training." I felt like I had been physically weakened by my bout with the stomach ailment. I didn't want the weakness to spill over to my mental acuity and tenacity. I needed to be strong. But today, only coffee and maybe a boiled egg or two, plus a couple of bananas. I wasn't there yet, I didn't want to challenge my stomach.

I walked into my usual coffee shop and ordered an Americano, black. My plan, which I was making up on the fly, was to go to the coast and find a place to walk by the ocean. I considered the possibilities. Big Sur? Half Moon Bay? At no point, even after the call with Janice, did I feel any sort of regret for what happened at MindSmash or anywhere else. I didn't feel any pangs of longing for a nine-to-five as Janice called it. Those things were eating away at me, eating at my soul.

The hankering that I did feel, that was different. I felt a need to get started. If I never started, how could I finish anything? But what was I doing? If this adventure never had a beginning, how could it have an end? How could I change anything.

My smart phone buzzed and, surprisingly, I saw a message from Karen. I had ignored her even before I had the stomach problems. The message said she wanted to talk. Oh no, I thought, I didn't want to get entangled in something romantic. Romance meant involvement and involvement meant time, emotions, activities. I mean, I had enjoyed spending time with Karen — I found her engaging, mysterious and beautiful — but I didn't really see a purpose. I wasn't feeling very needy, not from a companionship standpoint. Physically, even, I was doing okay by myself, for the time being. I didn't want everything else that always came with a relationship. I guessed she had seen something in me that made her want to spend more time with me — some conceit shining through? I tried to put myself in her position. A difficult task, if there ever was one, a man trying to figure out the inner workings — the thought process — of a woman. I felt like a ship, lost at sea during a storm, getting tossed here and there. No anchor, the sail was torn. I had no base of knowledge, no base of information, to even start to understand what she wanted to talk about. I knew how I thought about things, in the past at least, and I projected my way of thinking onto her.

But how could it be accurate?

When I thought of romantic relationships, and even imagined one with Karen, things were simple. Did I love being around her? Was I attracted to her, physically? Could I 'love' her? These were pretty simple things, and I based the answers on how I felt. If I liked how I felt, it would be a simple, "You and me babe, how about it?" It wasn't a rational exercise, not for me. It wasn't a technical calculation. All of the answers were in the affirmative — Karen was great. I still didn't want anything. The time was wrong.

But what was it that caused her to message me? I was just a guy. Reasonably smart, reasonably successful, reasonably handsome, reasonably funny, reasonably fit. But, there are plenty of guys like that. There are plenty, also, who are smarter, funnier, better looking, stronger, can run farther, chop more firewood, whatever. All of that stuff. So, what would cause her to give attention to me? Was it that she thought that I was the best she could do, at least for now? Because a woman, a girl, she could always head off to greener pastures, right? That was the current theory of liberation. I didn't even know Karen's exact age, but looking at her, she was at least five or six years away from hitting the wall. That's a lot of time to find new boyfriends, especially if she kept a presence on-line where there were an endless number of sycophants throwing the kitchen sink at them. The whole dynamic was insane, and I was off that carousel for now, whether the ride was with Karen or anyone else. I would sit things out for a while on the sidelines, I wasn't worried about settling down.

Right? Right. The whole situation was a quandary for me. I didn't know how to react to her contacting me. I didn't have a plan as to how to respond to the attention, given my wants and needs at this particular time. Those were throttling me back, I hadn't even really thought about this topic for quite some time.

Minutes went by like this, I was thinking about Karen, about relationships — a manifestation of exactly what I was trying to avoid for the time being. I didn't want to spend my time like this. Maybe I was concealing my feelings for her? What feelings?

I realized it wasn't going to be easy to push the topic out of my head — Karen had a nice presence. I decided to respond to her, partly so I could stop thinking about all of this stuff.

So, my curiosity got the best of me and I messaged her, with a quick apology saying that I had been ill (which probably struck her as phony, despite its general truth) and asking her to let me know when she wanted to get together.

My smart phone rang with a call, almost immediately. It was Karen.

"Hi, Karen."

"Brandon, can you meet me now?"

"Umm, well, yeah, I think so. Where?"

"Rodney's on fourth," replied Karen, referencing a diner in downtown San Mateo.

I paused for a just a second without saying anything.

"What, do you need to freshen up or something? Come on, Brandon, I'm the girl."

"Okay, ummm... yeah, see you in a few minutes. I'll probably be there in ten," I said.

"See you in a bit."

ASSASSINATION PLOT?

**

I beat Karen to the diner. I sat down at a table and ordered a water and a coffee. So here's the thing: I can't say exactly what I was thinking of Karen at the time she walked into the restaurant. If I am totally honest, I would admit I was dead wrong with the entire train of thought I had undertaken, about thirty minutes before. The entire scenario I had concocted in my head — the one about Karen seeking a romantic relationship with me, was a figment of my imagination. That wasn't what this was about, not at all. But I'll get to that.

As I sat waiting for Karen, my mind wandered. I took a breath and tried to get myself to slow everything down. I didn't need to be thinking about thirty things at once, wondering about this and anticipating that. "Settle down, Brandon," I told myself. There was no set pattern to these occasions, I thought — and there was no pattern, really, to my thoughts about my investigation of the 'system.' I had found that my mind was less regulated — more prone to wild streaks and tangents — since I had been out of sales.

There used to be a specific time for everything, it helped me sort my thoughts, it helped me partition my day — and those partitions also affected the inner workings of my mind. Since my day was less regulated, I filled the space dancing around in my own head. I didn't like the feeling, to be honest. Again, I found myself questioning my own sanity — and I had a strict personal policy against doing that.

In the old days, I would wake up in the morning and drink my coffee and read the stories the corporations pushed into my phone. A mish-mash of events, politics, sports and opinion pieces. And advertorials, of course. It seemed like the merger between mass-produced corporate product and 'world or national news' had been completed. There was no difference between the two things, and the items that the media wrote about always seemed to make a strong case for some geopolitical activity, for a degenerate social change, or for the purchase of some corporate product — sometimes all three at once. The social change component was hard to swallow — no behavior was too strange for them to try to normalize, and they pushed the behaviors over and over again, year after year. No lie, no amount of harm couldn't be sold with the right amount of repetition. People just gave up and stopped being revolted by whatever was being pushed on them. They calculated that it wasn't worth the energy; life is short. I think that is the wrong calculation. But, trust me, that's what happened.

Look what they had done to people! Even in the diner, at this very moment, everyone was staring at their respective computer device (in the form of a smart phone). Everyone stared at their screen, except one old woman in the corner, sitting by herself and reading a book. Poetry? The others were zombies chained to smart phones, as everyone, seemingly, had become in a few short years following their introduction. One day, people suddenly had a device in their hand, a short time later, it seemed as if they could not live without it, without the information pulsating on the screen — without the validation of posting pictures or text to their digital accounts. It was surreal — and it seemed irreversible. Many had transferred their identity, their entire personality, to the device and the digital accounts it contained. It was hard to say whether the device was more human — if connection to other humans is counted — than the device's holder. Or maybe neither was human, maybe they were, individually and collectively, something else.

I marveled at the social change.

In my current state — unemployed, no nine-to-five, no

office, no cube, I had friends but those, by and large had nine-to-fives and busy lives. Actually, not by and large, they all did the nine-to-five thing, mostly for mega-corporations, for Globo itself. Separately, many had wives or girlfriends and were busy posting on digital media in their spare time. To top it off, a number of my friends had moved away from California which had become a crowded polyglot with the wokest of all woke politics, perhaps, ever seen. How woke can you be? California was trying to find out. I thought, sometimes, of leaving. But retreating from my homeland — even in its current version — never sat well with me. Where would I go? Who would I be? Brandon, or some strange, rootless version of myself? I had to stay and fight it out. I had to figure out why things were as they were.

Here I was, right now, doing the very thing I was growing weary of. Thinking in circles about topics without any possibility of resolution. I just told myself not to do this!

I could go on like this forever, or so it seemed. Thankfully, Karen walked in and sat down. I was granted an escape from my mental merry-go-round, but now I expected I would have to run the feminine question gauntlet. I clenched my teeth, involuntarily, not knowing what to expect from this conversation. I didn't have any angst about it, as I had no expectation and, while I liked Karen, I didn't have much skin in the game. We hung out a couple of times, so what?

As she sat down I reflexively moved my hair to each side, out of my eyes. My hair had gotten pretty unruly in the last few months and I had forgotten to shave for at least a week.

She smiled and said, "Hi, Brandon. Thanks for meeting me."

I smiled back, casually, and replied, "Of course, Karen. How's your morning going?"

"Well, I've had better mornings but we don't need to go through that, I need to be honest with you about some things," she said, staring at me intently.

I paused. Caution overtook me, I had no idea where she was going with this. My rambling thoughts, from earlier, about our interactions, about our relationship — it wasn't even a relationship, so whatever it was — ran through my head again, speeding through my mind like a getaway driver.

"Okay, well shoot," I said, still casual.

"Listen, there's something going on and I wanted to get your thoughts on it," Karen said, with an intense look on her face and what I thought was worry in her eyes — something I hadn't seen in our time together at the bar and at the mall. She was carefree on those days, now I was seeing something different. It looked like concern, maybe even fear.

"What is it? What's going on?" I asked, staring back at her. My mind, wandering all morning until this exact moment, became clear and focused. This didn't seem like a relationship talk, I'd been through plenty of those and this wasn't starting out like one. My face flushed with this recognition. I felt a twinge of embarrassment based on my presumption and all the ridiculous thoughts I had in my head. Karen may not have thought of me, at all, in the way I had imagined. I breathed out in a quiet puff. "Hold your horses, Casanova," I thought. I almost smirked due to the tsunami of self-reflection and semi-embarrassment blasting me in the face.

"I have to say... I'm not trying to drag you into this situation. I need a fresh look at what's going on. I needed someone to talk it through with. My girlfriends aren't right for that..." she said, trailing off at the end and not looking me in the eye for the first time during the short start of the conversation.

173

"Okay, got it. You can talk generally or you can trust me to keep the details confidential. It's up to you, Karen."

"Well, it's my dad. There's a group of people trying to kill him," she said, meeting my eyes again as she spoke.

I processed what she said and tried to pick up on what was being said by the look, the emotion, the strong connection from her soul to mine via our eye contact.

"What?" I replied, sharply. I was thrown, and I know my face conveyed that fact to Karen.

I was wondering, these past months, about my grip on reality. Now, in a flash, I wondered about Karen's. That type of thing is for spy novels, Netflix, whatever. It's not normal, everyday stuff.

"Yes, I'm certain of it. He doesn't believe me, of course."

"Have you ... have you gone to the police?"

"They're in on it. We can't trust the cops or the feds. They're all corrupt. Not the day-to-day ones, sure. They would be fine, many of them are honest and try to do the right thing. But this thing with my dad is being watched at a high level. If we went through regular intake - with the cops -- their eyes would be on us in no time. And the group after my dad, it's a network with ties to the government and big corporations. Freelance enforcers — paid by the NGOs."

"Why would they be after your dad?" I asked, trying to understand the situation. I was skeptical, of course, but I didn't allow that to show through in my countenance. It seemed ridiculous, but I was sitting here and had to say something.

"Brandon?"

"What?"

Karen looked confused. The waitress walked over, for the second time, but sensed that we were engrossed in conversation and not ordering yet, so she walked away.

"He said he told you some things... I guess I don't know how much, though."

"Who did?"

"What do you mean?" she asked, exasperated.

"Who told me?"

"My dad, Brandon, who do you think we are talking about?" said Karen, flustered.

"I know, Karen, but... who is your dad?"

"Ha! Oh, man! I thought you knew... Dr. Lowd is my father."

I didn't respond, not right away. At first it was comical, with the miscommunication about Dr. Lowd's identity — but, with the confusion ironed out, the silence was soon marked by dread. I'm certain I had a stunned look on my face, more so than the one a few moments before. A few seconds and my feet were back underneath me. Out of nowhere, I thought about the hole in the ground, the one behind where Karen and I had parked at the mall.

"I had no idea he's your dad, I thought you just knew each other!" I exclaimed.

"I figured he said something before he introduced us... I assumed! Also, with our age difference, I figured you would realize my dad and I weren't random friends. But never-mind that, I thought he told you," Karen said loudly, laughing again.

A moment of levity always helps a dire situation.

"That's funny. But, the other stuff, that's not funny. What

makes you think they are after him?"

"Well, someone that worked for my dad, years ago, tapped into some communication that makes us pretty certain. The guy hasn't worked for my dad for years, but they kept in touch, and he came upon the conversation accidentally in his government job. He's not corrupted, my dad's friend. It's a group of ex-CIA and ex-Mossad guys working in reconnaissance and enforcement for global money, the banks and the big corporations — which are in some ways the same thing. You know the things my dad calls Globo... I'm sure he told you."

There was a pause and I let her comments sink in.

"Why would you come to me? I mean, we're friends but I don't see what I have here. It's not that I don't want to be involved. I don't want to pretend I have some ability to offer protection when I don't. We should go to the police. If something happened..." I said, trailing off in thought.

"Well, no, don't get me wrong. I'm not looking for protection for my dad, like a bodyguard. He's supposed to be working on that — even though he's completely discounting the threat, at least when he talks to me. He's a stubborn guy. I'm not here to talk about physical protection. I wouldn't do that to you."

"Well then, what is this about?"

Never in my life had I encountered such a strange situation. I went from the sincere thought that I was contacted by Karen to discuss 'us' — Brandon and Karen. You know, whether we would hang out again and spend more time together. Instead, I was hit with information I never expected. I thought of Dr. Lowd as an interesting, albeit eccentric, fellow. Now, I was faced with the surprising disclosure that he was Karen's father and may have been in physical danger.

Why all of a sudden? Dr. Lowd had been railing against corporate and government corruption for longer than I had been alive. He was getting up there in years. Why would the corporate-government complex take notice now? Why would Globo kill him now?

I would have been considerably amused — it seemed so far-fetched, like a wild, paranoid conspiracy theory — had not the story Karen told involved a shadowy assassination plot. Assassination didn't sit well with me on a Tuesday, or on any day of the week. I was ninety-nine percent sure there was no plot; there would be no assassination. I mean, how could there be? But the one percent — creeping doubt — was ominous and it hung in the air. It wouldn't go away.

"They're going to murder him, Brandon. They're gonna... they're gonna kill my dad. I'm sure of it. We need to do something. I'm not even sure what I'm asking for."

I stared at Karen's eyes and swallowed. I stared at her, speechless.

FORTY-FIVE FOURTEEN

❊❊

The sun shone through the diner window causing a soft warmth to hit my right side and Karen's left. I couldn't help but notice that Karen looked quite fetching, despite being frazzled by relaying her suspicions of an assassination plot against her dad. Her cheeks had a really nice shape and she had lovely skin. Her eyes stayed focused on me.

I broke up the heaviness of the conversation, temporarily, by asking if she wanted to order anything. The waitress came back and she ordered a cup of tea. I added my coffee to the order and that was that. Metal and glass clattered in the background as the kitchen staff went about their business, preparing eggs and bacon and sausage and biscuits and all the rest.

"So tell me, what do you know about the plot? Tell me everything."

At this point, I hadn't done a deep dive on any assassinations. JFK, RFK, MLK... even Lincoln. I mean, I knew about them, of course, but I hadn't tried to trace them to check if the official story worked.

Karen started slowly. I could tell she was in an emotional state, and as she spoke I could tell she thought the future, as it relates to the safety of Dr. Lowd, was bleak. It was a long story, and I won't recount all of it here. Karen spent time on background, fleshing out Dr. Lowd's views that the world-government death vice — the one tightening its grip on humanity — was created between an endless propaganda loop focused on promoting the interests of global capital. She sketched it out on a napkin, in fact.

The loop, as described by Karen resulted in money for the corporations and mind-control and money for their partners in government.

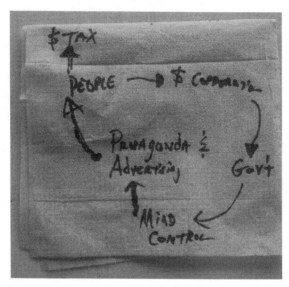

"Karen, this is all important. I basically knew Dr. Lowd's — your dad's — position on these things. Can you tell me carefully why he is in danger now. Specifically, what has changed."

"Okay," she said, taking an exaggerated breath. "For years, they were able to marginalize him by calling him names. They called him a crackpot, an anarchist, a conspiracy theorist. They had him in the margins, tucked away. People were afraid to listen to him, they didn't want to be associated with those names. Sure, he had a big following, still, but nothing happened."

"I'm following."

"But, in the last five years or so, things changed in this way. He was able to speak directly to people, unfiltered, unlabeled — online. His speeches were posted, some by him, some by his fans. They started getting millions — literally millions — of views on every video. The people heard him directly, the pre-emptive labeling as a conspiracy nut stopped working. Nobody listened to the gatekeepers, they heard my dad directly — and they believed him.

What he said about the corporations, government, about Globo — it all hit the target."

"Okay..."

"His message caught on. People agree with him. Once you see the connection between the international governments and the international mega corporations, you can't stop seeing it. But nobody ever seemed to do anything. That frustrated my dad terribly."

"Here's the thing Karen, that's what I've been investigating. The 'system.' I still don't see why they — you know, some shadowy group — would kill your father. The 'system' is too strong for him to take down anyway. It's entrenched; it's too strong for anyone to destroy. There is no way to break that loop. It seems like they would just laugh at his efforts to bring them down. There's nothing anyone can do," I said, pointing to the napkin.

"These aren't the type of people that like to take chances. They want to stamp out any glimmer of hope. Anyone who gains traction pointing out the programming that's taking place is eliminated, if they can be. My dad still got millions of people to pay attention to Globo. Even if things can't change, there is no reason for these people to take the risk. They have unlimited resources to enforce their dominance."

"Right, let's say that's true. What specifically makes you think they are targeting him?"

"My dad has a guy — Tony Karichek — who helps him with some of his tech stuff. The guy is real sharp, he's like a Serbian or something — doesn't matter — but he's so technologically savvy. He's got all the stuff, you should see his workplace, it's insane. Anyway, he noticed some monitoring activity on one of my dad's video servers. He traced it to a specific IP address. And then he got lucky — the guy doing the monitoring wasn't piping in on a virtual network. He used his own."

I nodded slowly. She was getting there.

"He tracked the guy down, and, long story short — don't ask me how — he was able to beat the encryption and mirror the guy's phone and capture his communications. He did it for my dad — he's been with him for twenty years and loves my dad."

"Okay, so he's in the phone..."

"There was a lengthy conversation in a normally encrypted chat — he never could have hacked the encryption, but the mirror worked wonders, all the activity showed up on the phone."

"I'm granting you all the tech stuff. I'll take it as true. What did it say?"

"They talked about how much damage my dad's messaging could do to the governments and the corporations. Three times they said they needed him forty-five fourteen. They called for a hit, Brandon. These guys can do it."

"You lost me. Forty-five fourteen?"

"D-E-A-D."

My face tensed. I could feel my cheekbones tightening. One eyebrow raised up, my left one.

"So what do we do?" I asked, the skin of my cheekbones tensing up. Karen's eyes were imploring me, but to do what? I'm a corporate sales guy. Secret spy assassination stuff is way out of my area.

My morning speculation about a relationship conversation was all wrong. Now, I was wrapped up in a possible murder plot. Suddenly, the cubicles, the Globo sales jobs, the entertainment, the corporate food, all of it — seemed comforting. A couch and Netflix! Movies about Nazis chasing down Jews or homosexuals, cartoon-ish bad guys reinforcing Globo-good-guy-dominance and glorified Weimar-style degeneracy — those seemed fine. Maybe I was a coward, but I didn't want this. I wanted out.

For only a moment! Out of nowhere, my resolve stiffened. I looked at Karen and something, some instinct, kicked in.

"Why don't we go talk to your dad?"

"I don't think that's a bad idea. Hey, Brandon, there's one more thing I need to tell you."

"What's that?"

"Tony mirrored your phone. I'm sorry, but I wanted you to know. They didn't send me any information... in case you were messaging girls or whatever. I'm just being honest with you. And I'm sorry."

"Well, I guess it's a good thing I don't send inappropriate pictures! I wouldn't want your dad to see me before you do," I said, volunteering a bawdy joke.

"Brandon!" exclaimed Karen, rolling her eyes.

"I mean, I wouldn't want your dad to see me at all. But seriously, thanks for telling me, I appreciate you letting me know I'm being spied on."

"They wanted to be safe. I realize it's invasive but hopefully you understand why they would do that, given what I told you."

"Yeah. I would be more upset if I didn't already know the government was tracking everything I said anyway. They capitalized on nine-eleven to create a massive, illegal surveillance state. Big Brother... he really is watching. So, what's another couple people reading my stuff?"

"Ha, I know. I just wanted to be transparent."

"I don't send anything very interesting anyway," I said, defusing the situation as much as I could.

"Let's go see the Doctor, Brandon."

We paid our tab and walked out to my car.

"Leave your car, I'll bring you back later," I said.

"Sounds good," said Karen, following me to my Audi.

We got in, and took off down the road. I turned down the volume on the music I had been playing, some rock from the seventies or eighties, Dire Straits getting down with *Sultans of Swing*. The guitar on the live track I had downloaded was out of this world. Knopfler on a little, old red strat, making it cry and sing. We were on a mission, it was no time to groove out even to a tune like that (I did, anyway, but only a little).

I followed Karen's instructions to get to Dr. Lowd's house. It was on the east side of downtown Burlingame, a little ways from San Mateo.

We had shared a lot at the diner, everything I recounted above and more, so we drove mostly in silence, with the music on low. I think the nature of the conversation drained us. We needed to regroup. There was no one around. The setting was really perfect for an assassination, I thought. It was a quiet neighborhood and yes, Dr. Lowd was a vigorous man, but he was not getting younger, in fact the opposite was happening day by day. I worried that the people Karen described could get to him easily, too easily. The capabilities of the CIA and Mossad were not to be trifled with.

I slowed my train of thought down, on purpose. "We haven't even established Karen's story, we can't assume anything," I told myself. I relaxed. Of course, Dr. Lowd had not been murdered. Being around Dr. Lowd's theories, his reading of the 'system' could make a person — his daughter — paranoid. I started to question everything. This was a longshot. I didn't know how old Dr. Lowd was, in fact, sixties, early seventies, whatever. Too far fetched! The text messages had to mean something else. A coincidence.

Focused on my thoughts, I made a "phmmpf" sound as I breathed out, dismissing the assassination plan almost entirely.

Karen looked at me because of the noise, but neither of us said anything.

Let's confirm he's okay and I'll get on with my day. None of this is real, none of this is true. Paranoid fantasy was blending with reality and it had taken over Karen's mind — via this Tony character, whoever he was.

We parked and walked toward the door. When we reached it, Karen knocked. We waited.

No answer.

"He's always home, working at this time. Writing. Sometimes he's on the phone. Every once in a while he watches a movie. He's got to be here. He heads to Oswald's in the evening to socialize. He does the same thing, almost every day."

Karen knocked again. Nothing. She glanced at me and made her eyes slightly wide as if to say "Something's wrong." Then, she tried the door. Surprisingly, it opened. It was not locked.

Part of me was pleased that the door opened. The other part of me was displeased, because I made a quick calculation: had Dr. Lowd been gone, he would have likely locked the door. Had he been home, he likely would have answered Karen's knock. What was going on here?

We stepped inside. I followed Karen, who walked at a normal pace, looking around. She made a right at the hall and then a left, heading purposefully towards a specific area or room. Given the time of day, I assumed it was the office or the study we were looking for.

Karen peered into a room and gasped. She clasped her hands together and rushed in.

"Oh my God!" she exclaimed. "Dad!" Her voice was steeped in urgency and despair. I followed behind, stepping with more determination after I heard the screams. I focused on taking methodical steps to help myself keep calm, expecting the worst.

When I arrived at the door, I saw Dr. Lowd's body slumped over on his desk. His head was resting mostly on the desk but partly on top of the computer keyboard. There was an empty, broken glass on the floor. There was no apparent blood or wound.

"Brandon, call 911!" Karen shouted as she went to try to assess Dr. Lowd, physically.

I dialed my phone and did my best to describe the situation to 911 dispatch.

Karen was still by the desk, and I didn't notice it when she grabbed a small digital device, a thumb drive, off the desk — it was sitting near Dr. Lowd's hand. I say I didn't notice, but I would come to find out about the drive at a later time. I'll get to that. She slid the device into her pocket and continued assessing the scene.

Minutes later, the police and an ambulance arrived, rushing in to see if Dr. Lowd could be saved or resuscitated (the short story is he could not). They questioned us and we told them the story of our entry and all of the details, including that Dr. Lowd was Karen's father. Karen looked as if she were going to faint the entire time. A knowing glance, though, between us told me Karen did not want to go into her suspicions regarding a murder plot against her father, not with the police.

When we had recounted the story to the emergency personnel and things were settling down, I looked at Karen. Her eyes were red and wet with tears and they flashed with sadness and despair in the Northern California sun shining through the windows of her father's home. I didn't know what to say, but felt I needed to say something. I said the first words that came to my mind.

"Karen, I think we should go. I want to get you out of here," I said, deciding direct communication was the best policy.

Karen stared at me, looking as if she were going to cry. But she didn't.

"I'll never know his last words," she whispered.

"Let's go. Now. We can go to my place. They have all our information, they will let us know what they find. We're doing no good here. You don't need this."

The police and medical workers continued to do their work documenting the scene. There were more questions than answers, but one thing was certain: Doctor Hogan Lowd was dead.

Karen didn't say anything, but turned her glance to the floor and started walking, slowly, toward the front of the house. I followed.

We drove to my place and walked in. I hustled around a bit and moved some things... things I hoped that Karen wouldn't notice (I wasn't expecting any visitors and hadn't cleaned in some time). I told her to get whatever she wanted out of the refrigerator. Water, tea, juice, whatever. She replied, "Thanks", meekly. I saw her pour herself some water.

"Go lay down in my room if you want. Anything you want, just use it. I can go on the computer for a while. We'll figure everything out," I said, trying to sound reassuring.

"I think I will."

Karen walked to my room. I didn't see her again for four hours, and assumed she was sleeping off the shock. The "forty-five fourteen" was real... and the good Doctor was dead. It was a bad day. Just as bad was the fact that we had no idea what was next.

HELL IS EMPTY

**

Somewhere in Antarctica

As decreed by Ranald the Repellent, the ship was prepared and inspected by the young giants — they were told to check every inch of the hull and the surface of the ship for flaws — and the food and other essentials were loaded by the female giants. The male giants were in charge of loading the heavier items for the journey. Ranald insisted that the tasks be performed, immediately, as he wanted to maintain some semblance of discipline with respect to the female giants' behavior.

Gerd ate way too much, Runa drank too much grog and moonshine, and Inger filled her head with filth written by a particularly degenerate group of human women who hated themselves and hated women who disagreed with them. If left to their own devices, they would do these things instead of their chores.

A firm hand was needed in this regard, he believed. This wasn't a pleasure cruise and there was no way the female giants were going to enjoy the ride while the male giants did all the work. He told the female giants, in no uncertain terms, to have the ship and its cargo readied by first sun. He told them the task was to be completed, with no excuses, before dawn — under the penalty, for the female giants, of a spanking over the knee. There would be ten strokes for non-completion. The penalty for the young giants, in the case of non-completion, was a removal of their access to grog and moonshine.

So, the older male giants drank grog — with a few gallon-sized shots of moonshine mixed in — well into the night and the female giants and young ones — Boromeo the Brash, Tyferius the

Troublesome and Chasdon the Long — dutifully prepared the ship and stowed its cargo. When Ranald the Repellent, Vilfred the Vile and Eindride the Low rose from their short slumber, everything was ready. No punishment was doled out — no spankings, no restrictions on food or drink — and everyone's mood for the journey was most excellent.

Everyone, at their own pace, boarded the ship for the journey. Mauve loaded three racks of penguins and a couple dozen crabeater seals onto the ship. He set the rest of the penguins free from their respective racks, releasing them outside, and did the same with the extra seals, taking them all the way to the water in a huge wagon.

"Live good life dear seal, make merry. Work hard long days find food," he said as he tossed each one into the water.

The penguin rack and the seal pens in the castle were totally empty. After he had released all of the creatures, he made a hand motion, one which looked as if it was intended to provide a blessing to the animals.

One penguin, marked with a special design on its front, did not wobble off to freedom after he was released by Mauve. It followed after Mauve for almost a mile, squawking.

"Special penguin friend, you make journey but not as food. On shoulder. Humph, Harrumph, Ha Ha, Muaaahhh!"

Mauve picked up the special penguin and put it on his shoulder. The look on Mauve's face showed satisfaction. Looking off in the distance, Mauve smiled, with the upper right corner of his mouth pulling further toward his cheek than did his left. He made a little noise.

The female giants brought stew and other vittles for the journey. The female giants dressed modestly, but sharply, for the long journey. Bonnets and blouses, covered with an ample amount of furs for warmth. Runa, secretly, had stowed a vest under her garments with containers of moonshine attached. She intended to supplement the grog on the boat with something a bit stronger, and the moonshine was at least sixty percent alcohol. Ingrid brought a stack of notebooks, full of what Ranald would call toxic feminism if he knew the term.

Ranald, for his part, sat in the Captain's chair on the deck of the ship, staring at his upside-down map — the same one he used to flee from Spain so long ago and sail southward to Antarctica, where they had spent hundred of years in retreat, in exile, disfavored by their old master, the Dark Beast. This time, the plan was to sail north, around Brazil and then cut directly over to dock in New York, at the southern tip of Manhattan. The others, Vilfred, Eindride, Mauve, the female giants and the young giants (except for Boromeo) had no way of knowing (for sure) that Ranald was a terrible, incompetent captain. They had only a sneaking suspicion. Ranald studied it with an intense look on his face.

Ranald may have been the worst sea-faring giant ever to exist. He had no idea which way to go; he had no idea how to repair the ship; he had no idea how to operate a ship. But, remarkably, he was blessed with a tremendous level of confidence in his missing skills. It was inexplicable, really. He fancied himself a giant Vasco de Gama or a big, aggressive Ferdinand Magellan. A great explorer. It was like a functional illiterate sitting down to read Homer and expecting to feel like Keats upon so doing. Because the others were almost entirely in the dark regarding Ranald's ineptitude, morale was extremely high for the journey.

Everyone had packed their necessities — and they lived simply, these weren't too many things. The focus of the packing was food to last for the journey and their weaponry. They didn't have room to pack non-essentials, and there weren't many of those in the ice bunker, anyway.

The oldest young giant, the offspring of Vilfred the Vile, went by the name of Boromeo the Brash. He was reckless, as his name suggests, in almost every characteristic of his life. But not in matters pertaining to travel. There was no real explanation for it, but if he was in some sort of vehicle for transportation — a sled, a ship, a glider — it was as if he were a different giant. Boromeo was the only member of the expedition who could identify Ranald's deficiencies as a captain. Boromeo knew how to reinforce the ship in case of damage, he understood navigation, in his satchel he had a compass and a sextant and he was fully capable of setting course based on nothing other than the night sky. He looked at Ranald and breathed in. He wanted to address him, but not in a way that drew Ranald's ire, which would mean a bruised set of buttocks.

"Uncle Ranald, are you sure you have everything in order?" Boromeo asked as politely as he knew how.

"Run along Brash, or I will give you a smack so hard you will forget what penguin tastes like," snarled Ranald.

Boromeo the Brash decided to not pick this battle with Ranald. His face showed restraint, indicating he would monitor the journey's progress and make changes by stealth rather than mutiny. Boromeo was not going to challenge Ranald's designation as captain. Instead, he would check his work on the journey, and help, subtly, when needed.

All of the giants lumbered about, making last minute preparations and organizing things. When, finally all the giants (the three brothers, their females and the younger giants), Mauve and his two demon-brothers, the Wolvine, and all the supplies were loaded on board, they set sail.

Ranald had the map upside down, still. Technically, he tried to set sail the wrong direction, but luckily, there was only one direction with water: north. They shipped off, and the journey had begun.

Scarcely had the ship proceeded two days on the sea, when about sunrise on the third day a great many whales and other monsters of the sea, appeared. Among the former, one was of a most monstrous size, even for the giants. It was a massive blue whale. As it surfaced, it seemed to look at the ship. The whale seemed to make eye contact with Ranald the Repellent. It did no harm to the sea vessel, tapping the bow of the ship with its tail softly, as if to say hello. The tap was also a goodbye of sorts, as the great whale turned away after the tap and continued its travels. With the food stock full at the outset of the journey, the giants did not consider trying to spear the whale for food.

Several miles into the journey, the group broke out into a ancient chant, one developed by an ancient group of giants while they traveled from the southern tip of Africa up to the northern part of Denmark, one of the earliest groups to establish an icy outpost, closer to the top of earth.

Makalaki Makalaki Roll Roll Roll!
Heading toward the Boreal Pole!
Makalaki Makalaki fight fight fight!
All the way up to the Northern Lights!

Aside from the crankiness of "Captain" Ranald, the level of cooperation and good-feeling on the ship was remarkable, and it seemed as if the last few hundred years in Antarctica had socialized some of the giants' tendencies towards violence and conflict away — not always, but much of the time. Perhaps they were like the wolvine, now? Their natural state, now, seemed to tend toward peace and cooperation — or controlled verbal conflict with a physical tussle only on rare occasions — a drastic change which made the group almost unrecognizable from the group that worked as enforcers for the Dark One. Looking at the group, with their weaponry (an axe belonging to Ranald, a hammer for Vilfred and a club for Eindride), no one would make the mistake of thinking their ability to bring decisive damage to any target had gone away, completely. They could still rain down death and destruction when they wanted to.

A few more days into the journey, the females prepared an incredible feast, with the help of Mauve. Eindride, with the help of Chasdon acting as targeteer, had harpooned a medium-sized grey whale. The entire ship blessed the whale, thanking it for it's sacrifice, and Vilfred had lowered Boromeo down by rope in order to carve some chunks out of the top of the whale's body, while it was still swimming alongside the massive ship, in tow, attached to the harpoon. With about fifteen percent of its body carved away for food, the whale's face indicated disapproval and discomfort. It knew something was wrong. But the whale's face didn't show anger with the turn of events, with the loss of mass — there was acceptance, but still a sense of hope.

Mauve had roasted the whale meat over an open fire in a special stone pit made on the starboard side of the front section of the deck. The female giants prepared a great number of sides — they had brought antarctic pumpkins which grew to a massive circumference, and they seasoned the pumpkin with tarragon and a number of special Antarctic roots. Two of the young giants played music, strumming a massive guitar and singing ancient giant folk songs, which told stories of ancient battles, ancient tradition and lore.

Everyone was allowed to drink unlimited amounts of grog that evening, a rarity for anyone other than the Repellent, the Vile and the Low, and the feast offered a very enjoyable outlet for pent-up energy.

The female giants and the young giants took particular advantage of the open flow of grog on the ship. Runa the Believer supplemented two barrels of grog with a large jar of moonshine, then another. Gerd the Wide ate more whale, seal and pemmican than she ever had before. Inger the Inquisitive rarely partook of grog or spirits, and as a result her tolerance for their intoxicating effects was notably low.

Full of moonshine and grog and free of inhibitions, Runa climbed up on the ship's railing. She balanced herself, precariously.

"Runa, stand down from there! Now!" yelled Inger, ordering Runa off the ship's railing, upon which she was walking as if it was a tightrope.

"I'm the Queen of the world!" howled Runa, balancing less carefully than seemed appropriate.

"Get down! The water is full of hungry beasts. They will tear you apart if you fall in there full of disorienting drink. You won't be able to get out quickly. Can you even swim?"

"We won't need to find out, I can't fall. My balance is stellar."

A salty wind blew across the deck of the ship and the boat rollicked gently back and forth on the starflower-blue ocean water — but Runa maintained her balance.

"Come down!"

"I feel a connection to the whole world when I am up here. I can see only sky and ocean. It is as I was meant to be."

"That's outlandish," replied Inger. "You're not a bird or a fish."

"Did you hear what I said, Inger? I'm the Queen."

"Ha!"

"I broke the second moon into pieces and made the stars. I broke the moon! That's what I did!"

"That's a lie! You broke nothing. And you're not a Queen, you're a wench. Think about what Ranald does to you. And you're not smart, not right now. You've had too much to drink," replied Inger, with emotions ranging from jealousy to fright.

Runa, visibly drunk, still toed the railing as if she were doing a high-wire act at the circus. She stood on the ship's railing, admiring the wide open vista, breathing it all in.

Inger became visibly upset with Runa's irresponsible actions and she walked away.

"Fall in if you like. Someone else can save you. Your big lummox of a husband can do something, for once, besides eating and belching like a volcano during the rapture," Inger said over her shoulder as she walked back toward the fire, clutching a large notebook under her arm.

"I don't care what you do, Inger! I'm the Queen of the world!" yelled Runa with a feverish grin.

Runa the Believer didn't end up falling into the Atlantic. In fact, no disaster or mishap occurred, whatsoever. Eventually, she rejoined the group for the remainder of the feast. When the feast subsided, and the group had satiated their hunger, they released the remaining portion of the whale, who, looking on the bright side, still had about eighty five percent of himself intact. They wished it good luck on its survival. Under Boromeo's direction (while Ranald napped in his Captain's chair), the young giants strapped the sails in the most aggressive position — for maximum speed — and continued sailing north.

Ranald woke an hour later, and was pleased that the ship was still sailing north — he guessed that were the case, at least. He sat back, taking stock of fate. He lit up a big pipe that contained a mixture of elevating roots and antarctic tobacco, a hearty form of the weed which relaxed the mind and energize the body, concurrently. When Ranald smoked his pipe, he mellowed out almost entirely. Puffing. Looking. Relaxing. Pretending to make calculations regarding the course of the ship. A flock of seagulls flew overhead, seemingly circling the ship to see if there were any scraps of food they could pick off the deck. One of the young giants, Chasdon the Long, chucked a spear at one of the birds. The spear grazed the bird, which squawked as if it had actually been hit.

"Long distance!" yelled Chasdon with a big grin.

"It is evil to kill a seagull for no reason!" yelled Runa, addressing young Chasdon.

"I didn't kill him, so neener neener," replied Chasdon as a look of mischief was added to his still-present grin.

"You'll go to hell if you don't watch out!"

"Hell is empty, Runa," replied Chasdon.

"Phhmpt. How do you know?"

"I look around; I see all the videos from Tyferius' device. The things going on — in Europe, in America. The Devil is here, on earth. He brought all his forces with him. That's why Hell is empty."

Runa's face changed and she paused.

"If anyone knows he is here, always, I suppose, it is us," she replied, acknowledging Chasdon was correct. "The videos you bring down from the sky... you think they are real?"

"I know they are and I can see what he is doing. The Doctor — he is right, even though he speaks less about the Devil than we do. He always speaks of the corporations - but in many cases they are the same thing. He is responsible for unleashing the forces that have brought about a corporate Dark Age for humanity. It is the only way. I fear he is stronger now than ever before. He will be harder to root out of his stronghold. His new weapons are too strong."

"I hope you are wrong, Chasdon the Long."

During this conversation, the seagulls took on more altitude to evade any further attack. They still followed along with the ship. From a safe height, they all let loose a bombardment of droppings on the ship, as much volume as they could muster up from their internals. Ranald, seeing watching everything transpire as he smoked his pipe, yelled at the young giant, Chasdon, to swab up the mess. Runa joined Ranald in scolding Chasdon.

"You caused the incoming, Chasdon!" yelled Runa, changing her tone entirely. "Swab up the bird slop or you'll feel my hand mar your backside."

Chasdon performed the task in a hurried fashion, cleaning up all of the bird droppings from the deck without objection.

A blunt object of force, masquerading as a sea captain, Ranald was working through an inner conflict, as he did most days. His normal desires were to hunt, to have a home — and yes, to rampage and go berserk at times, destroying his enemies. Seafaring life was different. It required patience. And it was a solitary experience, even when traveling with a group. The group, as massive as they seemed in comparison to most other creatures, was simply overpowered by the presence of the ocean, the sky, the sun, the moon and, at night, the stars. Ranald's impressive size was nothing compared to these things — they suggested a higher power such as the one Runa always spoke of, at least after her conversion. They suggested the presence of God. But the suggestion was unnecessary for the adult giants. They had lived in heaven, they knew He existed! They met God, but were cast out when they sided with the Dark Angel in olden times. Those facts are written elsewhere. Due to all of these factors, Ranald was more contemplative than usual while sailing on the ship.

After smoking his pipe, Ranald strode up and down the deck, as he often did. The planks of the ship, despite their incredible sturdiness, creaked slightly under his massive weight. He paced his normal route. He alternated between staring at the deck and off into the horizon.

Tyferius approached Ranald, walking with his right shoulder forward and his left leg back, creeping forward without regular pacing. He looked as if he wanted to tell Ranald something, but he also felt the need to be in position to defend against a right cross or slap, should Ranald throw one at him for any or no reason.

With a high voice, Tyferius exclaimed, "Starboard, Captain Ranald! A whale! A pod of them!"

"Ayyy! Keep an eye on them! Chasdon, ready the spears and the harpoon in case they get too close."

A couple of the whales spouted their mist and re-submerged. The whales, a minute or two later sauntered off toward the sun, ignoring the ship.

The ship sailed on, covering one mile, then the next. Clouds rolled in, suddenly, and the ocean became disturbed. Inger, who was scared to sail even in perfect weather, went down below deck. The ocean swells grew larger and larger and the ship was tossed on them, to and fro, like a bouncing rubber ball. Ocean spray was pulled up from the surface of the water, a swirl of salty, damp mist. The seafaring crew was on edge... driven to the ocean for the chance to counter the Devil himself — and running all related risks, brought about by nature itself. They were at the mercy of the waves. But, without tragic event, the ocean eventually calmed down. The smoke-grey clouds dispersed themselves. Ranald looked out to the horizon with a steady gaze, straight ahead, to the north as he loaded up another pipe.

RAPID BREAKDOWN

**

While Karen slept in my room, I was logged onto my computer. I used my mouse, my keyboard and my fingers to explore a voluminous amount of material on Dr. Lowd — link after link, site after site, article after article.

Dr. Hogan Lowd — the deceased — had quite an interesting background. I didn't want to bother Karen with a million questions about her father, but for obvious reasons relating to the recent events, I felt the need to learn as much about the Doctor as I could. I was involved! If the police investigation was inadequate — as many of them are when the subject is political — I wanted to be able to play a role in helping to figure out what happened to Dr. Lowd. To catch the perpetrators, to bring them to justice, that was my goal.

The entire time Karen slept, I researched Dr. Lowd's background on the internet. A controversial figure, there was plenty of information to read about him (also written by him). He was a true iconoclast. He spent his life running against the wind.

Lowd was a true medical doctor. He wasn't one of those 'doctors' allowed in from the third world who simply read Google articles to make their fake diagnoses and collect a fee. He understood the material, he had synthesized it. He was also an attorney, although from the internet and the timeline of his life description it was clear he hadn't spent much time practicing law, formally. His medical school degree was earned at the University of Michigan. After a short stint in a general practice, Dr. Lowd enrolled at the University of California at Berkeley for law school. He was one of only two students in the history of Berkeley Law to win a moot court competition twice — the other being a younger student who went to Berkeley thirty years after Lowd by the name of Maddox Malone. Following his time there, he spent the next three years, it seems, writing prolifically. He wrote one book and numerous articles. The book was on corruption in government, and focused on three specific anecdotes proving the corruption was real — but that it always went ignored when it was perpetrated at a high enough level. I'll come back to those if I have the time. His articles covered a variety of topics, but usually fit into three general categories: government malfeasance, corporate malfeasance and the rapid social breakdown of traditional society (with the final genre of articles featuring more prominently around the turn of the century as the pace of America's decline quickened).

Hogan Lowd was born in Providence, Rhode Island, to Dietrich and Anastasia (née Tolstoy, no relation to the author) Lowd, both of whom were immigrants, Dietrich from Germany (pure German ethnicity) and Anastasia from Russia (pure Russian ethnicity). When Hogan was three, they settled in Connecticut, Dietrich worked in a grain mill before opening a bakery. Hogan worked in the bakery and was also a delivery boy for the local paper in New Haven.

Hogan, gifted with a naturally sharp intellect, received a scholarship to a prestigious boarding school, Boston Preparatory School for Boys. He went on to attend Princeton University for his undergraduate degree. He graduated, having studied at the Woodrow Wilson School of Public and International Affairs, earning his degree in 1967.

Judging from his writing, Hogan Lowd held John F. Kennedy in high regard. He was particularly interested in the circumstances surrounding Kennedy's assassination. He attended Berkeley, seemingly expecting the 'liberal' campus would have an anti-corporate bent. Even at an early age, Dr. Lowd, as evidenced by his writings, argued vehemently that unrestrained corporatism and consumerism — modern-industrial society, essentially — were destroying lives.

But, again as evidenced by his writings, Lowd clearly became disenchanted with Berkeley. He considered it a fraud, a phony — complicit in muddying the waters of a corrupted regime. He saw a link between the talking points — the uniform opinions held by the faculty and transferred to the students, top down — and the partnership he saw between modern 'democracy' and the corporations running roughshod throughout it. He soured on Berkeley, writing "the Berkeley establishment provides cover, through rhetoric that did not match up with any actions, protecting a society based on hyper-capitalism married to a toxic brand of crypto-communist de-constructive language. The resulting stew is a toxic environment where nothing good and beautiful can survive, for long."

He argued that this late stage American cess-pool, the product of a marriage of active hyper-capitalism and free-wheeling communist language (a secular religion had been created to spot - isms and -phobias everywhere), was evil and should not be sustained. Essentially, he argued for the deconstruction of the American Empire through a split and a re-start.

I read much more about Lowd, but this summary shall have to do for now, as I want to carry on with the story and not let it get hijacked by Lowd's biography. To do his background justice, another book would be required. So this background will suffice for the purposes of my story.

Karen, having had her fill of sleep, walked out, coming to my side. She shook her head slightly and breathed deeply.

"He's gone. I knew it," she whispered.

I didn't know what to do. I had nothing to say. So, I stood

up and gave Karen a hug. I held on to her for a while.

"I can't forgive myself," she whispered. I couldn't see her eyes, but tears were welling up inside them, again. I could tell, I sensed it.

The situation filled me with considerable melancholy. I told her nothing could be done at the moment. She had to go on. We would take stock of the situation and see what we could do. I said things like that, one after the other. Getting the sense that I was rambling and speaking in platitudes with no meaning, I decided to shut up.

Tenderly, continuing to hold on to me, she said "Thank you for being with me."

I didn't say anything, but I made a little sound, a huff of breath, and I held on. I held on for dear life; for hers, for mine. What was I into? What were we into?

* * *

There was no easy way to look at things. We were in poor spirits. Obviously, the loss hit Karen quite hard and I was secondary. But I felt it too. I felt a bond with Dr. Lowd in a short time, I admired him. And I felt close to Karen, she was mysterious and charismatic at the same time. I'll never forget how she looked with her wind-blown hair the first night I met her — the night Dr. Lowd introduced us at the bar. I have a still image of her, at that precise time, fixed in my mind, and I think about it often. It is something I'll never forget, no-one can take it from me.

There was a notable disconnect between the sadness and loss we felt and the beauty of the early fall Northern California day. I noticed it as we walked outside, heading to the car, seeing as we had decided to go for a cup of coffee.

It was an afterthought, my mind was elsewhere. But still the beauty of it affected me. Blue and green, with the customary splashes of yellow. A slight breeze graced my face with its comfort. Death had struck, however it happened, but still the sun shone and I could, somehow, feel a beautiful, hopeful presence around me.

We didn't speak a word on the ride to the coffee shop. I drove, concentrating on my turns and my surroundings. With my mind racing, zigging and zagging here and there, hopping between wonder and worry and fear and sadness and hope, I knew I could easily be distracted. We didn't need to add a careless accident onto the list of problems we were facing.

When I parked the car, Karen sat still for a moment. She slowly turned to me, resting her left elbow on the center console.

"Thank you for being there for me today. It has really helped me," she said. I could see the sincerity in her eyes.

"Anytime, Karen. I can't believe it happened," I said, with sadness and disappointment coming through in my voice, even as I tried to block those emotions from passing over my vocal chords.

"They are monsters," she replied. "Corporate monsters, tied in with the government. And everything is so thoroughly corrupted, we have nowhere to turn. No one to help. The law is compromised by their group, their club. If we went to the police for help they would stonewall us and give any information they found to our enemies. And they would tell Globo we are looking into the death. It's best to just leave it alone and do what we will on our own. And I don't know what there is to do. They have all the money, all the real money. It's the loop my dad talked about. Corporations, global government and capital. I feel like a rat in a trap."

"You're not a rat, though, Karen. You're a person, a woman. I feel like my mind is spinning. I feel like its a hallucination. I don't know what is real, anymore."

"It's real, Brandon. I couldn't save him. I wish it were a lie."

That line caused me to think of something to say, so I replied, "I have a friend, a guy I met not too long ago, who always says 'it's all a lie.' I'm thinking he's right about many things. The one thing that is true is the power and viciousness of Globo."

Karen didn't answer. She didn't even look at me. I think she got lost in her thoughts.

"Let's go inside, Karen," I said. "We need a pick up, and I need something to help focus my mind."

We ordered our drinks and sat down at a table. I sipped my Americano and Karen did the same with her cappuccino. A few moments after we sat down and took our first respective tastes, she excused herself to take a phone call, saying, "This is my friend, Lisa. I'll only be a few minutes."

For some reason, when she took the call, and with my mind feeling the sharpening effects of the caffeine in my drink, I decided to contact Rory, having thought about him as we parked. I sent him a message, using my smart phone.

"Rory — it's Brandon. Dr. Lowd is dead. His daughter suspects foul play. I'm with her, right now. I wanted you to know."

Surprisingly, my phone buzzed with a response almost immediately.

"These are not secure comms. NO MORE MESSAGES WITH SUBSTANCE. The GC got him, that's my guess. Come to the store if you and his daughter want to talk about it. But I won't be back until Sunday, I'm on a three day hike with Lucille, doing a beef bone broth cleanse in the mountains."

"Okay, I'll talk to Karen," I responded. I remembered Rory speaking of the globalist cabal, and I was relatively certain that's what he meant by GC.

I realized, right at that moment, the only way out — the only thing I could do with the rest of my life to try to make a difference — was to go further in. Into the belly of the beast! I needed to find a way to bring the fight to the corporations, the global government — all of the things making life miserable — and meaningless — for so many people. People who, thanks to constant propaganda — a form of mind-control — engaged in behaviors adverse to their interests.

But how? That was the question, and finding an answer seemed impossible.

Karen leaned in toward me, before I could say anything about Rory's message.

"What made you do it? What made you question the 'system,' Brandon? Was it a girl? Come on, you can tell me... Did she break your heart?" she asked. The change in topics allowed her to smile, it seemed that it gave her some separation from everything at hand.

"Nah. It wasn't a girl... I mean, I thought a lot about what caused it. But it definitely wasn't a girl. It was a job. Or a collection of jobs, really. I was just wondering if that was all there really was. Muh cubicle, muh products. Especially when the corporations started all this nu-speak. I think I burned out."

"What do you mean?"

"Well, I don't know exactly when it happened, but they just manipulated the meaning of words. Everything became weird. You know, the euphemisms and the sayings used to obscure truth. And, I looked around and suddenly everything seemed to be controlled by a mega-corporation, a big brand. It's the same stuff your dad talked about. I just wasn't happy at EquiPark, MindSmash, anywhere. I started questioning everything."

"Do you think you figured it out? I mean, what was your big takeaway... you've been looking into everything for a while."

"The 'system' never stops. If you are not vigilant about protecting a place — a way of life — it will be taken from you. You have to protect it all the time, every minute and with everything you do."

"Complacency and compromise, that's how," Karen said.

"Yep. A little bit here and there. Then before you know it you couldn't stop Globo if you wanted to."

There was a momentary pause in the conversation before Karen spoke again.

"So it wasn't a girl..." she said. It seemed as if she was trying to elicit information about my dating life. So I gave her some.

"Definitely not. I mean, I dated pretty consistently. But things never lasted. Maybe a month, maybe six months, maybe a year. Then, we always parted ways. I just never got the right feeling. But that didn't get me started on the 'system.'"

"So, no white picket fence?" she pressed further.

"Well, I think I'm looking for something that doesn't exist."

"What do you mean?"

"Have you met a single girl who's not on digital media all the time? I just didn't want to have a relationship on Instagram or Facebook. It just always seemed weird to me, and its a huge part of modern dating. Digital posting."

"There's a word for it, but I won't say it."

"Yeah its..." I replied, cutting myself off.

"I don't have any of that garbage. I would feel ridiculous creating content for Mark Zuckerberg or whoever," agreed Karen.

"Really?" I asked. "Not one account?"

"Zero," she replied, flatly.

"Amazing. Anyway, it's not real... it's crazy how it all happened so fast and everyone adapted to those websites," I said.

"It really is. It's interesting. You're a romantic, Brandon Brooks. Don't meet one of those every day."

"I don't know."

"Romeo, Romeo..."

"Stop it, Karen," I said, laughing.

The conversation trailed off for a minute and we sipped our coffees.

"We're always talking about me, Karen. What about you? Your thoughts on the things we talked about?"

"Like what?"

"Well, your thoughts on the 'system' or on Globo? Or, how is it possible that you're single? You're smart and beautiful, Karen," I said, not caring if she took the comment as an expression of interest. Maybe it was, maybe it wasn't.

"Well... thanks... and yeah... uhhh... I don't know. I mean... I think I just had a vision for what I wanted that didn't translate into what was out there. If that makes sense..."

"Well, it does. On a really general — like riddle-speak — level."

"Well, more specifically... it's not that I wouldn't date. It's just that I don't... not in a couple years at least... because I haven't met a guy I really like. That's all. See, I'm an open book," she said, smiling.

"Okay, that was, uhh, totally more clear. You're still a mystery, Karen Lowd."

"I don't try to be. Really. I am how I am," she replied, smiling.

"Well, however things work out for us, they will work out," I said, purposely saying something in Karen's manner of roundabout speaking and smiling to myself.

"Maybe we both should stop looking for perfect and go with good. I'm not talking purely about dating, that would be a horrible thing to say while sitting here. I'm just talking about life."

"Good enough for me."

The entire conversation was making me think about things I didn't want to think about. The future. My future. It was better to just go through my days, one at a time. I tried to stay busy with my investigation, with whatever was occupying my time. And usually, I did fine like that. I stopped looking at Karen from across the table and took a deep breath. I didn't know what the future would bring — and now was not the time to worry about it. It was time to take things day-by-day. And it was time to figure out what Globo was really up to. Our survival — and maybe even that of humanity itself... of beauty, purity and light — was at stake.

NEW WORLD ORDER

**

A cloud of gloom and defeat hung over us at our table. There wasn't much to say. I thought about trying to start a conversation on another topic, but the idea seemed so contrived as to render the execution of the plan impossible. So I sat in silence.

Minutes and minutes went by, we sat there, taking occasional sips of our coffee drinks. We seemed to be on the verge of either an incredible battle — a battle for our very souls, for the world — or heading towards complete stagnation and impending death, whenever it might come. A weighty malaise set in on the both of us. Anyone looking at us could see it smeared all over our faces.

Karen broke the silence.

"We look miserable. I feel bad for dragging you into this..."

"You didn't drag me into anything, Karen. I knew your father independently. And, I was on my own journey of recognition before any of this happened. You know that, don't be hard on yourself."

"Yeah, but I still feel bad. I would feel horrible if I ever put you in any danger. These people, they will never stop until everyone is controlled. I'll be a target, because of my father. I don't want you caught in the crossfire."

When her lips pressed together after she spoke the word "danger" I felt a wave of exhilaration. I took stock of myself. Was it possible that I, Brandon Brooks, an unemployed corporate dog — one who started noticing and questioning — could become a warrior in the fight against the 'system?' I could shoot a weapon. I could handle myself in a fight. But there's always someone better armed, better positioned, better prepared. Especially if they had more resources — like the power of the government or unlimited capital. The 'system' could squish me like a bug. It could destroy anyone at this point. With that thought, a wave of despair came over me. How can you fight a target, one clearly present, but so well-hidden at the same time? How do you fight a 'system,' one run by shape-shifting corruption and greed?

Karen must have seen the despair and disappointment wash over my face because her demeanor changed. She strummed her fingers on the table and I detected a very slight frown on her face. For good reason, the whimsical, carefree Karen of prior times was gone. Then, two things happened which changed the entire atmosphere at the table, in a flash.

The first came from Karen, and the second came from my smart phone.

"Oh, Brandon!" she said, excitedly, as she reached into the pocket of her tight jeans. "I almost forgot..."

She pulled out the little device, the thumb drive, she had grabbed from Dr. Lowd's desk.

"I think my dad, when he realized he had been poisoned — or whatever, poison is my guess — grabbed for this. It was near his hand, on his desk. We need to look at its contents."

Before I could respond to this welcome distraction, my smart phone caught my attention, with a buzz. It was a message from Rory.

"I'm cutting my trip short. This is too big. I'm already miserable and cranky from the bone broth deprivation. I'm literally starving. We're coming back tonight. They said an old guitar was all he could afford. Tomorrow, 9 a.m."

Karen saw me read the message and perk up. Rory, writing in his goofy conspiracy code, was obviously suggesting a meeting at the shop in the morning.

I replied to her, first, saying "That's great. Let's check out the hard drive tonight. Why don't you stay at my place? You don't need to be alone. I'll sleep on the couch, you can have the bed."

"You really are sweet. Okay, let's have a slumber party. I really appreciate it, and I don't want to be alone. And my friends, they are separate from all the stuff with my dad. We can check out this drive and maybe even watch a movie or something, take our mind off of things."

"So the message was from the guy I told you about. Rory. He's canceling the rest of his stupid bone broth hike. He invited us to his shop in the morning. He knows stuff."

"Ha! He knows stuff, that's great. Why was he doing bone broth? I don't even know how to frame the question." said Karen.

"It's Rory. He's goofy. You've never met anyone like him."

"I'm my dad's daughter, you'd be surprised who I've met," she said, with her first big smile of the afternoon.

"Let's roll. We can stop for some groceries and bunker up for the night. Thumb drive and a movie if we can find anything good. Let's watch a Mel Gibson flick."

"I love Mel Gibson — that's a real man."

"Hey!" I said. "What in the...? He reads lines on camera, Karen!"

"Look at him. The aesthetics. Iron and sun."

"Ugh," I replied, waving my hand.

Karen smiled.

* * *

The grocery stop was carried out efficiently, and we also went to Karen's place so she could grab her things. She went inside and came out with a massive bag. "We're not hiking Everest," I thought, but I kept it to myself. Women were incredible, wonderful creatures. But different! And that's what makes the world go around, the differences between men and women. Those things can never be erased, I thought. Not even with non-stop propaganda and brainwashing. People will recover, even if things seem bleak for a while. The differences would survive and thrive, and humanity works best with men and women living naturally, together. A man can never truly emulate a woman, and vice versa — despite, of course, having a common humanity. The wonders of life! I was fine with it all, I accepted it. I embraced it, even though I chuckled at Karen's enormous pack.

We made it back to my place by seven. The evening was enchanted. Everything was all right, the mood was as light as could be hoped for, given the stunning event of earlier in the day. We ate small grass-fed steaks — prepared perfectly by the local high-end grocery store which had recently been purchased by a global mega-corporation. The products were passable, for now — and we also added a selection of vegetables to the meal for good measure. Then we turned to the hard drive. When we connected it to my laptop, we were both surprised to see it contained only one file. A rich text file, but one we couldn't open because an encryption key was required (and we didn't have it).

We spent the next thirty minutes trying to guess the encryption key, to no avail. There was frustration in the air.

"Let's not frustrate ourselves with this all night. We have the file. I'll talk to Rory tomorrow and see if we can approach this in a way that makes more sense than guessing. He knows stuff, remember?" I said, smiling. "Maybe there's a way to crack the file other than guessing the code."

"I love this guy and I haven't even met him," said Karen, smiling. It was one of those smiles forcing its way through sadness, but nonetheless it was good to see.

"He's a piece of work. Let's make popcorn and watch a movie. First, sweats! I hope you brought something comfy."

Hanging out with Karen over dinner felt strange. I had never — not once — done this with a woman before: a private meal without a romantic relationship of some sort. And, Karen and I didn't have that. Had I become a beta orbiter, circling around Karen? I dismissed the thought outright, that wasn't what was happening here. These circumstances were unusual, and it called for an unusual response; I wasn't losing my edge or my masculinity. I walked into my room and put on some cotton sweatpants and a long-sleeved t-shirt. I left the door open so Karen could use the room to change. She did, putting on, somewhat surprisingly, a Juicy Couture sweat-suit. It looked comfortable, but I would have pegged Karen for something simpler, if I were being honest.

We flipped through the digital selection of Mel Gibson movies. There was one called *Blood Father* and it looked interesting, but I couldn't risk the possibility of Gibson playing a father who died in the movie. It didn't seem far-fetched, given the title, and subjecting Karen to such a plot-line would have been a bad call. So, we went with *Conspiracy Theory*, starring Uncle Mel and Julia Roberts. With our popcorn popped and some Irish butter drizzled on top, we escaped, for a couple hours, into the flick. It was topical, for sure, and we sat on the couch with the popcorn bowl between us, like friends should. A couple times during the movie our hands touched while we were grabbing popcorn — a strange feeling for a friend. Strange indeed. This was all so new for me!

After the movie, Karen touched my shoulder and told me she was exhausted from the emotions of the day. She was ready to head to bed. I went in my room and grabbed a blanket and a t-shirt to use as a pillow (I hated normal pillows because they are disgusting bacteria-bags) and then came back to the couch. Karen went in my room and climbed in the bed.

I laid down on the couch, staring at the ceiling. Sleep eluded me, for at least an hour. My thoughts swirled around in my head, filling it and emptying it at the same time. I swam!

"Brandon, get a grip on yourself," I half-whispered, half-thought. "Take a breath, go to bed. Let the light be your guide."

I thought about saying let God guide me, let God help me make my way — but I wanted a bigger hand in things. In my perfect world, God would provide the light showing the way, and I would follow the light, myself. I had no idea if He would cooperate, how could I know? It was a matter of faith and, at times mine felt strong (other times, shaky).

As soon as I had these thoughts, however, I started to question them. I had always believed in God, but in recent times I had been more reliant on Him. What did this say about me? I hoped that it wasn't just over-compensation for trying times — with quitting my job and investigating the system and all. I hoped that it was deeper than that.

The thoughts of the 'system,' Dr. Lowd, Karen, tomorrow's meeting with Rory — they didn't go away, they continued to swirl. It was a strange feeling, because my thoughts were not linear. They were not sortable and they were not progressing towards any understanding, any realization, any clarity. Mercifully, velvet sleep overtook me.

My dream began as if stardust had been sprinkled over me. It was a wonderful start! Something exhilarating floating in the air, lightening the mood, giving me an endless sense of peace and wonder and a view of some of the most beautiful scenery the world had to offer. A massive snow-capped peak towered above me to my left; an imposing peak no man had ever dared to scale. A dusky, grape-and-orange-and-banana colored sky hung peacefully above me. A beautiful, empty, sandy beach straight ahead. And the ocean, the wondrous, mysterious, massive ocean, to my right. There was no corporate plastic in the ocean of my dream. The scenery escape from the regular landscape of fast food restaurants, gas stations, convenience and specialty stores — the poisonous fruits of the global, mega-corporate 'system,' constantly being advertised and sold. For a moment, I became free of those things, and I seemed to return to a state of grace, a state of wonder, a state of harmony with nature.

I walked along, taking it all in, on the land which was elevated above the beach, maybe fifty feet above. I looked for stairs leading down toward the beach. The dream was going swimmingly, restfully. A pack of armadillos played over to my left, they were just buzzing around doing fun armadillo stuff. A porcupine napped to my right — peacefully, I had no fear of him prickling me with his quills.

But then something happened... the easy, peaceful feeling was ripped away from me. In the dream, I was looking too far up on the horizon, looking for stairs or a path or something to get to lower ground — I wanted to go to the beach, as I recall. I looked ahead at the expense of checking my closest surroundings. I took an ill-fated step forward and plummeted, falling at the fastest rate gravity would allow — nothing to brace me and nothing to slow me down or for me to grab onto. After ten seconds of this, my back and rear hit onto a smooth, tube-like slide structure and I was plummeting down it, at an angle approximating sixty-five degrees. I was careening, purblind, through the tube — destination unknown. This went on seemingly forever. I endured the plummeting feeling, so awful, so disturbing, but had no way to shake out of it. Until finally, splash!

The miracle I longed for — stopping my fall without a death impact — happened, after all. But what now? I was submerged, under water. Would I drown? I took stock of the situation, opening my eyes. It was surreal (as dreams always are), but I could somehow breathe under water and I could see clearly. Presumably, I was in the ocean, I suspected, as the tube I fell in through the man-hole sized opening was only a couple hundred yards from the water. And I was traveling long enough to reach it, for certain.

It didn't seem like the ocean — it seemed more like an aquarium. Clean, crisp, transparent water. Beautiful fish, brightly-colored and perfectly-finned, moving effortlessly through the clean water. I breathed and floated, I watched and enjoyed the scenery, the fish, the plants, the toothpaste-blue water streaked with a blue-green brightness caused by refracted rays from the California sun shining down from above. A luminescent orange fish maneuvered into my space and nodded his head at me, or so I thought. He wandered off, heading in the direction of a larger, yellow fish who was swimming alongside a white fish with red stripes.

I was enjoying the dream again, I had almost forgotten about the disturbing fall, and I watched nature in motion. Beauty, light, grace. The natural order of things. This was what made life so wondrous and whimsical and such a joy.

I blinked (in my dream) and a new world order — right there in the water — met my eyes with an unforgiving harshness. An ugliness I could never imagine while awake. My previously clean and beautiful natural surroundings were replaced by a polluted muck. The water had somehow become murky with dirt and other particles, corporate plastics, waste and toxins were everywhere. The fish were ugly, and they were all the same gross hue. God must have abandoned these poor creatures, they had to be the work of the Devil. The fish, their skin or scales or what not, were a little lighter-colored than excrement and a little darker-colored than caramel. Instead of bright, inquisitive — even happy — faces I had seen on the yellow and orange and white fish, these all looked dysgenic and foul. Crooked faces, ugly features. Fat. Dull eyes. They were Goblin-fish! Or another name I won't write here out of a duty to propriety. Were they mutated by the corporate plastics? Some other awful influence? What did they eat to get so fat? And their color! Their color was disgusting! They were not beautiful, not these fish. I longed for the yellow fish, for the orange fish. I blinked, in my dream, hoping they would come back. No luck! The corporate plastics floated around, and they seemed to increase, moment by moment. A plastic cup from Starbucks — actually, three of those. Styrofoam containers, from McDonald's. A bag of Cheetohs. An empty Coca-Cola bottle, emitting visible toxins in real time. Those are a few examples, and I will refrain from listing the dozens more I saw. Corporate garbage and packaging everywhere. Ugly fish. Spoiled, stinking, foul water. My dream, once beautiful, had become an industrial nightmare!

I sensed motion behind me, and I saw Karen splashing into the muck, hurtling from above, then submerged. She came through the same hole from which I had arrived. We made eye contact and a deep, knowing disappointment was communicated, without words.

Dr. Lowd's dead body floated into view, and our shared disappointment was replaced by a look of horror. It took complete hold of our faces, twisting them with grief. I looked away, then looked at Karen, who was looking down, away from her father. We surfaced momentarily... and we heard big, loud voices calling our names from the tube above. They said they were coming to help us... coming to save us from the cesspool. We could hear loud footsteps. But whatever or whoever was producing the sounds never arrived. We lurked about, just treading water and looking for a way out. For no reason (or from the cumulative effect of what had become a nightmare), I awoke with a start and a deep, desperate breath.

A dream, coming true, makes life magnificent. Nightmares are the same, if you replace magnificent with unnerving, even horrifying. I had both a dream and a nightmare during the night's sleep. But which one would come true? The answer, my friends, would keep things interesting.

ENTER THE LASER

❧❧

The good news is that the nightmare was over. The bad news is that it woke me up way earlier than I intended to rise. It was too early to start the day! My mind was quite foggy and the vivid dream — involving Karen, who was in the other room — allowed for a strange state of semi-consciousness even after I awoke. It was as if I had been awake during the dream and, now, the reverse was true — I was physically awake and felt as if I were sleepwalking even though I wasn't moving around. Staring at the ceiling, I remained on the couch for a while, but I didn't want to risk going back to sleep. I didn't want to see those God-forsaken dysgenic Goblin-fish of my dream, not again.

I thought of a solution, but it required me to lift myself off the couch (after a short pep talk). The solution was caffeine, so after another minute I walked to the kitchen area, where I brewed up a fresh pot of coffee. I guessed it might be an hour or two — or three, depending on how hard the fatigue had hit her — before Karen woke up. So, I sipped coffee and thought about things, woke myself up and such. I glanced at my cell phone and noticed an unread message.

Before I could read it, Karen walked through the bedroom door and into the living area. Unexpected, but a nice surprise.

"Good morning," she said, rubbing her eyes and stretching her arms in the air.

"Hey, you're up earlier than I thought. How'd you sleep?" I asked.

"Good for a couple hours, I think. Then, not so good."

"I hear you, same thing happened to me," I replied, deciding not to tell her about the mud-colored fish and the rest of my dream. "Want some coffee?"

"I do, absolutely."

I poured her a mug full of coffee. Karen took a sip after sitting down and rubbing her eyes.

"Are we still going to your friend's place?"

"That's the plan," I replied, checking the unread message on my phone, which was from Rory, received at 5:53 a.m., in which he asked if we were still coming up to the shop. I responded to Rory in the affirmative before continuing, "I didn't expect us to be up this early... you know, with everything. But we can go, whenever. Rory's already up, he messaged me. Do you want to shower?"

"I don't need to, but I wouldn't mind."

"Go for it. I'm going to throw on a hat and some gear, I'll shower when we get back."

Karen finished her coffee and walked back to my room, closing the door. She must have enjoyed the shower, because she was in there for a while. She emerged right before eight a.m. and looked as if she were ready to go — tank top, shorts and tennis shoes, with a small (by her standards) carry-bag.

We loaded in my Audi and drove off, heading north, towards Rory and Lucille. About halfway through the drive, my heart sank.

"Did you bring the thumb drive?" I asked in a rushed voice.

"Of course I did, Brandon," replied Karen.

"Ha, thank God. I forgot to ask before we left."

"You're a man. I get it."

"Stop that," I said, smiling. "We'll never settle the battle of the sexes; let's not try."

I looked over at Karen, who noticed my glance. She rolled her eyes and put the back of her hand on her cheek, then straightened her tank top. She smiled, warmly. Our relationship was strange due to the fact that we had been through a lot together, but had only spent a few days in each other's company. It created an odd dynamic between the two of us, shifting between a comfortable familiarity and its opposite.

The drive went smoothly, with the Audi gripping the turns and ripping along the road, slightly above the speed limit. I wanted to make good time without attracting the intervention of the government, which was always looking for revenue from things like speeding tickets. No amount of money was good enough for the state, they could always grift and spend more! We didn't say a whole lot during the drive. I had the car stereo playing a mix of classic and bluesy rock. I figured a conversation would too easily revert to things we had already discussed. Dr. Lowd's murder, the thumb drive, the 'system.' So I didn't press the issue, and I didn't say much. Not at all. Karen, presumably, felt the same way, riding without speaking, enjoying the tunes (judging by her body language).

We reached our destination, and suddenly I realized this trip would have an out-sized effect on the rest of our lives — most certainly Karen's, and, on my current path, mine. The content of the drive, the threat of the Global Cabal — or whoever murdered Dr. Lowd (at this point, despite not having any conclusive toxicology reports, we were assuming foul play) — we would have to take action in response to what we found out.

I parked and we walked into the shop.

Rory met us with a loud roar, taking all tension out of the

room immediately. "I'm sorry about your dad, Karen. I really am. He was a great man!" he hollered, from a ways away.

Rory — exuding energy of life, talking loud, yearning, desiring... something. Going in every direction at once. He was a candle burning at both ends, burning bright, giving off light and life and positive energy. Inside the candle, I remember thinking at the time, there's probably a stick of dynamite.

Lucille, using an opposite approach, made like a turtle much of the time, waiting for Rory to lure her out of her shell. At this moment, she didn't say anything, not immediately, but instead walked over to Karen and gave her a hug, whispering something in her ear.

There seemed to be no point in dwelling on the death. It happened, it was done. We had to move forward, and everyone seemed to recognize this fact.

Rory, wasting no time, said, "Did you bring the computer drive? I've got the Laser coming over in about half an hour."

"Settle down, Rory. Settle yourself down," Lucille chimed in.

"I've got the drive, but what is the Laser?" Karen replied.

"Rory, you need some bone broth, man," I said. "Take the edge off."

"Ha, I know. Look at this belly! It has a presence," said Rory, poking fun at himself.

"That's too big, man. Too big," I teased, stating a fact.

Rory scowled at me, but playfully.

"You shouldn't have cut your hike short. A thousand miles on bone broth and bananas would get the belly thing under control, down three notches."

"I beg your pardon?" said Rory. Rory had a good poker face, and I was unsure if he was still playing around or growing tired of the ribbing, so I stopped.

"Who or what is the Laser?" asked Karen, repeating her question from moments before.

"My hacker, that's who. The best there is! A technological wizard!" exclaimed Rory.

"Does he have a real name?"

"I told you, it's Laser. He comes from a heritage family in west Russia. Orthodox. A long line, pure Russian blood. His sister is one of the most beautiful Russians I've ever seen. Blonde hair and green eyes."

"Stop it with the sister, Rory! How does she come up every time you talk about Laser?" asked Lucille.

"It's probably not the only thing that comes up," I said, before deciding it was time for me to quiet down.

"Alright, alright. Can I get you guys anything? Coffee?"

"We had some before we left but if Karen wants another one I will join."

"I could go for one," Karen said. "I'm on the struggle bus."

Rory hustled off to get coffee and we sat down in the front area of the shop, where there were four leather chairs set facing each other. A table sat in the middle of the chairs.

There was some surface level conversation, but nothing of substance was said, even when Rory returned with the coffees. I glanced, a couple of times, at Karen. I had to admit, her face looked very pretty with the inter-crossed rays of light entering through the front window of the store. She crossed her right leg over her left and I had to tell myself to stop — STOP — looking at her.

Things went on like this until the front door opened and a man walked in, wearing a black hat, black t-shirt, charcoal shorts and white sneakers. A black backpack was strapped around his shoulder and clasped over his stomach. He was a fit, handsome fellow — excellent physiognomy, eugenic — and I both hoped and feared his arrival (and successful de-encryption of the file) would allow us to proceed along this journey, wherever it may lead.

"I'm the Laser," he said, greeting Karen and me. "Hey Rory, hey Lucille."

I drifted off for a moment, in my own thoughts, away from the conversation. I was on a roller coaster again. For a moment, I abandoned all hope. I longed for the comfort of one of my old cubicles. Any of them! I didn't want to fight the 'system' any more. I didn't want to be involved in murder plots and counter-plots. I was done. I cannot lie, I thought about walking out of the shop. Going corporate! Sending out some resumes. Cutting my hair and shaving my face. My consciousness veered left then right. I had no plan, no foundation. Maybe my brother Timothy, the simpleton, was right? Maybe I was a no-good 'conspiracy theorist?' I started to doubt myself, my sanity. When I dwell on things, at length, though, nothing good happens. I learned that about myself. So, I refocused myself, by paying attention to the conversation. Laser and Rory were speaking among themselves — I lay in wait for what was to come.

In the minutes following Laser's arrival, energy peaked. Adrenaline was flowing with the arrival of the Russian hacker and caffeine had also been thrown into the mix. Karen had handed the Laser the hard drive and he plugged it into the laptop he had pulled out of his backpack. His fingers clicked and clacked at his keyboard as he tried to de-encrypt the file. Minutes later, he looked up and addressed the group.

"The file — it's not cooperating. I hacked the initial layer of encryption but there is a reverberation in the encryption and it kicks me back over to a new level of encryption, every time. So, I hack it and it re-encrypts. Who's file was this?" asked the Laser.

"My dad's," answered Karen.

"I'm going to have to take it up the ladder... heighten the process... and crack the file. We gotta go up one level. I have a partner in Russia — the Camel — who can, I hope, hack the file at the same time I do it. Then we can beat the reverberation as it will open up before it has the chance to re-code itself and hide again. Does that make sense?"

"That's why they call him the Laser, boom!" hollered Rory.

"The Laser-boom? Who calls him that?" asked Lucille.

"Is that really why they call him Laser? And now we have the Camel?" asked Karen, who was still stuck on the nickname. "We need to figure out what is going on with all these nicknames."

"Just go with it, Karen," I said.

"The Laser, why do they call him the Camel? Please tell me, it's killing me," Karen persisted.

"Nobody cares, Karen," I said, making sure to smile so it didn't seem rude or harsh. Karen shook her head went silent, but her face didn't indicate any ill feelings towards me for the comment.

"No, Brandon, it's okay. I will let others answer for my nickname, but we call my friend the Camel for a simple reason. He can go all day without having to go pee. That's it, no big deal," he said, turning his attention back to his computer screen.

Karen and I looked at each other with wry smiles. She whispered something to me about saving on toilet paper. I said, "Toilet paper is disgusting... and guys don't... nevermind." This, somehow, was real life.

The Laser put on a headphone and microphone and clicked around on his computer. Soon, he was speaking Russian into the microphone, presumably talking to the Camel on Telegram or some other encrypted chat app. Obviously, I won't try to transcribe the conversation here, as I don't have any knowledge of Russian. They chattered on and Laser continued to click on his keyboard as he spoke.

Suddenly, the Laser yelled, "ни фига себе! The file is open!"

We all let out sounds of approval and acclimation.

"Here's the message, guys. It's short. Why don't you guys take a picture of the screen and I'll scrub the file and kill all traces of this IP address?" suggested Laser, as he turned his laptop screen toward Karen and me.

The rich text file was shorter than I expected. It read, in full:

KAREN, BRING BRANDON BROOKS
I CAN'T TELL YOU WHY
SYSTEM'S FINAL PUSH, SHORTENED LIST, THEY ARE COMING FOR ME
PETTY DESTRUCTION WON'T WORK, NOT ENOUGH TIME TO GET THE PEOPLE TO NON-COMPLIANCE
ANTARCTICA MOBILIZED TO HELP
BE IN NEW YORK ON NOVEMBER 26, 2020
TD FEDERAL RESERVE, LAST CHANCE
THEY ARE CONSOLIDATING WITH CENSORSHIP,

FINAL GLOBO CHOKE-HOLD, ENDING HUMANITY
PERMANENT GLOBAL CORPORATE-GOVERNMENT
LATE-STAGE CAPITAL COMMUNIST FUSION
MIND-CONTROL, BIG FOOD, BIG CHEM, BIG PHARMA,
BIG WEAPONRY, BIG TECH — 100%
IT'S HAPPENING, KAREN.
GODSPEED, I LOVE YOU. HL

We both read the message. Rory, Lucille and the Laser read it as well. Karen snapped a photo of it, using her phone. Everyone sat in silence. Karen was crying, but not sobbing or otherwise making noise. Tears just quietly streamed down her face.

It seemed no-one knew what to say, so no-one spoke.

The morning had kept rolling on through all of this. By this time, it was mid-morning and, after reading the message and watching Karen break down in tears, an ashen sense of gloom overcame me. It blocked out the soft fall-season Northern California sun coming through Parker's Mortuary. The room seemed to darken. In fact, it did darken, I wasn't certain if the cause was the sunlight being blocked by a cloud or if the darkening happened in my mind. Was I losing my grip? I had no way to know. I did worry I was starting to have a hard time differentiating between what was real and what was taking place in my head. There was a major disturbance in my world-view! The sense of anticipation — a mixture of excitement and dread — for the opening of the file was gone. Replaced by sadness caused by a clear indication Dr. Lowd had been murdered and uncertainty regarding the request — out of the blue — that we go to New York. What for?

Karen, usually energetic, seemed frail. She seemed smaller than usual, more vulnerable. She was still crying, and after a few more moments, she excused herself and headed to the restroom.

"CALL ME RANALD!"

**

Somewhere in the south Atlantic Ocean

The next few days of the giants' voyage on the ship were unremarkable. The mystery of the ever-changing sky loomed up above, with the sun pushing its red, yellow and orange rays down through the firmament until they finally reached the ship and the ocean, where they were appreciated by the giants. Clouds came and went, different colors streaked and pulsed through the lively sky. It was still cold, and, when direct sunlight hit the boat, the giants cherished each ray, which provided only the slightest hint of warmth as they splashed onto the skin, the furs, the deck of the ship. But any ray of sunlight was better than nothing. Through this stage of the journey, somehow, the ocean managed to be both plentiful and desolate at the same time. Sharks, seals, fish, whales and other water-beasts surfaced now and then. Even with these visitors, the Brobdingnagian ocean still seemed empty, even unreal. At times, a terrible, freezing wind (which wasn't an antarctic wind anymore but still felt like one) swept across the bow of the ship, pelting the giants with a good reason to go below. But no one went below, they stayed above, sailing north, hoping warmth would come to them. When it didn't, they begged Ranald to allow another bonfire on deck.

"Ahoy! Stark Mateys we sail, we sail with the wind heading due north!" Ranald yelled, trying to sound like a sailer, with his stuffed pipe dangling from his mouth and his fraying-but-trusty map held in both of his massive hands, upside down.

The rest of the giants, having no enthusiasm for Ranald or his speech, ignored it.

Ranald glanced around, noting that his words drew no

response. This upset him, so to fill the air he yelled "We sail!"

"Everyone already knows," said Vilfred, sneering.

"I know. Why is he telling us that?" asked Eindride.

"You look like an idiot, Ranald!" yelled Vilfred the Vile. "Pretending to be a sailer. You look stupid, you don't know what you are doing. It's a miracle we haven't hit an iceberg or otherwise been capsized due to your limited intellect."

"Ha Ha Ha Hooo!" laughed Eindride. "Take him to task, Vile. He is role playing! Who made him captain? No-one did! Yet he clings to the map like it is the Devil's pile of gold."

"By thunder I will mop the deck with the both of you," yelled Ranald, his massive white-skinned cheeks reddening. "I'll swab it with your lifeless bodies 'till it's as clean as the heavens!"

"You'll do nothing of the sort and you know it!" replied Vilfred. "You haven't fought for stakes since the old days, and I hone my skills every day. I'll knock you into last century!"

"Belly up!" yelled Ranald, challenging Vilfred to a fight. In truth, despite Vilfred's mockery, Ranald cast a formidable presence. Strong jaw, light eyes, long, thick hair, a massive muscular frame, a sword strapped to his belt — Vilfred could mock him, but Ranald was a force to be reckoned with. Brutish, for sure, but impressive. A fight between the two — and they broke out with regularity — would be, as always, an even match.

"Be careful or I will old boy! You're not too big for me."

"BELLY UP! Or I'll take you down regardless," replied the Repellent, not letting the matter drop.

Vilfred was willing to let the first challenge go. But the second challenge, issued in an even louder voice and with a condescending sneer, could not be ignored — not so long as Vilfred maintained a shred of honor and a masculine demeanor. He bellied up to the Repellent.

The female giants, the young giants, Eindride, Mauve and the Wolvine all turned their attention to the impending fight.

The wind howled, and it was one of those days where the sun and the moon were present at the same time. There was a presence in the crisp air, a presence of anticipation, the presence of impending battle, of gain or loss (or both).

Ranald stamped his right foot back a few feet and threw a left jab at Vilfred. It connected on the Vile's chin. Thwap!

"That's what you've got, is it. It's not enough! It's not going to do the trick!" the Vile yelled, smiling as the impact was absorbed with no lasting effect.

The Vile lowered his left shoulder as if he was going to make a bull rush attack on the Repellent. But he didn't! He raised up to the same level he had been at before the fake tackle and threw a right cross.

"Pap!" the punch connected with the Repellent's jaw. His face flowed to his right, as the punch's impact, including the follow through, was realized.

"Now try to spew your sailing nonsense! Your mouth won't work any more!" hollered the Vile as he charged at the Repellent, whose face registered shock — but most certainly not fear. The charge was successful, and the Vile tackled the Repellent. They both crashed down to the deck. The Vile drew his fist back, intending to start raining blows down on the Repellent when, without warning, outside events intervened.

"Whampfttt!"

A jarring impact, from below — from the ocean — rocked

the ship. It tipped the ship significantly, maybe twenty degrees to the starboard side, throwing all the large occupants off balance. All three of the female giants fell. The Wide plopped on her ample rear, and the others, Runa and Inger, went down face first, and their bodies actually crashed into each other as they fell. Mauve, the young giants, Eindride and the wolvine all maintained their footing. Ranald and Vilfred were already sprawled on the deck of the ship.

"It's him!" yelled Ranald, still laying flat on his back from the fight with Vilfred. "It's the great white beast! We saw him centuries ago! He must live forever! Ayyy! I'll wax that lubber and fry him in his own blubber!"

"Humph, Harrumph, Ha Ha, Muaaahhh!" laughed Mauve, a simple creature who loved danger. Mauve was smart enough to realize that if the whale capsized the boat, they would all drown and freeze, in whatever order. Yet still, he laughed! His special penguin did not find the incident as amusing, and it let out a pathetic whimper. That stopped Mauve's laughter and he gave the penguin a little rub on the belly to calm it down.

Ranald and Vilfred untangled themselves from each other and stood up. The female giants also re-established their footing.

"He doesn't know we switched sides! He doesn't know we chase the Light like him!" added Vile. His comment was in reference to the giants' shared belief that the whale was a force for good, for beauty, for God — they had reason to believe it (from old times) — but for the sake of brevity the story will not be included here. It is written in other lore, to be sure. Find it and know it, if you like.

Panic set in on the ship! Giants were never afraid — that served well as a general rule. But in the middle of the ocean, that rule did not seem to apply. Only Ranald was an accomplished swimmer — and, obviously, even he couldn't swim hundreds of miles in the freezing water. His range was probably up to a mile before he would die of cold and fatigue. Like Mauve, the wolvine and especially the female giants, knew if the ship was capsized by impact from the massive white whale they would die. They would sink, while their internals were being frozen, to the bottom of the ocean where the meat would be picked off their bones by sea creatures. Even Mauve's demeanor changed after his special penguin's whimper. Every living creature on the boat, judging from their faces, was picturing a gruesome death. What a way to go out!

Ranald, taking matters into his own hands, moved with determination to the port side of the ship (which he thought was the starboard side). Without any deliberation, he threw himself off the ship with a tremendous leap, yelling "Call me Ranald!" as he disappeared over the side. While plummeting, Ranald brought his knees up to his chest to create a cannonball splash on his impact with the surface of the ocean.

SPLASH! A massive wave rose from the ocean where the giant cannonball met the water!

Vilfred and Eindride instructed the young giants to ready the rope, so they could retrieve Ranald out of the water, on the off-chance he survived the events to come.

An incredible battle ensued! At the outset, the whale used a ramming strategy. But he couldn't get a clean impact on Ranald, who frog-kicked his way out of the whales path. Ranald, after looping under the immense creature, decided he would use the tail of the sea-beast to try to pull him to the surface where he could pummel him into submission. But the whale was too big and too slippery — the plan failed. The whale, realizing Ranald's initial plan had failed, whacked Ranald on the left side with his tail, trying to crush his backbone. When the tail connected, the impact stunned

Ranald, but only for a second — his back was bruised but not broken. The air was expelled from his lungs by the impact, and he swallowed gallons of sea water when he gasped, involuntarily, trying to replenish his oxygen. Ranald's face, usually stern and commanding, showed more than a trace amount of fear. Ranald surfaced for five seconds, coughed up some of the water and gathered himself. He then dove under again, propelling himself to the front side of the whale with several strokes of his arms and a few powerful kicks from his legs.

He made his way through the water until he was close to the whale, who was heading in to ram him again. He held out his left hand to brace himself from the impact. With his free right hand, he punched the whale in the eye. Wham! Wham! Wham!

The whale sprayed salt water from its blowhole, seemingly out of frustration, "Phhhsssssshhhhhttt!"

"I am friendly to you now! But I can't have you attack the ship! Learn your lesson!" he yelled, when he surfaced for a breath between punches.

All in all, Ranald punched the whale nine times on three trips under the surface of the water, then Ranald resurfaced for good; he was out of energy and struggling for breath.

Still, he managed to find his voice. "By God, we are not working with the Dark One any longer! Believe me, you beast!" he yelled, his head pointed toward the sky to try to prevent swallowing water. "Cease your attack or I will continue to strike at your eye until it is destroyed!"

Everyone on the deck watched the battle below intently. Tension gripped the face of everyone on the ship, which leaned dramatically to the port side, as all of the giants, the nook-demon and the wolvine were standing on the same side of the ship, staring

234

over the rail. The ship leaned, but the weight of the group was not enough to capsize the ship, which sat in place, drifting only slightly, in the water — Eindride had instructed the young giants to lower the sails when Ranald jumped into the ocean so as not to leave him behind.

The whale, whether persuaded by Ranald's words, defeated in battle, or simply having lost interest in capsizing the ship, swam away from Ranald and the ship. To Ranald, it was as if the whale had heard his words, or received a signal from something or someone, and departed. The whale, Ranald surmised, was not angry or disheartened by the combat. He swam away with determination but not discontent.

The young giants lowered the thick rope to the surface of the freezing water. It took Vilfred, Eindride and all the young giants pulling on the rope to hoist Ranald and his soaked furs back into the ship.

The female giants waited for Ranald to strip all of the wet clothing from his body, then they covered him in dry furs. The young giants went to work preparing a fire on the deck.

Gerd the Wide exclaimed, "Oh Ranald, you are the bravest! You saved us from that humongous beast! We would have died a frozen death! A most miserable death! Wonderful Ranald!"

"Bite your tongue, Wide!" interjected Vilfred. "Too much enthusiasm in your praise for my brother. Even his wife is not gushing like a ridiculous river. Watch yourself!"

"Oh drat!" said Gerd, starting to cry. "You're so mean!"

"You've made her cry, you buffoon!" hollered Eindride. "You are worth nothing, there is emptiness where your soul should be."

"Fight me!" yelled Vilfred.

"By the light I will!" replied Eindride, emphatically.

"Belly up!"

"Stop! Stop now! Fire and music!" yelled Ranald. "Fire and light! And Grog!"

The fight didn't happen. Eindride retreated — without apology — but not pursuing his angle any further. Gerd the Wide went below deck, crying and blubbering. She would, likely, console herself down below the deck with a heaping mound of pemmican mash.

Eindride looked as if he would speak again, but then he didn't.

The young giants continued to prepare the fire. The female giants retrieved their instruments after Runa went down below deck and persuaded the Wide to come back up.

When she resurfaced on deck, Vilfred berated her again, yelling, "You've hit the pemmican mash again, haven't you. Put on the Yellow Letter! Put the Yellow Letter O on your furs, you wildebeest!"

Runa, her face flashing with anger, spoke in an angry grown, "You are not trim, Vile. And anyone would eat piles of mash if they were betrothed and married to someone as awful as you. Something to get through the pain. Gerd, ignore this awful beast."

"I'll throttle you, Runa. Watch it, I will."

"You'll do nothing of the sort, Vilfred," said Ranald. "You'll not throttle my wife without killing me first."

Things went on like this. Constant bickering, but no more physical conflict. The relief from the safe end of the encounter with the white whale was enough to calm everyone down.

A few minutes later, the bonfire was started by the young giants and the female giants were playing their instruments, with Runa and Ingrid strumming guitars and Gerd beating mercilessly on drums. Everyone else sat down in their chairs. Grog flowed, barrel by barrel, brought out from storage by Mauve. Eindride, who had a gritty but pleasant-sounding singing style, sang in a deep, slow melodic voice.

> Riding on the waves of destruction
> Northbound sea ride, grizzly demon tail
> One ship and fifteen weary riders
> The wolvine howl, we broke outta frozen jail
> All along the world's most epic journey
> The ship sailed on, leaving ice behind
> We pass the whales, we carry swords and shields
> This time we will set the Devil aflame
> Times like these the mighty sword beats the pen
> Our bellies full of penguin and seal
> Watch your back, oh Evil one
> Here we come!

SHUT IT DOWN!

❉❉

Everything was fine. Everything was in shambles. There, in Parker's Mortuary, we all sat, deep in our big leather chairs (other than the Laser who sat near a table on a wooden chair), deep in conspiratorial thought. Dr. Lowd had spoken, from the dead. What was the reference to Antarctica? What were we to do in New York? There was no detail provided in the message, which left us with more questions than answers.

The mood in the shop shifted, slowly, from one of sadness to one of impending adventure or impending doom — depending on whose face was carrying the message. Rory was staring at Lucille and Karen and I were staring at each other. Karen had stopped crying, her eyes were no longer swimming in tears, but she was still blinking more than usual, seemingly to make sure to prevent more of the same from welling up and rolling down her cheeks.

Lucille seemed to be looking to Rory for guidance or for assurance; for something, it was hard to tell what it was. I focused, for a second on Karen's nose, which had just a teeny bit of a snub to it, in a cute and endearing way. As everyone looked at one another, and the Laser looked at his laptop screen, an energy built up in the room. Nothing could have seemed more daunting than, days after a murder (we suspected foul play even if it remained unproven), being charged with going on an undefined mission to New York.

I wished the Doctor had given us more information to work with.

Once a city chock-full of opportunity, a symbol of freedom, of glossy capitalism, New York had become crowded, rat-infested, diseased and mono-cultural, for the most part. Globo had won the battle for New York, as well as almost everywhere else. The dominant force in New York was international capital and the machinations of the mega-corporations. The place, now, was the perfect distillation of everything Dr. Lowd opposed for years... the things I opposed, since I started noticing. Yes, there were still holdovers — neighborhood restaurants and coffee shops and bars. Some businesses remained independent. But the endearing characteristics of the city had been smashed by the global pull of the big-capital operations — mega-corporations and all the accompanying signs of late-stage, degenerate capitalism — they were all located there. Third world people, whether they had American papers or not, outnumbered the heritage Americans in New York. It was a rotten Babel, a teetering-tower containing garbage, rats, and random people from wherever, doing whatever. To the keen observer, it was now a symbol of the unchecked evil of global government, global money, global corporations. The people living there were cannon fodder, there to feed the 'system' — which could never get enough of what it took from them.

The energy built and built, yet no one spoke. I stopped looking at Karen and looked around the shop, with thoughts racing through my mind.

A red guitar hung on the wall, next to a white one, which hung next to a blue one. Other knick-knacks and wares — old records, clothing, other stuff — were positioned around the room, for sale. The entire time we had been inside, however, not a single customer had walked in to look around.

Minutes went by and a queer dullness crept in the room as the energy started to stagnate. Everyone seemed to fidget around more as they felt it.

Would someone attempt small talk? Or would someone bring up the message from Dr. Lowd? There was no way to know, and I was frozen with indecision. The mention of New York, without enough context, seemed completely arbitrary.

It was Rory, who spoke up.

"Look, we don't have a choice. We have to go to New York! How can we not? Just read the message."

"The meeting, or whatever, is on Thanksgiving Day, Rory," said Lucille. "We told the Pattersons we would go to their place and bring the dogs."

"Tell the Pattersons to pound flour and blow smoke."

"Rory! You are an obstinate...!"

"We're not choosing the Pattersons over this. Tell them or I will. How can you even suggest that?" interrupted Rory.

I braced myself as I noticed that Karen looked like she was going to speak. My face held, flat and expressionless. My nerves were shot.

"Rory's right. I have to go. But I don't want anyone to feel like they are obligated to come with me. He was my father. No one else needs to get into something they don't have anything to do with," Karen said, plainly.

"Whatever this is, I feel like it's mine too. I'm part of it. I knew Dr. Lowd. How can I miss this? For what? To send out a resume for a sales job?" I said.

"I'm going," interjected Rory. "Dr. Lowd was one of my idols. I may not have known him well — other than seeing him speak and reading his writings, but I am part of this. I don't know what we are looking for, but I'm going along."

"The Pattersons..." whimpered Lucille, smacking her lips. "They make an incredible stuffing."

"Tell them to save some of it for us and we'll head over when we get back. It's simple. Not like you need any, anyway," said Rory.

"Oh my... Did he really say that? You're fatter than me, Rory! You and your stupid bone broth! Still fatter!"

Rory laughed enthusiastically, patting his belly. It was obvious he loved Lucille very much. When a man really loves a particular woman, when he is wrapped around her finger, it is always very plain to see for those who pay attention and have experience observing matters of the heart. What was refreshing to see, for me and, I think, for Karen, was that Lucille was not calculating — she loved Rory back in the same manner he loved her and she wasn't in it for anything else. She wasn't keeping score. She wasn't measuring Rory's shortcomings against what he had to offer her. He wasn't the hottest, the smartest, the coolest... she just loved him, she loved Rory. That was my impression, anyway. It was one of those rare, old-fashioned love affairs between those two. I wanted the same thing for myself, but I had learned you can't chase it. That type of thing either found you or it didn't.

"Guys... really," said Karen, her eyes flashing with a mix of humor and exasperation.

"We're going, that's the end of the discussion," I stated as firmly as I could.

The Laser, who had been sitting there, saying and doing nothing, grabbed his stuff and said, "I gotta take off, guys. Can't go to New York, but reach out if you need any tech support while you're there."

"Thanks again the Laser, I'll get back in touch," said Rory. Everyone else said some words of thanks to the Laser, who then walked out, presumably to do Russian hacker stuff.

"What day should we go?" asked Rory.

"Let's go Tuesday," said Karen. "We can avoid the very heavy travel on the Wednesday before Thanksgiving."

"Okay."

It was already Sunday.

"Plenty to do between now and then, and only in a day and a half," I chimed in. "Let's split up and get some good relaxation in today. We can confirm everything tomorrow. But we need to be well-rested. We have no idea what awaits us in New York."

"It won't be nothing!" yelled Rory.

"Too loud, Rory," said Lucille.

"It's okay," said Karen.

"Bone broth, Rory. Stick with it. See ya Tuesday," I said.

We parted ways, agreeing to keep in close contact until we traveled on Tuesday. Karen and I walked out of the shop towards the car. As Karen got in the Audi, I saw her make a pained expression. It was fleeting, a second later and her face was fine again. I didn't mention anything.

We settled into the car for the ride. The silence was killing me, and my reaction was to blurt out the first thing that popped into my head.

"Are you okay?" I asked. Right when I said it, I thought about how stupid the question was.

Karen sat silent, but didn't seem upset with the question. She gave me a quick look, with wide eyes. I made a mental note to be less careless with my words. I would let Karen bring up her feelings, and I would only ask questions pertaining to activity between us, not to her mental state.

We drove along the windy Northern California highway, heading back to San Mateo. I was playing the Rolling Stones as we drove (*Tumbling Dice*). It was upbeat music, but not too aggressive and the familiar songs made for decent background music in the event Karen decided she wanted to talk.

We passed some roadkill, a raccoon, on our right. Karen noticed it and grimaced.

"Poor raccoon," she said. "I feel sorry for him."

"Karen..."

Another thirty minutes passed as we drove.

"Hey, can we stop at the next gas station or whatever? I need to use the restroom," said Karen.

"Of course."

I continued to drive but kept an eye open for a stopping point. Along the way, I dodged a raccoon which was infringing on the road and wondered if it was any relation to the dead one a ways back. It was a lucky miss, as it would have, no doubt, upset Karen. We pressed on until I let her out at a gas station with a convenience store. I didn't go in with her, but instead I sat outside with the engine running. The Rolling Stones kept playing. I looked at the signs on the front of the convenience store. Chips, sodas, candy, hot dogs, corn dogs and beer. All of the brands were owned by one of about five mega-corporations that pushed junk-food on most of the world. All on sale inside, all basically toxic materials. I wasn't tempted, thankfully, those things weren't for me and hadn't been for a long time.

Karen emerged and I watched her walk back, her hair blowing in the soft breeze. She walked with her usual flair and energy, making me feel good about her and about things. "Everything was going to be okay," I told myself.

She settled in the chair.

"Hey," I said.

She turned toward me. I leaned over and gently pulled her closer to me. I kissed her, on her left cheek, quite close to her lips, but not close enough to be interpreted as a romantic kiss. I don't even know exactly what made me do it. I was feeling sentimental and caring toward her, toward her situation.

"You're doing great. Hang in there. If you need to talk, I'm right here."

"Thanks, Brandon."

"Anytime. I'm worried about you. All this stuff... and now we have the New York stuff right away. Which is fine, but we don't even know what it is."

"Yeah, that's a little stressful. I hate to even bring this up — I feel like such a loser — but can I stay with you again tonight? We don't have to stop for any stuff. I can bring the same bag to New York. I'm not ready to go home, not yet."

"I was going to suggest it, without trying to sound weird."

"Okay, great. I'll cook if you want."

"Let's get takeout. I know a place, Greek food. Olive oil everywhere. We can talk at home. Or watch a movie. Or go for a walk. Whatever."

"Sounds great, I really kind of like you right now. I'm not kidding."

"Wish I could say the same thing," I joked.

"Seriously, Brandon, it's not the nineteen-nineties, anymore. Negging only works with dummies," said Karen with raised eyebrows, feigning frustration.

"Who said I was trying anything?" I replied, caught red-handed.

"Oh. How convenient, another neg, right after I told you it doesn't work anymore. Well, maybe you're not interested. Not like I said I was, either."

I stayed silent for a moment.

"What did you think about the message the Laser opened up?" I asked, changing the subject.

"What a mess..." she said, making an exasperated face. "We're off to New York for a goose-chase, except there's no goose involved."

"Yeah, I was thinking the same thing."

"I love my dad but he was always not careful enough or else he was too careful. He never took precautions at the right level."

"I see what you mean. He didn't take enough precautions with his safety, but was very careful to make sure the message didn't give real information. We already knew all of it except for the New York request — and the weird mention of Antarctica."

"Yeah... We can talk about it tonight," said Karen with a funny look on her face.

"What should we plan. I mean, unless we are going to stare at each other and lob in guesses about the purpose of the New York trip, we need to do something."

"I know. I feel like a slug. I haven't been getting my exercise and I'm not used to that."

"I have a walk I do, down by the river. Remember? We messaged one time while I was there. We could do that. There's a one hour version and a two hour version."

"I'd love that," replied Karen. "Let's do the hour and then chill out at home. Let's have a glass of wine somewhere, or at your place. Would be good to relax tonight before traveling."

"Excellent," I said.

And so we did, after another forty-five minutes or so on the road, I parked the car in the usual spot, along the road next to the public bathroom and right under a street light. We were dressed comfortably enough. So, we pulled over and started walking, without ceremony.

It was a beautiful day, with a high sky featuring only a few clouds, pretty, puffy ones set against the mid-afternoon sun.

We walked for a twenty minutes before we were treated to the sight of a beautiful crane, standing on a rock in the middle of the river (which was really more of a creek).

"Look at him!" exclaimed Karen, with her girlish enthusiasm. "He's beautiful."

"It's true. I see him often."

"You do this walk every day?"

"I have for most days since I quit my last job."

"Why'd you do that, anyway? You never told me."

"It wasn't for me anymore. They had me do this big analysis project. Then, when I completed it they said 'well, thanks and we're going to keep pushing unrelated topics because we can.' It was weird. I sort of snapped and quit. They didn't break me... I was just done with it all. All at once." I paused, then continued, "Then all this happened," I said, waving my hand up to my shoulder.

"I can't imagine what you think of me," replied Karen,

grimacing.

"Nah. I don't think anything bad about you if that's what you mean."

"I don't believe you."

"I mean, what is life without some excitement? Uhh, meaning the trip to New York, not your dad's death."

"I know what you meant. I'm still in shock, I still can't believe it. I mean, my mom died two years ago and I know it sounds stupid but I never thought I'd lose my dad."

"I know. I never even knew my mom. Not really. You're lucky you had what you had for so long. I know you don't see it that way right now."

"I don't know how I see it. I'm in a fog. Thank you for being there for me. I can't say it enough."

"I'm not doing anything else. It helps me stop reading articles on the computer and obsessing about the 'system.' So I'm the one who should be thankful. That's the way I look at it, at least."

"You're so positive."

"Not always."

"Yes, always."

We laughed and walked on and after a little while longer reached the point of the walk where we were passing the white crane again.

Karen hadn't said anything for a while until she stopped walking and said my name. I stopped as well, and she pivoted on her left foot to face me.

"I need to tell you something."

I didn't say anything, but I did widen my eyes a bit to indicate I was listening.

"Our introduction wasn't on accident."

"Don't mess with me Karen."

"No really. My dad made me swear not to tell you. I promised I wouldn't. And I didn't, while he was alive, I didn't. I dreamed about it last night. All sorts of stuff ran through my head. But I knew I had to tell you, since they killed him. Even before the stuff about New York. I really don't want to get you hurt or in trouble."

"I don't understand. How did he target me? I go to Oswald's all the time. I mean, to get out of my place. I don't drink much when I go there, just so you know. A whiskey, neat, once in a while. Otherwise I get soda water. Your dad told me he did the same thing."

"He made me show up that night. You saw the girls I was with. They are not hole-in-the-wall kind of girls. I love them, but they are modern girls. You know, e-girls. I'm not being mean... but they are. They want to go places so they can post glamorous-looking shots on Instagram for clout."

"Okay..."

"I had to drag them to my dad's dive - I guess that's your dive too."

"I get that part, I guess. If you say so. But he didn't know anything about me. We had only spoken one time before we met. I'm not buying it. I mean, I'm not ugly, but I'm not Brad Pitt. I'm not stupid, but I'm not Nikola Tesla. I don't see the point of introducing you — his daughter — to me. I don't, sorry. Why would he bother? And you're younger than me, from the looks of things."

"Don't sell yourself short," Karen said, with a look I couldn't quite categorize. Mischievous? Flirtatious? What is going on here, I asked myself.

"I mean... uhh... what are you talking about? It's not like you're a spinster. You're smart and beautiful and engaging. Or are you saying he introduced us, but not romantically? I'm not getting it. I'm not connecting the dots."

"I don't get it all either. And I have no idea what my old man had in his head about the romantic part. He didn't say anything about that. But I wasn't joking when I said you were cute."

"Cute, I see," I replied with the biggest scowl I could muster. I looked down at my shoes. "What in the..."

"Oh come on Brandon, stop being a baby."

"Now I'm a baby! A cute baby. You went on a date with a cute baby."

"Yeah, and I wanted to kiss the cute little baby but he was too busy doing baby stuff. Too distracted, he didn't even try to kiss me."

I feigned horror, twisting my face.

She paused and then continued, "I was hoping you would believe me without my having to bring this up... but dad... spied on you, sort of."

"This keeps getting better."

"He had a connection, he wouldn't tell me his name or how it happened, but the guy either worked at the National Security Agency — you know, the NSA — or otherwise had access to their information. They had you on a watch list, one they shared internationally."

"A watch list? For what?"

"My dad said the focus was on the websites you were visiting. I don't remember all the topics, but my dad had a list of them. Monetary stuff, United Nations... stuff like that. Basically, anything the media and the people — you know, the people who don't question anything — call conspiracy theories."

"I call those people the dogs of the oligarchs."

"Why?"

"Well, because they are poorly-treated pets. And even though they are treated poorly, they are completely loyal to the oligarchs and their capital. I love dogs, but I don't like human versions of dogs."

"Oh... I'll have to think about that analogy to see if I think it fits. Makes sense, though."

"Well, my dad always, you know, watched the watch lists. It was a way for him to find good people, since he didn't have access to the same surveillance materials.

"They really are watching everybody. What did he say in the message. Consolidating power? Something like that?" I asked.

"He said consolidating with censorship. They want to shut it down. Shut. It. Down. He always said that, with the same tempo," Karen said, smiling, as she must have been re-playing a specific memory of her father.

"Have we ever talked about who the 'they' is? This is what they use to make people seem crazy. And see, I just said 'they' again."

"It's the government, in cahoots with the corporations and global capital. The cabal, according to my dad, centers on the capital — those are the people controlling the corporations, which control the governments."

"Cahoots? This is too shadowy for me. I can't imagine a group of people sitting around a table giving a single... you know... about what websites I visit. I can't."

"What's wrong with cahoots? My dad's connection said most of the hits, most of the views, came from a bunker on the fringe of Zürich, Switzerland. They tried to mask the IP address but the NSA is good at uncovering stuff. Even the people controlling them can't hide. Not completely, at least... they make mistakes too."

"I knew that before I ever met your dad. I would go to websites with articles, posts, whatever... about those topics. I was a few months into it before I ran into your dad at Oswald's. Right before I met you. The coincidences are pretty wild."

"All of the best people, original, independent thinkers, are on the watch list with the NSA and whoever is running them out of Zürich. These are all websites the government and their handlers wanted to censor. They wanted to shut all these websites down. But it's whack-a-mole. There are still resilient people out there and the government doesn't want to be too obvious about being a totalitarian operation. So, they don't lock everything down immediately. They wait for a pretense."

"So, if I'm understanding correctly, your dad co-opted Globo's watch lists as a way to identify fellow subversives?"

"Yes, allies."

"Clever. A way to find the few people who pay attention. People who noticed what they were doing and didn't have to be spoon fed anything."

"It's that pesky 'they' again."

"They. Them. Their."

We laughed.

"Exactly, he let them do the groundwork for him. Only, as you know, he wanted the subversion. He wanted the 'system' to come down. All the petty destruction, non-compliance stuff."

"It's so far-fetched, Karen."

"It's real. Think about it. You know it. Think about whatever research you were doing, whatever sites you went to. Tell me how my dad would know that if what I said wasn't true."

"Maybe your dad hacked my computer," I said, jokingly.

"My dad couldn't hack anything. You met him twice. You saw him. He looked like Mark Twain, for crying out loud."

"I love Mark Twain. If I ever write a book, I'm using a pen name."

"You're nuts, Brandon. But you know he didn't hack anything. When he used a computer, it was either from the library or one that he borrowed. He wrote on a typewriter."

"Maybe it's true," I said, nodding slowly. "I don't know anymore."

I felt dizzy all of a sudden.

"How else, Brandon? Think about it. My dad identified you through his contact. He did."

"Even so, why does it matter?"

"Because this is dan-ger-ous, Brandon," Karen said, exaggerating her pronunciation of the key word.

"I already know it. You keep telling me over and over like I'm a cute baby."

A flash of emotion crossed Karen's face, but it was quickly replaced with a smile when she realized I was joking around.

"Okay. I'm just funny like that. I don't like all this stuff. I feel trapped in it. And you're the one who has to hear about it. I'll try to stop."

"It's okay. I get it. I'm fine. How could we read the message and not go to New York? That's impossible, so let's stop worrying about it. I don't care how we got here, we're here."

"It's true, for me at least. I have to go. And I'm thankful, every day, to have you here with me."

"Wow, not bad for a cute baby," I said, flirting, playing the victim. I wanted to drop it, but I couldn't. That line of joking wasn't overly humorous — in fact, it wasn't even funny — but it was an easy mark to needle her a bit, to gaslight her by pretending like she had said something wrong. It was hard to tell if our wisecracks were the start of a love song or the opening notes to the score of a horror movie. But I didn't see any reason not to persist. Life is a winding road.

"Let's go have a glass of wine."

"Okay, we'll stop for a drink and then get take out. If you think about it we don't have much to do. Buy a plane ticket and a couple hotel rooms and pack a bag. We have to kill some time."

"I don't have cooties, Brandon. We can get one room with two beds. I'm not going to barge in while you're using the bathroom. I mean, how old are we anyway? Get over it."

"Fine," I said, shaking my head, but smiling.

Big Apple Mindset

❧❧

The rest of the night was uneventful; it was more of the same. Our main goal was to pass time, but we still managed to enjoy each other. We ate, we visited, we watched a movie. Another Mel Gibson flick... he was one of the only men in Hollywood who wasn't totally compromised, totally controlled. So, we watched one of his 'oldies' — *Mad Max*. I feared a breakdown of the global 'system' — of pacification, wage-slavery and propaganda — would lead to a dark period of lawlessness. Just like they portrayed in the movie, a post-apocalyptic scenario. Fighting in the streets, trying to expel all of the people who made the country a bad place. A period of violence was the downside of breaking free from Globo. I mean, I don't long for violence in any way, shape or form — but it's better than a slow boil that results in lower standards, lower quality of life, more products, more destruction of nature.

People once had strong visions of what they wanted their life to be — distractions and compromise with the Globo-induced reality make that type of thing a sad, distant memory.

But it was an open question as to how long the rebuilding process would take, after the corporations were reigned in and the merchants and capital-holders were removed from power. It was any-body's guess, but it would be a period of adjustment to go local again — local and natural. People were creatures of habit, and at present they were totally swamped by mega-corporations, government, the bonds of capital.

The night passed in enjoyable fashion and we retired to sleep — Karen in my bed and me on the couch.

In the morning (after sleeping surprisingly well and with no nightmares), I made a coffee before booking our flights and hotel.

Eager to have Karen awake (although for no urgent reason), I brought her a large mug of coffee while she was still half-asleep in my bed. I had already showered and gotten dressed. I was antsy, but not because we had much to do during the day — in fact, with the travel arrangements made, the real task at hand was killing time, not using it productively.

Karen stirred when I placed the coffee on the nightstand. I didn't want to admit it, but I liked having her here. I know the circumstances were not ideal — but when I imagined my life as it was in the weeks leading up to meeting Karen through Dr. Lowd, I felt an ache. I would have missed her.

"Oh, hi Brandon. Good morning. You know me well, already," she said, with a little nod at the coffee mug.

"Good morning. I got our travel stuff all set. I hope you don't mind, I went in your stuff to look at your ID so I could book the plane travel."

"It's fine. Thanks for doing that," she said as she took a sip of the coffee. "I had the most vivid dream. I can't remember all of it, but my dad was in it. There's this one quote he always would tell me about. He kept saying it to me as we went around, doing stuff."

"I bet your dreams are going to be interesting, for a while."

"Yeah, nothing to do but embrace it."

"What was the quote?" I inquired.

"It's a long one, but I know it by heart. Woodrow Wilson. In the dream, my father said it so slowly. Like a record playing at the wrong speed... 'Since I entered politics, I have chiefly had men's views confided to me privately. Some of the biggest men in the United States, in the field of commerce and manufacture, are afraid of somebody, are afraid of something. They know there is a power somewhere so organized, so subtle, so watchful, so interlocked, so complete, so pervasive, that they had better not speak above their breath when they speak in condemnation of it."

"That is a long quote. I wonder if it's true."

"In the dream it took forever because it was slowed down. But I know it by heart. It was one of my dad's favorites. He focused a lot of his day to day efforts on anti-corporatism and anti-corrupt-government. You know that."

"Yeah, he wasn't shy from day one, letting me know a bunch of stuff."

"It was a calculated risk. Remember, he had a list of the articles you were reading on-line. He figured if you were on their watch list, you were probably okay."

"True, I didn't consider it that way," I replied. "Hey, that one day at the mall... did you...?"

I trailed off.

"Did I what?" asked Karen with a mischievous grin, answering my question.

"Never-mind," I said.

"So... Woodrow Wilson — a creep — he still had access to the highest levels of political knowledge. He knew there was something — the power of capital — lurking in the background, calling the shots."

"That's exactly the type of stuff I was reading about after I started noticing how wacked-out our society had become."

"And, hence, you popped up on NSA radar and then my dad's. That's what happened, that's why he told you. You know the whole back-story now."

"They're tracking everything. Even some corporate guy —

me — reading blog posts. That's insane."

"Yeah, the Constitution isn't going to save anybody. When they are powerful enough, they'll just do away with it. The people will be so conditioned that they won't even notice. Wilson was right... the enemy is so organized, so subtle, so watchful."

"Yeah. A glimmer of truth from an evil — or possessed — man."

"It is. If you've ever seen pictures of his face, you can see that he's possessed by the Devil himself. You can see the Devil controlling Wilson's face, his being. You can see him right below the surface."

"I never believed in all that Devil talk. For thirty years, I just shrugged him off. But not anymore. The Devil is here, walking among us."

"Look at us, starting the morning off on a light note."

We both laughed. Karen sipped her coffee.

"We have our travel booked, we leave at six-fifty a.m. tomorrow morning. Let's not sit around and wait until then. That would be agony. Let's go to Big Sur — check out the sights. Old-time California."

"Wow, Big Sur sounds great. Let me finish this coffee and I'll hop in the shower and clean up this mess," said Karen, glancing down at her body.

"You're hard on yourself! Want to see if Rory and Lucille want to come?" I asked.

"Let's not. I have a feeling that we're going to get plenty of the 'Rory and Lucille Show' in New York. Plus we would have to wait for them to come down from up north. Let's just go, the two of us."

"Okay, makes sense. I'll leave you alone so you can shower."

While Karen was in the bathroom, I had the opportunity to take inventory of my mind, which was split. I was, to be sure, enchanted by my adventure. I was enthralled, sometimes totally subsumed by this journey I was on. I did things — or thought things — that would never have been possible in times gone by, with my old mindset. That was one side of me. The other side — the side clinging on to the comforts of the 'system' — was apprehensive. What if I needed a corporate sales job to survive and I couldn't get one because I was on this stupid NSA black-list? What if this whole path led not to the destruction of the 'system,' but to my own, personal destruction? Homeless, looking for half-eaten chicken wings? Worse, what if they killed me for questioning their 'system?' That happened, a lot, in other countries that had similar cultural revolutions. Mao? Stalin? Those guys just killed people who dissented. Why did Karen seem so un-phased by everything (other than her father's death)?

Sometimes, as was the case at this moment, these thoughts made everything seem so hopeless. So horribly hopeless. The blissful thoughts of destroying and replacing Globo with something better, something local... those thoughts always gave way to an enfeebling paralysis brought about recognition of Globo's strength and scale.

My vision for local community was a paradise — it existed in my mind when I could imagine life without Globo's tentacles everywhere — the present condition, the ever-present corporate blight and inertia of human habit left little chance for change. It felt impossible when I viewed it this way. My vision was doomed. All of this was for naught and I would disgrace myself and my family and go down as nothing other than a failed conspiracy theorist, dead in a gutter somewhere.

Gloom set in, clouds of a sort hung right over my head as if positioned by Satan himself.

I will leave the details of the ride, the conversation, Karen's requested stops (she needed to stop to tinkle three times which I found incredible), out. I have a story to tell! I will mention, however, that by the time we reached Big Sur, my personal gloom had lifted. I attributed this to a couple of factors. Karen's company, for one. She was delightful! Bright eyes, a willingness to joke around (even in difficult times), and a ready smile mean so much in life. And the passage of time, for another. I had an optimistic personality and it was hard for me to stay down for too long, but Karen helped in this regard.

Big Sur was like a mirage, it held so many sensory delights. The views, the sounds, the fresh ocean smells. I wondered if the entire area had been blessed, arranged to convey a new level of profound beauty. The sky was thick and damp, the waves carried a bounty of bubbly foam and some seaweed here and there. The charm, the rose-and-scarlet-colored tinge to the edges of the clouds, the pure beach, untrammeled, wind-swept, facing out toward the Pacific. It slowed everything down for me.

We walked out to a little cove area and sat down. We mostly stared out at the water, at the horizon. We enjoyed the moment, enjoyed the time together. An hour had gone by with no mention of New York, of Dr. Lowd, of Globo. Birds were plentiful, as were sea otters, playing in the surf. Humans were scarce (there were none around) and I appreciated the isolation.

I was startled when Karen grabbed my hand and held on. She glanced at me and I looked at her over my right shoulder.

"I'm not making a move on my cute little baby, I'm liking

this. It's so beautiful here. Touching you helps me feel our connection together and our connection to this place, to the ocean, the beach, the sky. I can't believe I've only known you a couple of months. Feels like forever, but in a good way."

"I feel the same way."

I was surprised by my cool reaction to Karen's touch. I mean, it wasn't new to me but something was different about Karen. I couldn't define what this meant, not exactly. But I knew clearly she was different from all the other girls who had been in and out of my life over the years. One a quarter, I would guess, on average. I didn't mind sharing deeply with Karen. I realized I didn't mind if she knew more about me than I had told any other woman, ever. My hopes, fears, dreams, my most protected thoughts and desires. Rightly or wrongly, I trusted her fully and implicitly.

More time went by in this fashion. We made no plans to leave, and our limited discussion stayed light in nature. We were jolted out of this rather blissful state of being when a horrid couple invaded our space, creeping up from behind until we could hear their loud conversation, which was really just the two of them haranguing each other over random disagreements. I don't want to issue a physical description of the couple because I have no desire to misinform the reader and, at the same time, I have no desire to come across as mean-spirited. I will say their verbal exchange was vulgar, intense, jarring. They bickered and fought with no regard for us, no regard for the beauty of Big Sur. A bright flash caught my eye as the woman waved her hand, in exaggerated fashion, at her scowling husband and the massive diamond refracted the sun's rays, right into my helpless eyes. I looked at Karen, raising my forehead and moving my eyes up and down twice. Without words, we stood and walked to the car, with the nasty couple taking no notice of us at all.

On the walk, Karen grabbed my hand again. I was okay with it, as I was before. It was nice to be with someone I found interesting and engaging. And, if we were to be murdered in New York in the next day or two, it was nice to have some pre-comfort before meeting my doom. It all made me feel good inside. This day — the experience of being surrounded by such natural beauty — this was permanent. If Globo killed us, it would be but a temporary setback.

"It's okay, it was time to leave anyway. Never-mind those people. That was a really nice morning, thank you for taking me," Karen said, quietly.

"I feel the same way. I love Big Sur. You wanna go eat?"

"Sure. You want to get some Sushi? I know a place back home if you can wait that long."

"That sounds great."

I used to be able to fall in love quickly. I don't know if I changed or if my definition of love changed. Or maybe I changed back? Something was happening. I mean, I'm not saying I was 'in love' with Karen. That's not what I'm saying. Everything she did — every gesture, every facial expression, every phrase — well, I hung on them all — like I did when I was young. I told myself I should ease off the throttle. But it wasn't a rational decision; it didn't work that way.

We rolled along the highway, heading back up north. The conversation ranged pretty widely, from small talk about the drive, to childhood stories, to our favorite conspiracy theories. Of course, Doctor Lowd came up often in the conversation. And the plane flight to New York loomed in our shared near future.

With the pleasant ride completed, we pulled up to Yakko

Sushi in San Mateo. I parked the Audi and we walked into my favorite hole-in-the-wall sushi joint. I hadn't been there since I went with April. I was coming to believe a lot of new things, but I didn't believe a restaurant could jinx a relationship. Besides, I wasn't technically in a relationship with Karen.

We walked in and didn't see too many familiar faces. But there was one — Sadaharo, the sushi chef, was behind the counter chopping and dicing and forming little dishes of sushi to pass to customers.

"Sit at the bar?" I asked Karen, without thinking anything through. That was just my normal protocol.

"Sure."

And so we did, walking over casually. There was no tension between the two of us, it was as if we had known each other for ten years. Everything was easy, everything was natural.

Sadaharo noticed me sitting down, "Ahhh, Brandon-san, rong time no see! Very beaut-i-fur woman, better than rast one! Hahaha!"

My eyes went wide and I froze, then I let my eyeballs peek over to my right to look at Karen's face.

"So this is where you bring all of 'em? Ha!" she said, smiling widely.

"Uhhh... he must be mistaking me for someone else. This is my first time here," I lied, but with obvious sarcasm which magically transformed the lie into a joke.

"Haha!" Karen laughed until her face reddened just a little bit. It must have been the delivery.

Sadaharo was totally oblivious, and he continued speaking. Before the words even came out of his mouth, I feared what they would be. "Giants rumbering! I terr you for sure. Chaos coming. Rong time coming!"

Karen and I turned to each other.

"How does he know about the giants?"

"It wasn't from me. Wait... What giants?"

"The reference my dad made. On the thumb drive. He said "ANTARCTICA MOBILIZED.""

"Yeah, I didn't get what that meant."

"I didn't want to tell you yet, I didn't want you to throw me out. But I don't want to lie to you."

"And?"

"He was talking about giants. Biblical giants, living in Antarctica. They used to be muscle... enforcers for Satan. My dad says they are switching sides and fighting for God against the Satanists. They converted..."

"Karen... I mean... I don't know what to say," I said, vexed. I looked up and down, checking my surroundings. I was trying to assure myself that this conversation was real... that I was actually here with Karen at sushi.

"I don't know, Brandon. Maybe the old man lost a step. Maybe we shouldn't go to New York."

I didn't even respond. Everything I had been through flashed through my mind, all at once. The investigation into the 'system,' the questioning, quitting my job, the dogs of the oligarchs fighting in the parking lot, my brother's Facebook posts calling me a conspiracy nut, the murder (we presumed) of Doctor Lowd. The thoughts tap-danced across my brain. I was stunned for most of the rest of the sushi dinner. I felt queasy; Karen must have noticed the change in my demeanor. We stopped speaking about the giants, about New York. Eventually we left, went home, and watched a Mel Gibson movie called *Payback.*

Karen, announcing that she was exhausted, retired to my room, and I brought out a couple of blankets to prepare to sleep on the couch.

"What have I done?" I thought. I changed my entire outlook... and now I was to meet up with 'giants' in New York to fight against the forces of Satan? If this wasn't rock bottom, I didn't know what was.

DAYS OF GRACE

**

Somewhere in the Atlantic Ocean, Heading North

The days out on the open ocean — heading north to start a new life in Italy, via New York — these were the days of grace.

They were simple days, on the ship, sailing, working, talking, eating, singing and drinking grog. There was conflict, to be sure, but fights between the giants were rare, and the ones that did happen manifested themselves in the form of pushing and shoving. Punching, not so much. Two nights had passed since Ranald battled the white whale in the ocean; that dangerous episode seemed like a distant memory. A tale they could tell their sons' sons, assuming, of course, some younger female giants — somewhere — had survived the G-A-F bacteria and could be found, with marriages arranged. Both of the previous nights entailed nice feasts, flowing grog, and massive bonfires in the stone-lined pit on the deck, carefully crafted to prevent too many sparks from flying toward any potentially flammable part of the ship.

At present, everyone on board, except the wolvine, were drinking from barrels of grog — the supply was still plentiful. The demons had been given the night off from their normal tasks and were allowed to sit around the fire with the giants. Mauve had a barrel of grog in each arm, draining them into his mouth at a steady pace. Ranald had decreed that this evening's feast and merry-making would surpass everything done before on the ship. Anticipation filled the salty air like a heavy mist.

"The notches on my axe are more than the notches of any giant in history!" claimed Ranald, seemingly out of nowhere. "I am so fearsome, I really am."

"Wait just a second, Repellent!" challenged the Vile. "My

hammer has been with me a long time. I've notched many villages and towns, destroying scores of enemies along the way."

"Ayyy. You have, but my notches are too many," said the Repellent. "At any rate, those are the old days. Those were our enemies then, when we were in the employ of Satan. Now, the same humans would be our friends."

"Is that possible? I think they would still run in fear. They have not forgotten our mayhem. It is recorded in their special books. We are a memorable force. And, I am certain I have more notches," said the Vile.

"Count them!" yelled Ranald. "I demand a fair and impartial count."

"Have the young ones count the notches. Boromeo! Tyferius! Count our notches!" added Vilfred.

The young giants took the weapons and over the next half an hour or so they dutifully counted the marks on the axe and the hammer. Each one represented a destroyed village or town. Each one represented hundreds or thousands of humans — often Christians — who had met their end in the form of an axe, a hammer, a club, or the teeth of the snarling Wolvine.

"What is the count?" asked the Vile with his customary sneer.

"Three thousand and seventy-two on the axe," replied Boromeo.

Everyone waited for a moment as Tyferius completed the task. He looked up and announced, "Three thousand two hundred and sixty-four!"

"And pride, it cometh before a fall!" exclaimed the Vile. "I am the master of destruction!"

Ranald's cheeks, peeking through his beard, flushed with red.

"Th... th... th... that may be so. But we don't know if the notches were applied fairly."

"Are you calling me a liar? Belly up!"

"There will be no fighting tonight, Vile. I am giving you a hard time. I will take the loss. You are the master of destruction. New times are ahead for us all."

Vilfred's face registered shock as he heard Ranald's words. Grace and humility were not often found among the group of male giants.

"That is the old power, though," replied the Vile. "I know we are on this mission — and destruction will result — but I am hopeful, like you have explained... hopeful we may find peace through strength. A new way of life, a new power, once this is all over."

"Nicely said, Vile. There is hope for you yet, to learn new ways and such. I think it will serve us all well. There are many things Runa has taught me — a woman, yes, but I am not afraid to admit it. She had the discipline to sit down and read the Word of God, especially early in the day when she is not run through with grog and moonshine. We can still find our path, even after all we have done."

"We are too serious. Tonight is time to make merry and rest," added Eindride. "We all know the stakes of this journey. We know the Dark One will put everything against us he can. Let us enjoy the fire and make some music."

"In a minute, Eindride," said Ranald. "We joined willingly with evil. There can be no doubt about that. Before we sing, drink and make merry, let us take a pledge to do everything in our power to fight against the evil which ruled us. It is time for an oath!"

"Oath!" came a chorus of yells from the rest of the ship. "Oath! Oath! Oath!"

"Repeat then, after me. Everyone, even you and... uh whatever their names are, Mauve," said Ranald, waving his hand to indicate he was talking about the other two demons.

Mauve nodded and his tail twitched with excitement.

"I will do everything in my power to stay faithful to this solemn oath," said Ranald, and everyone repeated him (as they did with all of the words he recited).

"I believe in the almighty God and I renounce Satan and his global soldiers."

"I believe in Jesus Christ, his son."

"After the Jewish Pharisees killed him on the cross for 'blasphemy,' he rose again."

"Jesus will come again to judge the living and the dead."

"We pray our sins may be forgiven and we may find peace in heaven through the Lord our God."

Cheers broke out at the end of the recitation of the oath. On the heels of thousands of years of raucous destruction — the giants were now Christians. It was an unlikely turn of events, but it happened.

With the demons enjoying the party, everyone responsible for getting their own barrels of grog, which they did with consistency.

Mauve, who — as a member of a separate species — was so happy to be included in the oath, laughed in his customary manner. Then, he started saying two words, over and over. Softly and then louder. He smiled. He was hoping to start a chant!

"New names... new names... new names... NEW NAMES!"

Everyone joined in until there was tremendous clamor on the ship.

Ranald raised his hand to calm everyone down.

"It is appropriate. Our epithets are dated. We can adopt new ones today. Vilfred will choose mine. I will choose Eindride's. Eindride will choose Vilfred."

"Ayyy!" everyone agreed.

There was a pause; wheels turned inside each of the giants' heads. Big wheels, turning slowly.

"Ranald... the Radiant!" shouted Vilfred, the first to choose.

"I like it. Thank you my brother. I appreciate it, very much."

"Eindride... the Steady!"

The crowd voiced approval.

"I am last it seems. Vilfred the Va..." said Eindride before interrupting himself. He laughed, once — enjoying his own joke even though it was not delivered. The crowd looked on, as if they were witnessing something like one of those all-too-common wedding toasts in the process of going completely awry. But Eindride gathered himself, apparently changing the epithet he had decided upon, and announced, "Vilfred... the Victor!"

Cheers cascaded across the deck. Grog flowed, barrel after barrel after barrel. The giants took up their instruments, the fire raged in the stone pit — and the food was plentiful. A fanciful feast on the open water.

The voyagers came to pass an island, unexpectedly. They passed on, without stopping of course. They steadily grew nearer to New York, minute by minute, mile by mile. The ocean ran on, full of mystery, impossible depth and, still, the occasional sea creature — both large and small — surfacing to take stock of the ship and its crew. None challenged them as the white whale had in the earlier part of the voyage, although a potential attack from a giant squid was addressed with a warning shot, in the form of a spear thrown by Chasdon which chased the sea monster from the area.

When the feast started to subside for the evening, everyone stayed gathered around the bonfire on the deck. Remarkably, everyone on board, toward the end of the evening at least, started to show restraint with the grog. No one was heavily inebriated.

The pleasantness of the evening impressed itself on the entire ship. The stars glimmered, the wind blew, but gently, the ocean air was refreshing and crisp — without a bitter cold.

It was Boromeo who spoke next: "Tell us the story, Runa, of how this came to be. How did you have the idea to guide us out of the dark and into the light? It is a major change for our kind — one that will never be forgotten as the history of our kind is written now and in the future."

"Ayyy. A fine idea," agreed Ranald.

"I will try to tell you, Boromeo, and everyone here. Lately, in the last few years, I have seen the light and the love adhering to beauty. My love for beauty overtook the pleasure we used to know from wickedness. He was always with us — but we were not with Him. We were ruled by viciousness and a desire for destruction encouraged by the Dark One. Ever-present beauty — all around me — became too much to ignore. The sky, the sun, the animals, even the ice-filled vistas we saw when we made our home at the freezing edge of the dome. He was always there, showing us his love, even with the things we did — the terrible things. One day, during a sunset, He called out. When I answered the call, I felt peace, through Him, and it was so deep it gave me the greatest joy I have ever known in my life. It was a belated joy, a belated love, but the fire it gave off burned so bright I wanted it always, and not only for me but for all of us. I saw the light, I smelled the wonderful fragrance of beauty and peace. I sipped from the chalice of His love and it gave me such warmth. I read the Word every chance I got, from this same Bible. I shared many verses, first with Ranald, and then with all of you. When everyone was receptive to the idea, I thought 'Why not?' And I hoped we could make this journey and give our souls over to God. When we did so today, a day brought about by grace allowing for the fulfillment of all of my dreams. May we find love and peace through Him — and a righteous anger when it is needed to fight against the forces of our old master, the Dark One. Through these things, we will find eternal life."

Even after Runa stopped speaking the others remained silent.

"So that is the story of how it came to be," said Vilfred the Victor, finally breaking the silence using a hushed tone. Everyone nodded, even the demons.

"A fine story, and all the better if it ends with us crushing Satan and his forces," added Ranald.

"It is no small task," said Eindride.

"We shall put on the armor of God and stand against the Dark One. We shall do the job that needs to be done," stated Vilfred.

"Ayyy!" agreed the others, almost in unison.

The boat sailed on through the beautiful night, steadily progressing toward New York.

◆

"WE BROKE THEM!"

**

Somewhere on the Fringe of Zürich, Switzerland

The air in the conference room was thick with money. The same was true for greed and hatred and jealousy. A group of men, mostly fat, mostly bearded, sat around a huge wooden conference table. Twelve men — all globalists — were seated in the room, lounging in over-sized leather-bound chairs.

"We have ramped up the propaganda calling for overturning the United States Constitution. And we are pumping as many people into the country — illiterates with no respect for America's founding — as possible. So, we will be successful, it is a certainty. It's a matter of time. It might take another year, it might take five. Or more. But it is done. Times have changed. It would take a miracle for them to reverse our grip. We have them by the throat. It is now a matter of when, not if," said one of the globalists, earnestly.

"Very few of the cattle — and these people are no better than cattle — can recognize anything. They are too busy buying stuff and distracting themselves with food, drink and tawdry entertainment. They care deeply about nothing. They poke around on their smart phones — phones we sold them. They can barely keep up with all of the content on their device, plus their wage jobs. But the ones that know ... we need to shut them down," said a globalist.

A squat man of mysterious national origin — showing no signs of clear ethnic identity due to his light brown skin, kinky reddish hair and warped facial features — entered the room and said, "Sir, Brooks took a flight to New York. We don't know why. We haven't seen any correspondence as to the reason for the visit."

"Shut. It. Down," chanted the globalists, reflexively. The men seated around the table all wore dark suits and expensive-looking gold watches.

Another globalist spoke: "We are close to ushering in a new dark era. Where every man and woman will work diligently — like a dog — to feed our global interests above everything. They work their whole lives to feed into our companies, into our governments — volunteer slavery — and it is the most remarkable achievement. Their armies serve our will. Their money fills our vaults. They live, day-to-day, to consume our products and media. Three hundred years ago no-one would have thought this possible."

Business-like expressions of acclimation sounded out.

"These people have no meaning, they have no use or purpose beyond their service to us. They are cattle, they exist to provide for our desires. For our corporations, our governments — and eventually our world-government. We are almost there. We cannot let interference from any of them cause an unexpected event. We can't take any chances," said a globalist.

"They can do nothing. What will they do, hold a picket sign to stage a boycott? We own everything. They can't fend for themselves. They need us for food, even for water," gloated another globalist.

Laughter and expressions of mockery filled the room.

"It only took us fifty years — admittedly, the media propaganda was relentless — but fifty years and we broke the European culture. America too."

"We did, yes."

"The richest cultural heritage in the world — and it's totally broken, totally destroyed. Look at the levels of deviance and decadence we have brought about. It was always inside them, we just needed to coax it out, into the open. Their great architecture, books, music, theater. Gone! Their best traditions, gone and destroyed, permanently. There is only malaise and despair, escape and death. We broke them!" said one of the globalists, adding a wicked cackle to the end of his monologue.

"The cycle, in the United States as in Europe, is unbreakable at this point. The corporations feed addiction and weakness into the people, who spend their lives growing our vast wealth. Not only can they never get out of it... they can't even see beyond it. There is no hope of breaking out."

"We won. Congratulations."

"Only a few notice what is happening... and we have them on lists. We know exactly what they are reading, what they are writing, what they are saying. We know where they spend their free time. We know exactly who they are. And, if they become a threat to us, we eliminate them. Thank you, Patriot Act."

More cheers sounded.

"We're getting to the point where there are so few dissidents we can take them out one by one. An accident here and an accident there."

"What can we do to twist the knife? With the winning over, what will we do for fun. Can we make sport of them?"

"We take their guns. America, I mean. We already disarmed the Brits — a once-great warrior culture now totally neutered. The only way the Americans can snatch victory from the jaws of defeat is through armed insurrection..."

"It's a long shot," interrupted another globalist.

The prior speaker continued, "If one of those nutty Americans got the crazy idea of starting a new country, staging a rebellion... that's the only chance they have. Their last hope. So, maybe we should just grab the guns. Then, if they decide to try to overthrow our corporate kleptocracy, they'll be fighting us with kitchen knives while we have guns and bombs and drones. Maybe we'll take the kitchen knives too."

Laughter broke out.

"Let's ban some books too, just for kicks!" hollered one of the globalists. "Anything good. Also, anything that criticizes global government!"

"Good idea."

"Anything else? Something to really humiliate them?"

"Ramp up the gas-lighting with our ridiculous gender propaganda — it is hilarious to see them argue until they are red in the face just to try to protect basic truths. I mean, think of the arguments!"

"It really is funny. When you have to argue over the most basic, well-known truths, there is no way you can get back to productivity."

"Hit the propaganda button, hard. Finish the degradation."

"Be ready, though. Similar propaganda has been coughed up before. Remember the Institut für Sexualwissenschaft in Germany. Those books were burned for degeneracy. Ramp up the propaganda, but keep an eye on the reactionaries. There are still some of them out there, straggling about."

"True, there has been blowback in the past... but the Americans don't have the spirit they once had. They got fat and lazy. They are distracted and they didn't notice what we were doing until it was too late. There will be no new Washington, Jefferson, Franklin, Paine. Those days are long gone. And, that reminds me, keep up the propaganda against the Founding Fathers.

"Yes, that was a nice touch!" interjected another globalist.

"That was a nice touch, I agree. Take everything from them. Their history, their country, their pride, their dignity. What's left of their freedom. Take it all."

"And take a moment to pat yourself on the back. None of this 'just happened.' We pushed it all on them. They shouldn't have let us control their television and newspapers and schools. It snuck up on them, a perfect example of how propaganda works. Repetition works. Take that to the bank," said one of the globalists.

"Our bank!" added another globalist.

"Britain... what a great accomplishment. They were once a disciplined and ferocious group. The masters of the sea. An empire spanning the globe, spreading civilization to the most forsaken Hells-on-earth. Churchill had financial problems, though."

"Churchill needed to borrow our coins! Kee kee, kee kee kee," shrieked a globalist, laughing wildly.

"That was all it took for us to push our capital in and take control of everything. It proves that every empire can fall — as America is right now. The weakest link..."

"Time is running out for the Americans. With facial recognition, 5G and our drone capability... before long, even with their precious guns they won't be able to expel us. The end of this cultural revolution will include aggression Mao could have only dreamed about. But take the guns, for good measure."

There was a pause in the room. A man sipped a beverage.

Another fiddled with his peculiar hat.

"We finally got Hogan Lowd the other day," said one of the globalists, casually.

"I wanted to take him out for a long time. He was a gadfly."

"Well, he's gone and we're watching everyone associated with him. We have operatives posting on Zuckerberg-Chang's Facebook platform about anyone associated with Lowd — we are relentlessly branding them as conspiracy kooks — we require our cattle to post on a weekly basis. We pay them, per post."

"How much do we pay them?"

"Fifty dollars a week."

"That's a bargain."

"Indeed. Did you think I would overpay?"

The weekly meeting of this group of globalists went on like this for another thirty minutes and then adjourned; the men walked out of the building and seemed to disappear into thin air.

* * *

My smart phone interrupted my conversation with Karen. It was a call from my step-mother, Janice. By this time, I was used to my brother, Timothy, acting out on Facebook.

I answered when she called, saying "Hello, Janice."

"Brandon, I'm not trying to start anything, but your brother just posted on Facebook about you. He said that you are in New York, trying to figure out who killed Kennedy."

"He did?"

"Yes, and I just hate to see this kind of thing happen between the two of you. It seems like he posts something crazy about you once a week. I don't get it."

"It's not between us, Janice. That's just Timothy. And I don't care about Facebook. Not a bit."

"Are you in New York?"

"Yes, and I have no idea how Timothy knows that. I don't post on any digital platforms and I haven't spoken to him lately. I told him once not to post about me. There's nothing more I can do, I'm not going to keep asking him."

"What are you doing there?"

"I... uhh... I'm with my friend Karen. We're... uhh, just hanging out. But it doesn't have anything to do with Kennedy. Not directly."

"Not directly? Brandon."

"It's a long story, Janice," there was no way I could go into Dr. Lowd, Karen, the giants, Zürich and everything else. I just swallowed my tongue.

"Everyone is worried about you. Your dad, for example. You know how he is. Big-foot? Loch Ness? Elvis? I can't even remember them all. He's relentless. I don't know what's going on."

"Just ignore it, Janice. Facebook doesn't matter. Digital media doesn't matter, Janice. It's not real. Someday, all the digital garbage on Facebook will be gone in a flash or a bang. What a sad and meaningless way to spend time. Facebook will be destroyed someday, I know it."

"It's real to a lot of people, Brandon. Be careful. Maybe you should talk to Timothy."

"I already told him to stop posting about me. In those exact words. He just won't listen."

THE TRUMPET SOUNDS

❋❋

Approaching Upper Bay, New York

The sun was peeking up above the horizon as the giants, the demons and the wolvine made their way out of the Atlantic Ocean and into the lower bay. They kept sailing to the upper bay. Steady as she goes, they crept forward a little bit more with Tyferius steering the ship. Time rolled on and they approached the pier just to the east of the Statue of Liberty, near Battery Park. The morning light ran down from the canary-yellow sun and danced nimbly on the water, with its reflection causing a wonderful glow to splash across the deck of the ship.

"Ay, take her slow my crew! No accidents!" yelled Ranald. Everyone on board the ship ignored him and went about what they were doing, each in their own way preparing to drop anchor.

"The castaways have arrived from the freezing cold to the less freezing cold! Intact!" yelled Vilfred the Victor.

The young giants took control the rest of the way, saying no words, but adjusting the sails to slow the ship down to a crawl. When they were drifting only a few feet away from the dock, Tyferius and Boromeo dropped the anchor, settling the ship in place. The ship was massive, made primarily of wood — it had been hand-crafted thousands of years before in the age of artisans. Above the front of the stern was a hollow (for minimizing weight) bronze statue of the Dark Angel. Satan himself, the giants' old ruler, leered over the rail, looking out, seemingly for followers, for conquests, for opportunities to do evil.

Ranald, having grown used to the presence of the statue over the years, had not paid it any heed for the entire journey. But once the anchor had been dropped, for some reason it caught his attention. He focused his gaze on Satan and wanted it covered up. It would send the wrong message to any passers-by; and more importantly, they were finished with Satan and his unholy ways. It was not as though Ranald was expecting any allies in the fight — except, he hoped, one — but, all the same, he didn't want to send the wrong message and create unnecessary enemies on the off-chance that there were any Christians left in New York.

"Runa, cover the Dark One with bedding, or with whatever you can use. He cannot be our front-piece as we work now for the other side, we fight on the side of righteousness, for the light."

"Happily," said Runa as she started walking below to gather a large blanket from one of the closets. Returning, she draped the blanket over the statue of Satan, and she secured the cover at the bottom with rope.

"Aye. Gone but not forgotten for his treachery!" exclaimed Ranald.

The beautifully-crafted ship stood out at the dock, the only other ships around were soul-less corporate freighters, made for utility and adorned with not a single piece of decoration. They were present only to move Globo's corporate products from point A to point B so that they could be sold for profit.

"Thanks and praise to Him, we are here," said Runa the Believer.

Vilfred the Victor, who had only recently awakened from his short, grog-induced slumber the night before, turned his head toward Ranald. "What do we do now?"

"First, we eat!"

"Good thinking, Ranald. Without food, we will not have the strength we need to carry out this mission," agreed Eindride.

"Gerd! Sandwiches for the warriors! We need strength to fight! Even though we all know how this will end. It always goes the same way, every time we have a detailed plan. This will be no different," predicted the Vile.

"And how is that?" asked Gerd as she started to walk toward the kitchen area.

"The mission will fail spectacularly. I can't predict exactly what will go wrong, but something will. And when it does, we will run riot."

"Pfft. This plan has been perfectly crafted. It is nonsense that you push," said Ranald, dismissing what he felt was a personal attack from Vilfred.

Gerd said something back to Vilfred under her breath, but it was not audible. She walked off and prepared two seal sandwiches for each of the older males, and one each for the young ones. Ingrid, without prompting, gave the demons and the wolvine each a helping of ground seal meat and blubber.

When the meals had been devoured, Runa knelt at the front of the ship, in silent prayer.

"Arm yourselves. Knuckles for everyone. The hammer for you, Victor. The club for the Steady. Spears for the Long. The other young ones, bring whatever it is you use. I don't remember. Armor of your choosing. Females, you can attack them with your yammering mouths — or stay on the ship, whichever you like. Ha! Ha!"

Mauve, who seemingly had a penchant for humorous attacks on the female giants, laughed loudly, "Humph, Harrumph, Ha Ha, Muaaahhh!"

"The purple demons will pull the drill. And prepare the wolvine with the harness and armor!"

Mauve chuckled, "He He He, Muaaahh," upon hearing the reference to the demons and the drill. He waved his tail back and forth, happy to be an important part of a mission involving risk and the possibility of a great victory.

* * *

The flight to New York had gone smoothly and we spent Tuesday mostly getting settled in and Wednesday walking around the city, trying out restaurants and talking. It was a mix. Karen and I had both been unable to sleep the previous night, our second in New York, also Thanksgiving eve. For me, in my bed, it was the pillow. My mind was calm but the pillow would not allow me to create anything resembling comfort. First and foremost, it was hot. Using my body heat against me, it absorbed and returned a level of heat that seemed as if it should be impossible. I tried abandoning the pillow mid-way through the night, to no avail. By then, I was too rattled to relax myself and get any sleep.

Karen didn't say anything about her insomnia, but based on her tossing and turning in her bed, just a few feet away from mine, I guessed it was her mind keeping her awake. It had to be her thoughts, dancing around like skeletons and ghosts at a wake.

Around six a.m., I couldn't take it anymore. I had hit my limit for staying in bed. I sprung out of bed — propelled by a natural energy.

"Karen, do you want to go get a coffee? I couldn't sleep and can't lay here anymore."

"I thought you would never ask," said Karen, who was wide awake.

"We can go down and look at the Statue of Liberty, just to kill some time. We have no idea exactly what we are supposed to do here, so let's enjoy it until a sign — something — arrives. I'm still having a hard time with our conversation about the giants. Let's not do that one again."

"I can't argue with that," said Karen with a touch of sheepishness.

"Grab your sunglasses, just in case. I've got my wallet, you can leave your stuff if you like."

"Hey... Karen... Happy Thanksgiving by the way."

"To you to, thanks again for coming."

"Should we get Rory and Lucille?"

"I don't know, it's early."

"It's just Rory. He's probably bouncing off the walls in their room, driving Lucille crazy. Let's get them," I said as I sent Rory a message that we would be walking down through the lobby for coffee and they should join us if they were up.

"Poor Lucille. I love Rory, but I'm not sure what it would be like to be married to a character like that."

"Well... we're on the same trip, Karen. So what does it say about us. I mean, without the marriage part."

"Not to get all serious but you always talk about marriage like its such a downer."

"You think I do?"

"I notice things too, Brandon," said Karen, smiling. "Why is that?"

We continued walking through the lobby while engaging in a lackadaisical debate about my attitude toward marriage. I denied any such attitude to try to head the entire discussion off at the pass, rather than engage on the merits. My nullification was proceeding effectively when the entire conversation was derailed. We both did a double take when we saw Rory and Lucille standing in the middle of the lobby.

"Ha! We couldn't sleep, we were going to go out ourselves when I saw your message!" yelled Rory, smiling widely, ear to ear.

With no small, family-owned coffee shops to be found, we settled for some mega-global corporate coffee from Starbucks. All four of us ordered large, hot coffees and began sipping eagerly — feeding our shared addiction for caffeine as we walked outside into the New York fall weather.

There were clouds overhead, and a late-fall chill in the air. The sun, partly or fully obstructed by the clouds (depending on the minute), steadily rose behind us, over our left shoulder, as we walked, with hot coffee in hand, down toward the vista point to see the statue. I had done this walk several times during my corporate days. It was nothing new to me, but it was always a pleasant journey.

In addition to the chill in the air, there was, besides a few sections of the sky where the sun managed to shine through, an oppressive darkness hovering above.

"You can just feel Globo here, can't you? You can just feel the mark of the beast," said Rory.

"It's everywhere. It's sad, really," agreed Lucille.

"They are watching everything. They watch people like us the closest. We haven't taken the mark. They need to keep an eye on us, we're the threat to their way of life," said Rory.

"They are probably listening to us right now," added Lucille.

"That's a conspiracy. Isn't that un-Constitutional anyway? They can't do that," I said.

"They do whatever they want while people argue about trivialities. They play with misdirection and distraction, Brandon. I've told you that. You know it yourself."

"You always talk about the mark of the beast but you never say what it is. You sound like a television preacher that doesn't have his sermon prepared," I teased.

"It's a requirement that is set up to exclude belivers — by that I mean Christians — from the marketplace. From commerce. To participate, you have to take the mark of the beast. In the scriptures, it talks about a mark on the forehead or hand."

"So... it's an actual mark."

"Well, it can be. It can be an actual mark — natural, or put there. I saw a guy on the news for implanting a microchip in his hand so he can buy stuff at stores with a scanner. That's obviously the mark of the beast. It can also just be symbolic — that's the case for most of these people."

"Okay, I'm following. And, you won't take the mark and you look down on those who do."

"Correct and yes."

"That's a doozy of a conspiracy, Rory. By the way, I did commerce for a long time. Sales, you know. There's nothing on my forehead."

"Everyone can be redeemed, Brandon," said Rory with a big smile.

"It's not a conspiracy, it's real," said Karen, siding with Rory and settling the matter.

* * *

On the Ship, Anchored by Battery Park

Each of the giants had armed themselves. The demons (having readied the drill) and wolvine (replete in full armor) were prepared for the mission as well.

"The time is here. There is not much land between us and the target," said Ranald.

"Did you bring the list from the Doctor, Hogan Lowd?" asked Eindride.

"Of course, it is right here, on this scroll. I will put Tyferius in charge of the list. We go straight for the gold at the federal reserve. After we take the gold, on the way back, we can wreak righteous havoc on those named on the list. We will teach them a violent lesson!"

Mauve laughed, "Humph, Harrumph, Ha Ha, Muaaahhh!"

"Can you just speak like a normal giant? Wreak righteous havoc? Who says that?" complained Vilfred the Victor.

"Be quiet, Vilfred. Stop complaining about everything. Your belly is full, just be happy," said Gerd, seemingly trying to elicit a 'thank you' for the task of making and delivering the sandwiches. It never arrived.

"My big question. How will we know the man and the woman that Hogan Lowd spoke of? How is this possible?" Ranald asked, addressing himself as much as anyone.

"They won't be there, Ranald," said the Victor. "Have you ever found a needle in a haystack? Your trust in this Doctor Lowd is over-blown. There is no way this will happen."

Before Ranald could respond to Vilfred, he was interrupted.

"Have faith. They will be there. I know they will," said Inger, softly. "I spoke with Runa about it."

"You base that on nothing, Inger. If not for Eindride — right there — and his massive club, I would spank the impertinence right out of you."

"You know nothing, Vile!" she replied, under the protection of her husband. "And, the spanking of human women for discipline would never be tolerated these days. You are a miserable wretch."

Vilfred paused. He ignored most of Inger's comment, saying only, "Use my dead-name again and watch what happens, Inger. You won't sit on your tush for a week."

* * *

We had stayed the night at the W Hotel in downtown New York. It was in close proximity to Battery Park, so our walk to the vista point northeast of the Statue of Liberty, after we got our coffees, was not a long one. When we arrived, we looked out, past the water, to Lady Liberty and chatted.

The conversation was all small talk, until Rory teed up the outrage and took a swing.

"I have no idea why they allowed the globalists to deface this beautiful statue with an awful poem. Those foul words were a contributing factor to their propaganda... helping to open up the borders with the Kennedy Act in sixty-five. You know, as a side-note, they let Emanuel Celler hang around in Congress forever," said Rory, ranting.

"Here we go," said Lucille.

"A real country would have term limits. He tried to open the borders in twenty-one if you can believe it. They told him to take a hike, because the globalists were still on the fringes. After all that time, he pushed his agenda through, using drunk Ted Kennedy as his dupe. If you think about it, the poem was a key plank in the destruction of the country — the slow death of the American Era, brought about by globalism."

"Rory, it's early in the morning, can it, would you?" asked Lucille. "Nobody wants the old school politics lesson, especially me."

Rory flattened his lips and closed his mouth. But only for a minute!

"Someone ought to rip that foul poem off the statue. Emma Lazarus was a filthy globalist, look it up. It was a beautiful statue and she ruined it... Just like the globalists ruin everything. Their ability to attach propaganda to everything and destroy our nation's heritage in the process is surreal."

"Rory, cool it. They killed the Doctor... there's a good chance they are listening to everything we say. An attack on Lazarus' poem is an attack on the Satanic vision of discord and destruction the globalists hold so dear. Just cool it with the anti..." I said, interrupted by Rory.

"I've got a deflector in my pocket, don't worry about eavesdropping."

"What is a deflector?"

"It's like a dog whistle, except it's made to block NSA surveillance — or any surveillance, really. It emits a high-pitched frequency — we can't hear it but it ruins the spies' ability to record and transmit anything for a fifty foot radius."

"Genius! Well, anyway, let's drop the Lazarus stuff. We know she was a horrible person. No need to dwell on it," I said.

"Yes, like I said," agreed Rory with a smug look on his face.

"We haven't really talked about the likely outcome of this

trip," I continued. "I know it takes energy — and money — to travel. So, speaking for myself, I just want to say I really appreciate you guys coming out here with us. I mean, nothing will happen, probably. We have to be prepared for that outcome." I didn't let on anything about giants. I'm not sure why I was embarrassed... Rory would have probably loved it and had all sorts of theories about them.

"Yes, thanks guys. The support is appreciated, even if nothing happens while we're here. At least we'll have good company," added Karen, as something caught my eye off to my left.

They appeared, seemingly out of nowhere. I recognized them, immediately. The giants — the same ones from the video I had watched some time ago. This can't be right... I thought the video was produced with CGI. They were real!

There they were... I saw them. They were real? I blinked my eyes, thrice, rapidly. The emergence was spectacular! So spectacular I was forced, even after the reality-check blinking, to pinch myself — you know, the cliché people use in order to check if they are dreaming.

The pinch hurt!

Wait... I think it hurt... Did it? Now I can't be sure. It was impossible to say, based solely on the pinch test, whether or not the giants were real. I discarded all thoughts of the pinch test, because these giants were so physically imposing, so menacingly impressive — that they had to be real. Like I said, there they were!

The coming events did not wait for a second pinch test. Rory, Lucille, Karen — all of us — we stared at the horde of giants, demons, wolvine. Ranald the Radiant strode purposefully in the lead, wielding his axe and wearing a metal breast plate over his customary furs and skins. A few more massive strides and he was standing in front of us, towering above. Vilfred the Victor carried his hammer — although he wore no armor, preferring to feel the full effect of any impertinent attack on his body (if anyone was lucky enough to strike him) before he would, inevitably, vanquish his combatant. Eindride the Steady stood slightly behind his brothers, carrying his club. The female giants trailed about fifteen yards behind. Off to the side, flanking the group to their left, were the young giants, Boromeo, Chasdon and Tyferious, who was holding the scrolls transcribed from the communication with Dr. Lowd. The wolvine bounded about, between them all. Pulling up the rear were the demons, towing a massive drill on a sled-like device. The plan, such as it were, was to abandon the drill after it served the purpose of exposing the gold in the vault and then use the sled to tow the gold back to the ship.

"Praise the Lord, it is them!" said Inger. "It is the man Dr. Lowd spoke of and sent . I recognize the picture. I told you, Vile."

"Use my dead-name again, Inger, and it's your hind quarters. My patience has its limits."

Runa, her eyes twinkling, exclaimed, "It is the time!"

A loud trumpet sounded in the distance. It played six tones, the first four each sounded a higher note than the previous one. Then the fifth tone dropped down, and the sixth note was the same as the fourth.

The giants' rough faces lightened. The sky brightened. Ranald, looking down, spoke first, "I am Ranald the Radiant. We all know Doctor Hogan Lowd. We are going to take the gold from the corrupted Federal Reserve Building of New York in the United States of America. Join us if you will! You can ride on the wolvine!"

He gestured to the horse-sized dogs with his left hand.

"We didn't know you would come here," I stammered.

"You knew about this?" asked Rory in a higher-than-normal pitch.

"Uhhh, yeah. Sort of," I said, addressing Rory. Then to Ranald, I said, "I'm Brandon. Brooks. And this is Karen Lowd, the Doctor's daughter, over here is Rory and this is Lucille. We are, uhh, the... rag-tag pushback." I looked at the massive axe held by Ranald. "We are happy to join you."

"Time to ride!" exclaimed Rory.

"Let not your hearts be weighed down. Victor, lift the humans onto the wolvine, chk chk!" he said. The sound at the end was an indication of some sort to the wolvine, probably meant to socialize them to the idea of giving us humans a ride without objection. I hoped and prayed that they understood it, noticing the size of their teeth.

"Do it yourself, Radiant!" answered Vilfred.

"You lazy, good-for-nothing grog-swiller. Still the Vile, I see. Do what Ranald said!" yelled Gerd the Wide.

Vilfred acquiesced to Gerd, lifting us, the four humans, onto the animals, one at a time. There was a convenient raised piece of metal on the back of each set of the wolvine's armor. We all immediately grabbed hold of them, like a handle, once we were on their backs.

Tyferius, acting as the navigator, cried out, "Now we cut over... one block east on Water Street. Then we walk right up Broad Street, with a dogleg to Nassau Street. There we will find the target and take their gold."

"To the Gold!" yelled Ranald. The giants marched, the

wolvine trotted like large horses and the demons pulled the drill behind, as fast as they could.

"Runa, Inger and Gerd — go back to Battery Park to wait for us. Prepare our victory picnic. A feast for the ages!"

"Sandwiches with seal and whale, and make them big!" hollered the Vile.

The female giants turned back and the makeshift army made its way down the street. The three older giants, three younger giants, and four humans, including me, riding on the ferocious, snarling wolvine. Mauve was leading a team of three purplish demons, pulling a sled with a massive drill, keeping an impressive pace. We were conspicuous, to say the least. I almost forgot to mention that Mauve still had his special penguin on his shoulder, adding to the spectacle. They bent their course toward Water Street and soon were marching up Broad Street, straight toward the federal reserve.

"Remember the instructions! No destruction until after we have secured the gold!" bellowed Ranald.

From my position on top of a wolvine (who seemed to take no notice of my presence), I was able to see New Yorkers parting like the Red Sea as we approached their positions. The pattern was, usually, a sped-up gait, followed by a hurried shuffle, followed by a jog and then a sprint until the passer-by was out of the way.

My wolvine was trotting alongside the demons and the drill-sled. I glanced over at Mauve, who looked up at a billboard and said, "I am vomit, grandparent cry." When I looked at the billboard, it reminded me of MindSmash — the billboard purported to advertise one thing, but looked to be pushing something else entirely. Mauve clearly disliked the tangential advertising involved.

We made our way up broad and took the dogleg toward Nassau Street. Soon, the motley army was in front of the Federal Reserve Bank of New York. The largest depository of gold in the world.

"Ready the drill, Mauve!" ordered Ranald as he stared at the stone exterior of the building. "Tyferius, view the architectural plan and position the drill so as to make the contents of the vault our own."

I looked at Karen, who had a far-away look in her eyes. I wanted to call out to her but my voice would not allow for it.

"The drill is ready, Ranald," said Tyferius, calmly. "The position is right!"

"Commence the requisition of the gold!"

Mauve and the two demons turned a switch on the massive drill, aiming it at the base of the stone wall. The plan called for them to drill down at a forty-five degree angle until they had reached the vault. Then, Ranald, with a downward wave of his arm, indicated to the demons that it was time to drill down.

Mauve, the purple nook-demon, started the drill's engine. With the aid of the other demons, he lifted the back of the drill until it was positioned at the proper angle. An unbearably loud whirring and revving noise filled the air on Nassau Street. Mauve smiled and laughed "Humph, Harrumph, Ha Ha, Muaaahhh!" He gave a hand-signal to the rest of us, making a circle with his thumb and second finger and raising his other three fingers. To commence the seizure of the gold, they pressed the drill into the stone target and pushed, holding the four handles and starting to drill down toward the vault containing the gold.

"Soon, the gold will be ours!" bragged Ranald. "We will bring the Dark One and his servants to their knees. We will starve them out! Their profligacy and decadence — it will be destroyed and judged!"

"HOO-RAY!" came a cheer from the other giants, including the young ones. Something told me they had plundered many times before. But, not likely on this scale.

It is hard to say how horribly wrong the operation — specifically, the attempt to burgle the gold from the Federal Reserve vault — went from this point forward. So, it will have to suffice to say that it did, in fact, go horribly wrong on several different levels, and all at once.

The drill, which was 'incredibly powerful and indestructible' (according to Ranald), broke immediately. The massive drill whirred and buzzed for a moment. It broke through a small amount of stone on the Federal Reserve building — it created a hole in the wall, about two feet deep. Then, all of a sudden, the drill bit stopped spinning, smoke started spewing out of its engine, and a massive crack became apparent on the back half of the machine. The demons looked around, confused, still holding onto the useless tool.

"Made in China?" asked Mauve, addressing no-one in particular. "The yellow man rip us off!"

Right after he spoke, Mauve's face showed tremendous alarm. His special penguin was no longer perched on his shoulder. Mauve, ran off to look for the penguin at a full sprint, with his tail waving as it followed behind him.

Two NYPD officers, having heard the commotion of the drill and spotted the rag-tag army on Nassau Street, had drawn their weapons and were aiming them at Ranald, who faced them down with both hands on the handle of his colossal axe.

"Freeze!" yelled one of the cops.

"I'm done freezing, I've been doing that for hundreds of years. Ha!" Ranald answered.

"Freeze or I'll shoot," replied the cop, who sounded hesitant.

"Your pathetic little weapon means nothing to me! Run off or the mayhem will start with the two of you laying broken on the street. I will crush your bodies until they are an unrecognizable stew of blood and bone. I'm warning you! I will summon the old days and you will be buried, if at all, with shame and contempt."

"Ranald, not the police!" yelled Lucille. "They didn't create the system!"

"We have no guarantee they aren't in league with the Dark One!" exclaimed the Victor, ready to start the violence. "Graft and violence run rampant in this time of trouble!"

The two police officers exchanged glances. They shared no words, but each seemed to feel an urgent need to retreat. They were used to dealing with petty violence from gang members, not an armed raid on the federal reserve featuring giants and demons. They started walking back, slowly, to their squad car. Ranald, in an act of mercy, let them live.

"What happened?" asked Ranald, addressing Eindride, looking in the direction of the drill and scanning the street for Mauve's location.

"Mauve went looking for his penguin. The drill broke. I know this is a shock, but the plan is not going to work," replied Eindride, thick with sarcasm.

Ranald, holding his axe in his right hand, threw a straight right punch at Eindride's shoulder, and it connected.

"Oof," went Eindride, involuntarily, as he was hit. "What

was that for?" he asked with an angry scowl on his face.

"I don't like bad news, especially when its already obvious to me."

The punch, delivered from one brother to the other, kicked off a storm of violence and destruction, which did not manifest itself in further intra-group conflict — it was focused outward, on their surroundings.

"Bring the thunder!" bellowed Vilfred.

"Put on the cloak of righteousness and break what you can! DESTROY THINGS!" yelled Ranald.

Eindride, instead of retaliating against Ranald, swung his club into the side of the Federal Reserve building, taking out one of the walls, completely. He brought his club down on two more walls, breaking them as well. The building started to collapse in on itself. With the drill rendered inoperable, there was no way to get to the vault, everyone knew that. Vilfred came in behind Eindride and dropped his hammer on three different sections of the building. With that, the federal reserve was reduced to rubble.

"Someone light it on fire!" yelled Vilfred as he walked away from the destroyed building.

We could hear the sound of sirens as they headed toward our location on Nassau Street, outside the Fed. Several helicopters flew in the air.

"Chasdon, defend against the flying machines!" ordered Ranald. "We can't get to the vault. The mission has failed. Get back to the ship! Tyferius, tell us the targets along the way — only hit the targets controlled by the beast!"

The wolvine, sensing the distress among the giants, started snarling and howling and running in circles. I caught a glimpse of

Karen and Rory, holding on to the raised metal on the armor. Rory's brow was furrowed and Karen's eyes were wide. I held on to my armor-saddle for dear life.

Chasdon the Long reared back and threw one of his spears at a helicopter. The weapon glanced the side of the helicopter but did no damage.

"Just a warning shot!" yelled Chasdon.

"Take out the Starbucks!" yelled Tyferius. "It's on the Doctor's list!"

Eindride and Vilfred heard the command. The hammer and the club smashed the entire Starbucks in no time at all. The entire structure was destroyed and the smell of mediocre coffee and burnt sugar wafted out of the ruins.

"Behind it. McDonald's! Corporate poison!" instructed Tyferius.

"Low quality! It's not grass-fed!"

The McDonald's met the same fate as the Starbucks. It was destroyed, thoroughly. Everything, including the garish canary-yellow modern plastic corporate M-signage, it was all leveled. The wolvine howled and galloped around in an excited state. The demons broke what they could with their knuckles and fists, after the main damage had been done by the giants with their massive weaponry.

"Head back down Broad Street!" yelled Tyferius.

The giants, demons and wolvine thundered down the street, heading south. By the time Tyferius yelled, "Chase Bank — Doctor Lowd says it is full Globo!", Mauve had re-joined the group with his pet penguin safely back on his shoulder. The demons had completely abandoned the cheaply-made, broken Chinese drill and the sled they brought to carry it and were now ready to join in on the chaos.

All three giants razed the massive Chase Bank building. Axe, club, hammer! Repeat! A lone man emerged from the rubble, bruised and bloodied, staggering about.

"Why? Why did you smash my bank? I'm the corporate manager! I have authority here!"

"Do you renounce Satan? Do you believe in God?" asked the Radiant.

"I'm a proud atheist..." replied the man.

"We fight against you and your dark leader now. It is a new era. Wolvine, Kill!"

A snarling wolvine — the one I was riding on, in fact, tore the man into several pieces. The atheist's head was positioned a few feet from his torso which was a few feet from each of his legs. A meaningless life of dissipation and nightly drunkenness had caught up with the man, who was utterly destroyed. His wrecked body lay in the street as the army moved on, still heading south. My wolvine followed after the group at a trot.

"The wages of sin is death!" hollered Eindride. "Ha! Runa taught me that one."

"Another Starbucks!" cried Tyferius at the top of his lungs. "Globo creep! Break it!"

"I've got this one!" yelled Boromeo. He reached underneath his fur clothing and grabbed a grenade. He had recovered about a hundred of the weapons from an abandoned military post in Antarctica — and he had strapped about a dozen of them inside his garment for this raid. The weapon looked like a peanut in his hand as he pulled the pin and threw it into the mega-corporate coffee store. The grenade smashed through a window and landed behind the counter, close to the supply of the Devil's own corporate soy-milk. A few seconds later, it exploded. The Starbucks was leveled, sections of it were on fire and it quickly became a smoldering ruin.

The wolvine shredded two of the people who had escaped the blast and the fire — it was obvious from their appearance they were Satanists; a third professed his belief in God and was allowed to run away in another direction — Ranald had commanded the wolvine to spare him with a simple snap of his fingers.

Our army which was simultaneously impressive (judging by size) and rag-tag (judging by organization) continued to head south, back toward Battery Park, back toward the ship.

We took the dogleg to the left on Wall Street and then proceeded on Broad Street.

"House of Morgan. Doctor Lowd says they are irredeemable Globalists! Smash it! Take down their money-counting structure!" roared Tyferius.

Axe! Hammer! Club! Grenade! Repeat!

The House of Morgan headquarters was quickly reduced to ruins. We didn't stop to celebrate the destruction, but kept moving.

"New York Stock Exchange. Dr. Lowd says it's the home of extreme, rootless capitalist exploitation. It is a stronghold of Globo, of the Devil. Tear it down!"

The club and hammer did much of the work, destroying the structure. Tyferius lobbed three grenades into the building. Soon, it was a smoldering ruin.

We kept moving, but not before a fat man in an ill-fitting

suit staggered out. Ranald confronted him.

"What do you say for yourself?" Ranald asked the man, who looked dazed from the chaos.

"I'm... I'm just doing my job."

"And what is that?"

Before the man could answer, he fell to the ground — struck down by fear itself. Ranald moved on, without giving the man a death-blow with his axe. He hadn't had the chance to finish the inquisition and had no desire to wait around to find out more.

The sounds of battle continued to echo through the streets of Downtown New York. The other giants, the demons, the wolvine... they all continued to wreak havoc on any Satanic outpost of Globo on the street.

"What about Pret A Manger?" whooped Ranald.

"Never heard of it. It's not on the list. Leave it alone!" replied Tyferius.

"Their food is terrible! They fed me a rotten sandwich that gave me dysentery!" hollered Rory from his seat on top of a wolvine... but no-one paid his demand for vengeance any heed, as the group had already moved on.

"Another Starbucks!" boomed the Vile.

"Smash it! Burn it! Make sure to get the entire soy supply!"

"Soy. I am vomit! Humph, Harrumph, Ha Ha, Muaaahhh!" yelled Mauve as the building was destroyed.

"New York Daily News! Trash of the highest order. Globalist, communist filth! Break it. Mauve, when it is broken, light the building on fire."

"Humph, Harrumph, Ha Ha, Muaaahhh!" Mauve laughed

and then said something to the penguin on his shoulder. When Ranald, Eindride and Vilfred had finished destroying the building, Mauve, drawing a match from his pocket, lit the rubble on fire, after finding a huge stack of unsold newspapers to use as kindling. The New York Daily News was gone, destroyed completely.

"Over here! Starbucks! How many of these things are there?"

"That one is getting old. But smash it anyway. They bear the mark of the beast and the penalty is death. Destroy!"

"ACLU. They hate free speech and work to subvert all things good and traditional!" howled Tyferius. "Doctor Lowd says they are a propaganda outfit, fully infiltrated with subversive communist globalists! They are part of the tight-knit group doing the subversion for the Devil."

"Break them! Break their backs! Destroy their building."

"Take it down, then head to the picnic! Wolvine, kill everyone in the building who comes out! They do the work of the Devil."

* * *

When we returned to Battery Park, the female giants had sandwiches waiting for the male giants. The giants hungrily ate them down, two each. Some scraps were set aside for the wolvine and the demons. Bellies were full. The female giants had even made small sandwiches for the humans, which we made short work of.

"Was the sandwich to your liking, Mr. Brandon Brooks?" asked Ranald, addressing me after I ate the sandwich.

"It was, Ranald. The proportion of bread compared to meat was perfectly done. Thank you."

"And the battle in the streets of New York? What did you think?"

I paused. I wanted to be respectful of the effort, but I suspected the battle would end up being a defeat. The globalists controlled the megaphone, and they would work to brand our efforts as armed robbery or terrorism.

"Well, we sent a message to global capital, to the global government and one-world corporations. We taught them a lesson, today. We taught them we would fight for a different way of life. We taught them we are willing to fight to the death, and we will no longer give the globalists quarter. We waited too long to fight back," I said.

"We lost! Our drill broke yet you talk about a 'message.' You are a dummy!" yelled Vilfred with a menacing scowl.

"It is a dark day for Satan. We used to be his best warriors and today, we fought against him and his forces on earth. Forces of possession. We fought Globo on their turf. We smashed an entire street inside one of his main strongholds," said Eindride, taking an optimistic outlook on the battle.

"We didn't get the gold, you idiots!" yelled Vilfred the Victor. "The human might be even stupider than you are, Ranald."

"This argument is going nowhere. Let us go to the ship and regroup. We will talk about what to do next."

Time passed, slowly. Sirens could be heard in the distance. The helicopters still circled above.

Karen steered her wolvine over to mine so we could talk.

"Globo's response was slow. Something is going to happen. There is no way that they let us do that without a response. They are gathering their forces," she said, speaking in a worried and hushed tone.

"I thought the same thing. We saw only two cops? That is ridiculous. Something is going on."

The sky was clear, which made the next occurrence quite remarkable. Out of nowhere, a loud boom of thunder sounded, which was followed by a lightning strike over to my left. It struck in a part of Battery Park that dipped down, just slightly. Not a ravine or even a gulley, but just a dip in the terrain. The lightning strike called my attention to the area, where I immediately noticed about a dozen vehicles of war gathering for a counter-attack.

At last, though, the response from the Devil himself had come!

In the area of the lightning strike, a small army of United Nations vehicles and infantrymen had amassed.

"The United Nations! On American soil!" shouted Karen, addressing me.

"Satanists. They finally showed their hand," I responded. Since I started noticing things, back at the start of my journey, more thoughts were forming in my head about the age old battle between good and evil — the fight between God and Satan. For the last hundred years, at least, Satan had been on a roll. But I knew, deep down, it was never okay to 'count God out.'

"It's okay to believe in God!" hollered Rory, seemingly reading my mind. "Fight the globalist filth!"

My respect for government, corporations, products, modern society — and most people — had been so diminished over the course of the story I have recounted here, but my faith in God had grown, filling the empty space. The relationship was inversely proportional. It was an interesting line of thought, but it was rudely interrupted by events in the present battle.

As those thoughts entered and left my head, a single bullet whizzed, inbound. It grazed my shoulder, drawing blood and causing a surface wound, but it didn't fully strike the target (me). Thank God! It would have smashed my collarbone and could have killed me.

"Sniper!" shrieked Rory. "They're targeting Brandon!" As he spoke, he stepped between me and the terrorists, as if to shield me from any further fire.

"We cannot stay here. Vilfred, take the females and the young ones and the humans back to the boat. Eindride, come with me to dispatch the global forces of Satan," said Ranald, pointing to the United Nations soldiers, a collection of third-world minions who wore blue helmets with the letters UN painted on each side in white. There were eleven or twelve vehicles in all, including four tanks and a bunch of all-terrain vehicles. Six United Nations soldiers appeared on foot, armed with automatic rifles. Some looked to be Africans, some looked to be East Indians. Some were ethnically ambiguous with no identifiable racial heritage. All of them were, inexplicably, standing on American soil, right here in New York.

"They can go without me. I want to fight. Back to the ship, all of you!" exclaimed the Vilfred the Victor. "Now!"

Everyone in the group seemed to start yelling at the same time. Chaos, which had previously been brought about by breaking, smashing, destroying all Globo strongholds — now came in a verbal deluge.

"I can see the sniper... over there!" exclaimed Eindride.

"Where?"

"See his face? He has rat-like facial features under his blue helmet."

"Ha! He will not be able to shoot that close to Brandon Brooks again. He will miss! Those people are sneaky and evil. We fought people who looked like him in the old times," yelled Ranald. "Let's go smash him!"

"Shut up, Ranald. While you are talking loud and saying nothing the rat-man is taking careful aim!"

Rory, for reasons I will never fully know, walked briskly to my front side, placing himself between me and the sniper, just as the next "crack!" was heard from the rifle. The bullet struck Rory in the next instant. It ripped through his chest, and I immediately feared for his survival. He fell on his back, with both arms spread — his left arm reached toward the water and the right back toward Downtown New York.

Lucille and I bent over Rory, trying to aid him in some way... but we didn't know what to do. Karen crouched as well, a couple feet away.

Rory gasped for breath and spoke in a raspy voice, "Brandon... Brandon Brooks — I never took the mark my friend. I never took... the... mark! Do great things. You as well, Karen. Lucille... my dear... I love you."

Those were Rory's last words, he struggled for another couple of breaths and then he was gone.

* * *

The mood had changed. Where before we had been considering the day's events a victory of sorts — now there was a different feeling. The globalists had taken another one of ours in the name of the Dark One. Death and defeat loomed over us. Ranald, Vilfred and Eindride, without hesitation, strode toward the United Nations' soldiers to exact revenge for Rory. And the revenge, it came. Each of them smashed several of the vehicles (including the passengers), and it was Vilfred who reduced most of the UN foot soldiers to meat pudding, using his hammer. The UN soldiers cowered and reeled and screamed at first but soon seemed resigned to their fate. Most were quiet as they died. Their weapons, which they discharged in a last-gasp flurry of hope, had no effect on the rampaging giants. All of it was over in a couple of minutes. The giants came back to our staging area after dispatching Globo's small army.

"We are very sorry about your friend," said Ranald. "Take care, Brandon Brooks. Also you... and you..." he said, meaning Karen and Lucille. "You are a tremendous warrior... we hope to cross paths again in the future. For our part, we will change our destination. We will find an uninhabited place and rebuild — we didn't get the gold so we need to modify our plans. The Devil keeps control of the money, still, which is most unfortunate. But we will endure, we always do."

"I told you about the plan, Ranald!" yelled Vilfred.

"Not now, Vilfred," said Ranald, calmly.

Still shocked, all the humans, including me, muttered words of thanks. For my part, I was still trying to convince myself that all of this activity was real. I didn't bother with a pinch test since the last one was inconclusive. The battle, the giants, even Dr. Lowd, Karen, Rory and Lucille. It had to be real. It was real! No matter whether our story of fighting the 'system' ended in victory or defeat... we had to go down fighting. We had to make the effort to change the course of history, to bring down Globo.

The giants, the demons, the wolvine — they all walked back toward the anchored ship at the edge of the water. As they walked, I caught myself wishing they would come back; I knew this adventure was ending and I didn't know when the next one would surface, if at all. Lucille, obviously shattered by the death of Rory, slipped away from the group. To mourn, I presume. I looked for Karen... she was standing off a ways, with a far-away look in her eyes. I felt warm inside as I looked at her, I had come to care about her so much in a short time. I decided I would give her a minute to reflect by herself before approaching her to see what we might do next.

If we didn't try, it would have been as if I lounged on my sofa, alone and un-showered, for all of Thanksgiving Day — drinking an entire bottle of HonkyTonk whiskey, eating junk food and watching an NFL game or YouTube videos about the moon landing, JFK, flat earth and anything else that caught my attention. And, without this event acting as a culmination of sorts (the Battle for New York) — it would have been as if I did the same exact thing for the months and months that passed (HonkyTonk whiskey and videos), ever since I burned out and quit MindSmash.

So what if we didn't get the gold and cause the monetary system to crash? The gold would have been nice, but with fiat money (which isn't real), the requisition, even if successful, may have had no meaningful effect on the 'system.' That was what we were up against. A monstrous evil so big, so powerful, so well-funded, so pervasive, it was likely invincible.

I thought, again, about my comparison to the bottle of whiskey and YouTube videos. It made me proud to think about what we had done. We came together and mobilized! We took action! If the 'rag-tag pushback' hadn't made this trip... if we hadn't tried... all of my investigations into the 'system' would have been for nothing. The articles, the quotes, the videos, the conversations, the notes — all for naught! What was the purpose of knowing all of these things — of all my important research into the 'system' — without taking action to bring about change? What would be the difference between that and a Thanksgiving Day full of whiskey and YouTube?

There would be no difference at all.

"Hey, Karen... Karen?"

* * *

About the Author

F.C. Fox is a pen name for Ryan William Morgan who is an American from California. *Dogs of the Oligarchs* is his third novel. He plans to spend 2020 on a cattle drive in Montana while writing *Thot Riot!* (the second Milo Tate novel) by the fire at night.

Made in the
USA
Middletown, DE